THE TALLY

E.G. WOLVERSON

A DARK TALE OF DANGER AND DIESEL FOR THE STUDENT LOAN GENERATION

Feed A Read

This edition published in 2012 by FeedARead Publishing.

Electronic edition first published in 2011 through KDP.

Typeset in VTKS Animal 2, Garamond, Courier New, Anarchistic, ITC Zapf Chancery and LFMolden.

Copyright © E.G. Wolverson.

E.G. Wolverson has asserted his moral right under the Copyright, Designs and Patents Act 1988, to be identified as the author of this work.

All Rights reserved. No part of this publication may be reproduced, copied, stored in a retrieval system, or transmitted, in any form or by any means, without the prior written consent of the copyright holder, nor be otherwise circulated in any form of binding or cover other than that in which it is published and without a similar condition being imposed on the subsequent purchaser.

All characters in this publication are fictitious and any resemblance to any persons, living or dead, is purely coincidental.

A CIP catalogue record for this title is available from the British Library.

*For the three Marks, the two Pauls, James, Alex, Michael,
Phil, Pete, Martin, Gaz, Andy, Kellie, Vickys #1
and #3, Rich, Liz, Radhika, Luigia, Elena,
Florian, Klaus, Mareike, Charlie James, Dan,
Bryce, Winnie and the rest of the uni gang*

And for Emma Lou, for rescuing me from the above

4

CONTENTS

Twisted	7
The Creeping Fear	13
A Life in Amber	27
Love's Just a Competition (and I'm Winning)	41
The Delicate Sound of Chunder	55
Treachery in the Pursuit of Beaver	63
Snakes & Ladders	77
The Jihad Drop	89
Escape to Danger	101
Educated & Trained	111
The Perfect Crime	125
The Fast Track to Fame	139
Destiny's Cruel Hand	143
αποκαταστασις	153
Future Nostalgia	157
Clogs'll Spark Tonite	171
By Inferno's Light	185
Just a Space Away	199
Last Man Alive	207
One of My Turns	227
The Truth	231
The Drunkard and the Tramp	251
When I Die, Don't Let Them Take My Eyes	255
Flight through Eternity	273
Forever Twisted	289
About the Author	295

TWISTED

NOW THAT'S WHAT THEY CALL A RIFF! THIS hook immediately tears friends, lovers and loners away from bars, tables and toilets. Gangs of friends and Wednesday sporting allies congeal into one smoke-veiled mass inexorably bound for the dance floor. Tight white dresses are sullied with sticky brown, purple and orange stains as not a single drink is left undisturbed. This is the kind of tune that, when dusted off and downloaded in fifty years' time, will carry many of those who hear it straight back to their student years. Alumni everywhere will put down their digipipes and newskindles, and just for a moment they'll taste the sickly sweet snakey b again. They'll smell the smoke and the sex and the decades-soiled student house shag piles as if their toxins were right there in the air.

But Tommy Briggs won't.

He isn't drawn to the dance floor like the proverbial moth to the flame; oh no. Tom's the *'Ah'll just stand near the bar for a bit, get battered, an' 'ope that somethin' good happens'* sort. Of course, 'something good' is rather a vague term, and more importantly, the concept of 'good' varies tremendously from individual to individual. One man's 'good' may well be another man's nightmare, and in this particular case, Tom's good is quite literally another man's nightmare; several men's, actually. Her name is Hannah Drake, and she's the love of his bloody life.

But sadly for young Tommy boy, this particular Wednesday night isn't quite as jam-packed with Hannah happenings as he would like, and in fact it's leaning worryingly towards the dull. Now this really is unusual because, on balance, his young life is full of an almost unbelievable amount of incident – though, in fairness, most of it does tend to revolve around punch-ups with randoms thanks to the machinations of the aforementioned Miss Drake. Or getting so drunk that he dribbles saliva down himself. Or being sick.

Presently, Tom is stood propping up the Union bar. Every so often he tries to rest his elbow on it, but each and every time that he attempts to do so, his arm slips in a puddle of spilt (and invariably livid purple) alcohol, causing him to skid forward comically. Each time he quickly corrects himself, takes another small sip of his pint, and prays that no-one noticed.

This happens four times before he gives it up as a bad job and decides to brave the human traffic meandering between the tables. Deep down in his heart of hearts, Tom is waiting for something to come along and stop nights like these happening.

No more damp shirt sleeves.

No more sick.

No more dribble.

Just a quiet life, an armchair, a fit woman and digital telly.

Having survived his shoulder-barge-strewn journey from the bar to the balcony overlooking the dance floor, Tom stops and leans forwards over the balustrade. His pint dangles precariously in his half-drunken grasp as he nods his head not quite in time to the music.

A Premiership-inspired bleach-blonde fringe, parted just off-centre, almost entirely obscures his features from the drunken partygoers below - not that many of them look up to spare him a glance. If they did, he'd probably be very worried; even were they drunken partygoers of the attractive young female kind. Whilst a bit of competition would certainly make Hannah think again, he'd rather risk not getting any action than be made to look a tool.

Tom's hands shake ever so slightly as he swills around the strange mixture of lager, blackcurrant cordial and what tastes like vinegar (but is passed off by the bar staff as cider) that lingers in the bottom of his glass. This way he doesn't have to drink it. This 'diesel', or 'snakey b', is a student poison that, even after almost seven months, he's not quite worked out how to keep down. Drinking it in such obscene quantities doesn't help matters.

Passing out in a pool of sick isn't the name of the game tonight though. We're well into the second semester and it's still nearly three weeks until the final instalment of the loan comes in. Half twelve and only a quid left in his pocket – that cash machine has stopped doing fivers. It's not enough for another pint, even in the Union. And so with his mind numb and his bladder swelling, Tom raises the glass to his mouth and drinks the most economic mouthful possible – the polar opposite of his usual practice. At half past he'll treat himself to a visit to the bogs and a hunt for his mates. Maybe even a hunt for Hannah.

Tom inhales deeply and then slowly releases the air from his cheeks. *Nights out are well borin' when you're sober.* There must be a hundred people down there dancing, or at least trying to. He reckons he knows nine or ten of them by name, but recognises the faces of all the others. They all look like slightly-tweaked templates and near-clones; a testament to a lack of imagination somewhere.

As Tom does his best to conquer his fears of rejection, peering out from beneath his floppy fringe in a feeble attempt to catch some hottie's eye, he is ignorant of a couple of salient facts.

Firstly, a group of young women is passing within a gnat's wing of where he is stood. One of their number is so very drunk that she almost falls into him, steadying herself at the last minute but still spilling a small amount of her purple snakey b down the back of his white combats. She barely notices; nor does he. Although neither of them knows it yet, their lives will become intimately tangled and before long... Well, you'll see.

Secondly, against what Tom perceives to be insurmountable odds, he *has* caught a young woman's eye, and she is staring at him right now through the tinted glass of the doors that separate the bulk of the club from the smaller Box Office and Cloakroom areas. Like him, she is waiting for something, although she knows exactly what she's waiting for: her coat.

Why is there always a bloody queue? Mind you, it would make little difference to her if there weren't one. She could be stood wearing her coat right now, but she'd still be waiting for her housemate, who as per usual is getting off with some fit guy on the dance floor, and as per usual is leaving her waiting to walk home with (well, a few steps ahead of) them. Jealousy and inadequacy are usually crushing her by this point, but tonight these familiar feelings are almost extinguished by the gravity of a pair of blood-red eyes that are sucking her in, threatening to swallow her whole. And she thinks that she might want them to.

Defying gravity's pull, she finds herself staring down at the dance floor, once again in the company of her jade-eyed companion, envy. Together they watch her housemate's fluid and sexual movements, enchanted. Most men would be a slave to such grace, but not this one. Not Will Surewood. His movements are so obviously cold and mechanical - a pre-rehearsed sequence of buttons to be pressed; a simple formula that, when inputted correctly, will trigger the desired result for his late-teen libido.

For Will, life's not so much for the living, but for the taking. His shallow, all-consuming selfishness is outweighed only by his grotesquely unbalanced hedonistic greed. Those of a cynical persuasion might think it ironic that the main driving force behind this young man's existence - the quest for physical pleasure and self-gratification

- is so often undermined by his unrelenting obsession with *more*. His fixation has such a deep hold on his soul that his fleeting moments of sexual bliss and ego-gratification feel like a *chore* because he's had to work so hard for them. Worse, he can't even enjoy them fully when he's in the moment because all he can think about is pencilling in his conquests' particulars on his 'tally', and / or where his next victim will be coming from. Pulling is more than a pastime to him; it's more than a job. It *is* him.

Will's two housemates that he came out with tonight would give anything to be where he is right now; a beautiful raven-haired business and marketing student's body pressed tightly against his, her fingers clawing sensually through his inevitably blonde highlighted hair.

Sadly for Romance, Will's tried and tested formula will once again pay dividends for him. This has three major consequences, each with a differing degree of significance. In reverse order of severity, the first is that Will will get *'another notch on the bed post', 'another brick in the wall', 'another one on the tally'*, or whatever the current Surewood parlance is.

The second consequence is that in the near future, this beautiful young woman will find out that she has chlamydia. There will not be any prizes for guessing from whom she contracted it.

Finally, and most importantly, it means that the housemate of tonight's conquest will be leaving the club alone. And, as a direct result of the same, she's going to die tonight.

THE CREEPING FEAR

'I SHALL SPEAK TO YOU SOON THEN. GOODbye.'

Jamal rolls his eyes and lets his head slump forward. The mobile phone remains pressed against his ear by way of an apathetic hand. 'Okay then Father, bye… oh yes. Worry not. I shan't forget. Goodbye then.'

His finger hovers above the red button anxiously. Every second spent on the phone will be a minute or so deducted from the end of his life. *You can't be too careful these days, what with mobile phones, x-ray radiation and all that what have you.*

'Did she?' sighs the wannabe teacher. 'Well… look Father, I really have got to go now. My supper is nearly ready… oh yes, I shall tell her. Bye then. Bye Father. Bye. Thanks… I shall. Yep. Will do. Bye then. Bye. Bye Father. Bye.'

Finally Jamal allows himself the pleasure of pressing that one little button. Instantly he can feel the air around his head clear of microwaves. He admires the disproportionately rotund bottom of his fiancée as she trawls through his dirty washing.

'Who was that then? Your dad again?' comes a bored voice from somewhere beneath a mountain of socks and skid-marked, implausibly nerdy y-fronts.

'Indeed,' replies Jamal perspicaciously, and then, after an uncomfortably long pause: 'He sends his love.'

The beautiful face of his wife to be turns to him, smiling warmly. 'Why don't you ever tell your dad you love him on the phone?'

Jamal scoffs. Why does she so love being his emotional superior?

'He won't be here forever, you know', she adds, the tone of her voice suggesting that she's won yet another little victory over her partner.

Jamal turns and walks out of the kitchen, rubbing the back of his hand rhythmically over the hairs on his opposing arm. His father knows that he loves him, surely to goodness? That sort of thing goes without saying these days. Besides, his father isn't an old man. There will be plenty of time for sentiment in the future.

It takes a good few minutes for Jamal to register that he is staring intently at his own reflection in the living room window, shaking his head; his dull grey eyes reflecting his own guilt back at him.

Jamal removes his key from the ignition and carefully folds up his *A-Z* before returning it to the glove compartment. After locking up the car, he takes a moment to look up and down the street of featureless, terraced housing where he now finds himself. Before today he'd dismissed rumours of the infamous 'Hull smell' as being an urban myth. How wrong he'd been! The simple function of breathing in and out is blighted by the taste of cocoa and burning equine carcasses that are already becoming embedded in his sinuses. A pained glance over his left shoulder confirms the propinquity of the biscuit and tanning factories, and in consulting page eighty-two of his diary slash personal organiser, he concludes that he is indeed where he is meant to be. The purple and white poster that catches his eye confirms it. In spite of a winter's battery at the hands of the elements, Jamal can just about make out the incongruously gaudy text:

> DRUNKEN STUDENTS COULD...
> GET LOST IN A BUSH.
> FALL DOWN.
> INJURE THEMSELVES.
> GET MENINGITIS.
> GET DEPRESSED.
> GET BEATEN UP.
> GET MUGGED.
> GET ALCOHOL POISONING.
> GET THEIR DRINK SPIKED.
> BE SEXUALLY ASSAULTED.
> DISAPPEAR.
> OR WORSE.
>
> CONTROL YOUR DRINKING –
> DO NOT LET YOUR
> DRINKING CONTROL YOU!

'Welcome to Hull,' Jamal mutters to himself. 'Just a letter away…'

As the house nearest to him is number 135, he logically deduces that the even-numbered student property that he has an appointment to view will be on the other side of the road. He gets half way across it before turning back and unlocking his car door. Without fully getting back into the small vehicle, he leans across to the passenger side and pushes the glove compartment firmly, just to double-check that it is actually shut and thus put his mind at ease. He's heard a lot about Hull in the media recently – none of it flattering, and frankly much of it very disturbing. That awful poster certainly didn't help to quash his anxieties about the place. Whatever he does, Jamal can't seem to quash the creeping fear that constantly gnaws on his adrenal gland.

He's half way across the road again now and he can't remember if he locked the door behind him. Pushing his spectacles back into position with his middle finger, he turns and walks back to his car once more. Locked. It always is.

At the third attempt, Jamal reaches the other side of the road. To his dismay, the number on the first door that he sees is 13. *13!* His stomach contracting in spasms of razor-sharp anxiety, he reaches for his mobile so that he can call the letting agency. No signal.

Jamal finds himself glancing around, his neck moving in sharp, clipped movements that can't be doing his neck muscles any good. Nervously he pretends to be texting somebody, just in case someone is watching him and thinking, *who is that strange fellow, stood all on his own?*

At the end of the road he is relieved to see what looks like a phone box. At least he'll be able to call the letting agency and find out exactly where this accursed student house is situated. As he gets closer, he becomes fascinated by the phone box - it looks more like one of those old-fashioned red phone boxes from years ago than it does any of the sleeker, transparent booths that you'd find in any other contemporary city. Stranger still, not only is its style redundant, but it's cream.

'How repugnant,' Jamal mutters rancorously, shaking his head. *It's like another world. Cream phone boxes! That would be bad enough in itself, without this lack of divisibility between odd and even-numbered houses! Where's the logic? Where's the order?*

Jamal has made the mistake of forgetting that fate has brought him to Hull.

Different rules apply here.

* * *

Somebody has gotten out of her bed on the wrong side this morning – or, more accurately, had gotten into the wrong bed on Saturday night. As the disgruntled History post-graduate checks her mobile phone to have the dreadful truth confirmed, what she can only describe as 'murderous rage' pumps through her veins instead of her usual brand of A negative. Amidst a flurry of uncharacteristic expletives that explode from within her, just two non-swear words are discernable: 'Will Surewood.'

Ben Davis, on the hand, wakes up every morning in a murderous rage. He can't help it; he's just put together like that. Today he's especially aggrieved, as he has to get up ridiculously early because his landlords are *bringin' a bunch o' beggars in to traipse through the 'ouse at abart 'alf one*. He might even have to put up with one of them moving in, as if Tom and Will weren't bad enough.

In all fairness to Ben though, he doesn't have much to be cheery about. His bedroom is a depressing place, even for a room in a student house. Just one small window to shoot his BB gun out of; four smoked-yellow woodchip walls; a manky old wardrobe; a chest of drawers with only two out of eight handles still present; and a bed which, excluding himself, is always as empty as the limited recesses of his microscopically minuscule mind. Everybody hates him - especially his parents and friends who, through fear of reprisal, are still forced to associate with him - and his abysmal luck with the ladies bothers him almost as much as the infinite regress of stupidity that he can sometimes *feel* holding him back.

Only recently he was drawn into a fierce argument with Will about his alleged virginity, and it wasn't that long ago that he was forced to defend himself against the allegations of Spadge – now an *ex*-housemate – who vied that he had only half a brain cell. Both conflicts ended as they so often did where Ben was concerned – quickly and efficiently, with black-eyes and / or bloody noses for his would-be tormentors. *Poncy students!* What do they know? He has a full brain cell.

It doesn't take long for something to raise Ben's spirits though. He's fortunate that he takes so much delight in the suffering of others because, with the world as it is, it's not often all that long before something comes along to put a smile on his acne-ridden Neanderthal face. Whilst doing his damnedest to put a bullet between the arse cheeks of the bin man, he clocks the generously-proportioned form of one of Will's latest conquests emerging over the summit of Black Hill, her face twisted into a mask of contempt that makes the historical tyrants of her studies look like errant schooboys. *She must 'ave found out 'bout vat ovver bird 'e's been bangin' this week - vat Anna piece.* Ben allows himself one of his most deplorable cartoon-dog laughs as he imagines this rather rotund, intimidating young woman remonstrating with his hungover housemate.

That'll learn 'im.

'It's the 'eadline wot matters', Will is explaining without looking up from his paper. 'Not the small print.'

Tom is half-listening, prising his eyes open in front of the mirror to see if there is any brown left in them at all. Glancing over his shoulder and realising that his best friend needs attention - after all, there aren't any women in the room to give it to him - he musters a half-hearted riposte. 'She was a reet munter.'

'Small print,' Will retorts, thinking about looking up but instead deciding to conserve the energy - it would be much better spent manoeuvring that sausage roll into his gob.

'Fat – chuffin' – 'effa,' Tom slowly replies, a note of genuine anger in his voice as he realises that his eyes are just two pools of grey nothingness. 'Dead man walkin'…' he mutters to himself dramatically, turning around to face his *'bestest friend'* and housemate.

'What you on wi'?' Will takes a hearty bite of the sausage roll, crumbs tumbling from the dizzy heights of his teeth all the way down into the depths of some cleavage in today's paper. 'What time's them people comin' for a butchers at Spadge's old room? I wanna gerra shower. Yer never know – they might be 'ot!'

Tom struggles to pull an important-looking letter from underneath a plate encrusted with the orange, fatty grease from rotting mincemeat. It takes him a moment to separate letter from plate, but once the struggle is over he quickly skim-reads the remnants of the correspondence. 'Their names are on 'ere. Lets 'ave a butchers: Mark Anthony Johnson, Jamal Prakash, Michael 'oskins, Mark Falkingham an' Chun-Fai 'Ashley' Ren.' He pauses for a moment, as if concentrating deeply. 'They better not nick owt.'

'Quality!' Will exclaims. 'That last one sounds 'ot, 'n' ah get extra points on me tally for foreign. Ah never done a Chink.'

The doorbell rings. Unable to tear himself away from page three and his sausage roll, Will waits for Tom to answer the door, who observably takes great delight in informing his best mate that 'this Chun-Fai is probably a bloke' as he does so. He also takes a moment to wonder why Chinese students often take an English name like 'Ashley' when they come over here to study. If he went to university in China and had to pick a Chinese name for himself, he wouldn't know where to start. He'd probably just have to go with 'Bruce'.

Will's eyes look up from the breakfast bar towards the door as he hears a girl's voice, becoming worryingly louder by the second…

'You fuckin' bastard!' yells the formidable looking blonde, towering menacingly over Will who suddenly appears very small perched on his stool. Her monstrous breasts at his face height seem poised to attack like two great weapons of mass destruction.

Grateful of the doorbell's second, not quite contemporaneous ring, Tom scurries quickly away to answer the door to a young well-dressed woman with dark hair and a forced smile. *She's fit as -*

'Hi, I'm Katie from *Studicom*. This is Jamal,' she says, indicating an awkward looking, thirty-something bloke with glasses and unsightly corkscrew hair. He appears to be of Asian lineage, and is wearing a tweed suit with leather patches on the elbows. Tom can't help but stare.

'He's here to view the vacant room,' fit-*Studicom*-Katie-girl says. 'With some luck he'll be joining you in September.'

'Y'alright mush,' Tom says, extending a modestly-tattooed forearm and trying to work out if Jamal's hair is an afro gone wrong, appalling taste, or just apathy.

Jamal accepts the handshake suspiciously. 'Hello. What are you studying then?' Jamal's uneasy greeting betrays his unfortunate lisp.

'Me? Er... politics, innit. Ah'm not that into it though if truth be known. Thinkin' a swappin' courses next year – means ah might get an extra year 'ere at uni. Bonus!'

'Oh. Am I to take it that you like studying here then?' Jamal asks, using that much-maligned 's' word again.

'Well...' Tom pauses, unsure of how to answer such a bizarre question. 'It's a good nite out 'ere, but like the course and that tends to spoil the fun a bit. Good life otherwise, though. Beats workin' for a livin' anyways! What will you be doin' up 'ere?'

Wiping his feet on the doormat that Tom has never noticed before, the prospective tenant looks around the hallway in fear and disgust. 'I have a place on the PGCE starting this September. Primary Years.'

'Orr! Ah was thinkin' a doing that when ah've graduated. You get six grand for it, don't yer?'

'Well yes, but it's very competitive,' Jamal snaps defensively. 'And it's not at all like an undergraduate course. You can't just do it for the money...' His voice trails off as he notices the state of the front door behind him. The wood around the door handle is splintered, and the handle itself is hanging on thanks to one hesitantly attached screw. He says nothing. Instead he just points at it, shakes his head, and sighs.

Tom raises an eyebrow and smiles awkwardly whilst Katie does her best to explain the merits of the super-mega-strength *Studicom* Yale lock and *Studicom*'s generous new 'all bills included / free unlimited internet' package to Jamal. For his part, Jamal pokes at the Yale lock, concluding that it looks about as safe as... well... *this poor chap here!*

The poor chap that Jamal is using in his simile appears nursing a red cheek, only moments after a flash of sound and fury too quick for anybody to properly register which saw the door flung open (nearly knocking Jamal out) and a blonde-haired, chubby young woman scurry past.

The second of Jamal's potential housemates stands on his tip-toes in nothing but his threadbare boxers. Still chewing on the remnants of his sausage roll, he cautiously pops his head out of the door before releasing a sigh of relief and offering Jamal yet another tattooed forearm. Jamal can see a pattern emerging here and he does not like it one bit - he signed up to train as a teacher, not join the Navy.

Katie normally maintains a healthy detachment from her job, and it's times like these that make her glad that this *Studicom* caper is just a part-time gig whilst at uni.

After about three minutes in this shithole she'd realised that she'd be lucky to let this empty room to a blind foreign exchange student with the personal hygiene of... well, this lot. She's got no chance in hell of letting it to this Jamal; she'd be much better off recommending to her boss that they shift the current tenants to a three-bed property next year and re-let this house to four students who already know each other (after a deposit-funded spring clean, naturally). She certainly didn't think that she'd be able to let it to this Jamal geezer. Still, she's had worse shifts. There's a half-naked semi-fit bloke to help brighten her mood, even if he does look like a right scruff. The other one ain't bad, either.

Following the ensemble through to the 'living' room (if indeed 'living' is the most appropriate word here) Katie is amazed at the juxtaposition of putrid squalor and state-of-the-art technology. *A GIANT plasma telly; about a million inch screen!* However students managed to move that in, let alone pay for it, she has no idea. She has to make do with a cheap portable with shit reception and no *Five*. This lot have a top-spec DVD player; a *PS2;* and one, two, three, four, five, six, sev-

'Wow! You have Dolby 7.1,' says Jamal, the rusty grey of his eyes suddenly alive with a newfound light. 'Oh my...' He sees something calling to him from amongst the debris on the coffee table – a shiny gold box with some sort of robotic face on the front. 'How did you... I mean... This isn't even out yet! I read on the web that they weren't going to release these on DVD until the prequels are all out!'

Will and Tom smile at each other. There may be a place in their house for this misfit yet. After all, there's always room for a man of distinguished tastes! 'Spadge got us it from Thailand; it's ripped from a laserdisc or somet,' Tom informs him.

Will cracks a smile. 'Clever them lady-boys, ain't they?' Katie finds herself intrigued by Will's voice itself, if not by the xenophobic bollocks that he's spouting. His dialect is Yorkshire through and through – not Hull though, she happily notes; he says *O*s instead of *ur*s. He'd say 'toad' instead of 'turd', for instance, which is more important than you'd think, given that just about every street corner in the city boasts its own giant 'turd' effigy. Strangely though, Will's voice has a definite Irish burr. It's quite possibly the weirdest voice that she's ever heard. In spite of herself, Katie starts to have thoughts that she cannot defend about the removal of those bedraggled boxers… until their wearer gives his bollocks an indiscreet scratch, shattering her fantasy completely.

'It pisses all o'er it!' Tom is shouting as he feels his chest tighten with both a pang of amused anger and an uncontrollable urge to 'correct' Jamal. How could he really come out with 'the original is better than *Empire?*' Tom's opinion isn't opinion – it is fact.

Jamal is holding out his hands and backing away from Tom. 'I'm sorry but you cannot beat the original – it's a cinematic masterpiece; outstanding in every respect. It will live on long after all the sequels and prequels are forgotten.'

'That's fatin' talk!' Tom says in jest. At least, Jamal *hopes* that it was said in jest.

'Aye,' Will butts in. ''ow can you beat the *"'ow's your father"* bit, ey?'

'It's *"I am your father"*, I think you will find,' Jamal points out.

'Ah should bloody 'ope you're not,' Will says, smiling. And then, just for a moment, he looks saddened. 'Although…'

But it is just a moment.

Less than enthralled by the riveting conversation, Katie finds herself asking if she can use the bathroom.

Just two more viewings this aft and then you're out with the girls for a nice meal and a few drinks tonight, she keeps telling herself. Trying not to breathe, she sandwiches her way into the broom-cupboard sized toilet and squats above it; after all, physical contact with that toilet seat is more than she'd dare. Pulling her knickers down to her knees, but no further, she tries to make herself go – not an easy task whilst holding the lock-free door closed with one hand and trying to squat.

Katie is disgusted to find the torn remnants of an old newspaper wedged between the wall and the empty toilet roll holder. Although she tries to look away and imagine that she is anywhere else, the huge front-page photograph of a girl that disappeared a few weeks ago ensnares her eyes. A fellow student.

There was an interview with this girl's dad on the front page. She hadn't known this girl that well, but she'd seen her in some lectures. This girl must've been what, twenty? Twenty-one? A shy girl; quite pretty, but lacking confidence. Probably the sort never to hurt anyone...

Hopefully it was all just a big fuss about nothing. She'd probably just took off to India back-packing or something and didn't bother to let anyone know. *Still. Makes you think. There are a lot of dodgy people about, and it only takes one nutter and that's it – game over.*

One miscalculated risk.

One stab in the dark.

In nearly three years of uni she'd heard of frequent muggings, several break-ins and even the occasional rape... *but this?* For some reason, it has really been playing on her mind a lot since she heard about it. Not in a major way; just the odd stray thought here and there as she wanders home pissed in the early hours. For some reason that she can't reasonably explain, she has a bad feeling about this whole thing.

She has to laugh at herself.

Cautious Katie!

When she'd spoken to her parents about it on the phone, they had explicitly banned her from being out after dark. In a way, part of her wishes that she was still young enough to have to heed their prudent instructions.

Worst case scenario: there's a kidnapper, perhaps even murderer out there. She'll be damned, though, if she is gonna let some sicko ruin the next few months of her uni life. *These times are for taking.* She'd just feel a bit better if she had a bloke like that Will on her arm when walking home at night. Hell, a corkscrew in her handbag would be something. Or, more pressingly, some loo roll would do... how can she be expected to wipe herself with the black and white image of this poor girl's face? *Animals! How can they live like this...?*

With a sigh of resignation and a sense of overpowering revulsion, Katie reaches for a pile of encrusted laddish magazines. Reluctantly she tears out the glossy centrefold and prepares herself for some pain.

'Yeah, we was out that nite an' all. Ah wouldn't worry 'bout it though, mate. She'll 'ave just done a runner or somet,' says Tom, his tattoo wrapped around his new friend Jamal's shoulder. For his part, Jamal is following the tribal pattern with his left eye, bewitched by it; he's hardly listening to a word that is being said. *How can they mutilate themselves like this...*

'Besides,' Will butts in, his lips embracing a hand-rolled joint. 'No-one would mess wi' us lot.'

Trying to take his mind off the disease that Jamal can swear he feels forming in his lungs, he manages to reply. It's a simple response to Will's statement; just one word taking the form of a question. 'Why?'

His query has a 'simple' answer.

A short, stocky figure appears in the doorway. Not all that clued up on his Yorkshire lingo, Jamal is still pretty confident that the appropriate expression is *brick shithouse*. Mercifully, he remembers not to say it out loud.

'Gristle.'

Just one word... but a most chilling one.

Enter housemate number three: Ben 'Gristle' Davis.

On a school playground in a small Lancastrian village, a petite school teacher with a fat bum answers her mobile phone. She does her best not to let the infants playing around her see, but within moments of hearing the familiar *William Tell* tone they are swarming around her feet.

'Jamal! Hi sweetheart... not bad. Miss Brown was ill again so I had no CSA in Maths... Yeah, but Harry was playing up again. Your whiteboard software worked a treat though for the oral mental starter... What? Already? The first one! Well what's it like, then? What date do you get the keys? Oh I'll have to come over at weekends... What? Sweetie... *Why are you crying?* Are you okay? What do you mean *Hell's Angels*? Oh you daft sod...'

The future Mrs Prakash frowns and stares up into the sky. Eastwards, she reckons – towards Hull.

'Alright my love. Well try not to worry; you've signed for it now. I'll see you in a few hours. Drive safe.'

She has a bad feeling about this.

A LIFE IN AMBER

IT'S FUNNY HOW LIGHT IT IS IN THE DARK,
muses Spadge as he stares at the ceiling, watching the moonlight seep in through the curtains and dance around his lightshade. Every now and then an explosion of whiter-than-white bright light illuminates the curtains, time and again forcing his face into a gross contortion. Taxi doors then slam and Spadge hears a series of exaggerated and empty goodbyes. It's another sleepless night for the Spadgeroonie.

Counting sheep! *Shepherds aside, has anyone in the entire history of the human race ever actually done that?* Spadge doubts it, not that it matters. He isn't seriously considering it as an option. He has a much more diverting means of slithering his way into the arms of Morpheus this night.

Nat. Anorexic Ems. Scary Kate. Her in Gran Caneria - that Scottish piece with the baby. Gemma…

Spadge lays there and forces himself to recall each and every unique sexual experience that he's ever had. Now Spadge has never considered himself to be a stud by any stretch of the imagination, but when he finds himself losing count after about twenty birds he can't help but feel a spasm of mannish pride.

But then he remembers their faces.

Eventually he gets to twenty-three. *Becky-Lee.* Of them all, she's the only one that he's truly proud of. A beauty. A stunner. She could have been a model. Well, maybe not a model but… y'know.

He tries to imagine her face. Her tits. Her arse.
Nah.
Too fit. It just doesn't work.

His mind wanders back to the hall of shame and to the grotesque parodies of womankind that lurk inside.
Scary Kate...
Cary Skate...
That one does the job for him.
The job in hand, that is.
But he still can't sleep.
Spadge lies awake, albeit slightly closer to the kingdom of slumber than he was, pondering on the epic question of whether to go for a piss and then clean himself up, or to simply roll over and let his mother worry about the sheets. His instinct is to roll over and risk a crusty stain, but those annoyingly efficient little neurons in his brain notice that he's also thinking about urine, and so they fire up the old memory cylinders on that subject. And now he's more awake than ever.
Oh Becks.
She could forgive him for dropping out of uni. She could forgive him for being carried home at four in the morning by complete strangers, shouting slurred abuse at her and vomiting all over the sofa. She could forgive his circular bouts of depression and mania, but the one thing that she could not forgive was the spray of something warm up her back in the night.
A girl has to have some respect for herself.

Seven-thirty! Rise and Shine!
'Oh for Christ's sake!' Spadge moans as he pulls his slightly crunchy covers tightly around him. Unlike most people, he can't even hit the snooze button. For one thing, he doesn't use your conventional alarm clock. Instead, he chooses to rely upon the sickeningly chirpy tones of his mother, beckoning him forth from the pleasures of unconsciousness to face another cold, hard day. He still hasn't forgiven her for eleven years' worth of schooldays,

and now here he is, twenty-four, being put through it all again. Only worse. Much, much worse.

Secondly, he couldn't afford even a minute's snoozing because he leaves everything to the last minute – get up at half seven; out of the shower by quarter to eight; an apple and a cereal bar bang on eight o'clock; and then at the bus stop by ten past in plenty of time to catch the eight twenty-nine bus. This way, he doesn't have to spend one second longer than necessary either thinking about or doing anything work-related.

He begrudges every single bloody second of it.

I'm flying through the infinite depths of interstellar space. The stars appear to be flying towards me in the form of little white pixels, because...

Because... that's what they are. I've just nudged the spacebar and it's turned off the screensaver. Bang goes another reverie. Here comes another call.

Some old spiel. No room whatsoever for any individuality. A fucking tape recording could do this job if it knew how to handle one or two possible customer responses.

Spadge stares vacuously at his monitor. He can feel the capillaries in his eyes caving in under the pressure - *no wonder* Happyloans *give their staff free eye tests!* He's not been there long and already he can feel his vision blurring and his forehead burning.

'Just before we begin sir, I need to let you know that all calls are recorded for training purposes. In applying for a loan we will search your records at credit reference agencies who will supply us with credit information as well as information from the electoral register. They will always record details of this search. We and other companies may use this information in decisions about you, your spouse or partner who lives with you or any other individual identified as being financially associated with you or any other members of your household. We will also check your details with fraud prevention agencies, and if we suspect fraud or money laundering this will-'

'What you tryin' ta say, kid?' the customer finally speaketh. And it was all going so well.

'I'm just explaining, sir, that as part of your application we are required to check your details with a fraud prev-'

'Are ye sayin' I'm tryin' to commit fraud, like?'

'No sir, of course not.'

It's weird working next door to a crematorium, Spadge thinks to himself. It's astonishing how, with just a little practice, one can detach himself so completely from the events unfolding around him.

'Oh... just bear with me a moment sir,' Spadge says nonchalantly as he sees his almighty team leader approaching with what look likes another new starter. *Happy-loans* have a high turnover of staff, astonishingly.

She's not bad actually, this one. *A cut above*.

Spadge presses the 'mute' button on his handset.

'Alright Spadge,' Jimmy B - the team leader - begins. 'This is Aley, she'll be on the phones from Monday. I'd like her to sit in with you for this week. She can start off by just listening in, then maybe she could just do the typing, and then hopefully by Friday we can get her taking a few calls. I'll leave the details up to you.'

'Hi,' Spadge says, smiling at her. She looks petrified. Sexy as fuck, but petrified.

'What's Spadge short for?' she asks him. *Cheeky bitch.*

'One sec,' he says to her, pulling out a phone-cable splitter and a spare headset from his draw. 'Pop this on.'

He releases the mute button, and prepares to induct another poor, hapless victim into a life of voluntary enslavement and ruin.

***

When the daily facts and figures are pulled off the system, they hover just below their targets but comfortably above the red; a life in amber only punctuated by a clocking on time, and a clocking off time.

When the thrice-daily drinks are ordered from what passes for a coffee machine, they hover around three raised wooden tables – not unlike those you might find in a bar. Unlike most bars though, the drinks served here taste of chlorine instead of alcohol, and the air is scented with defeat and perspiration instead of smoke.

Aley looks up at this odd, slightly ginger, slightly bald, wreck of a man. As she's got older she seems to have lost her ability to accurately assess another person's age. Back when she was eight she kicked arse at it - with but a single glance, she could easily identify those who were six; those who were seven; and those who were chic and urbane eight year-olds like her. These days, regrettably, the talent eludes her. She wouldn't be surprised if this guy was forty. Then again, she wouldn't be surprised if he was only in his early thirties.

'I really, really wouldn't drink that if I were you,' twenty-four year-old Spadge says to her, sipping his hermetically-sealed water purchased from the snack machine. Disregarding his advice and sipping at her bright orange "coffee," Aley starts to think that of all the people in this place, this guy may actually know what he's talking about. *Pity he's a ginge.*

'So what kind of music you into?' she asks Spadge, awkwardly trying to make conversation as you do when you start a new job and it looks like it's going to be shite. Again.

Spadge pouts and exhales deeply. 'Pfft… Loads of stuff, really. Pink Floyd, Bob Dylan, S-Club…'

Aley laughs out loud. 'S-Club?'

She half expects Spadge to come clean. A wind-up, surely? How can you like both Pink Floyd and S-Club 7?

On the contrary, Spadge looks deeply wounded at her mockery. 'S-Club are awesome. I mean, I've got an open ear for music, generally speaking, and I do like a lot of what people say is 'good music' - stuff with meaningful lyrics and that jazz. But everything has its place, I reckon. You know what I mean?'

Aley nods. She doesn't know what he means.

'I mean, you can't knock a bit of *Street Spirit* when you're lying in bed dying, but if *Street Spirit* came on in a nightclub the place would just empty! There's always gonna be some wanker at a house party who plays nothing but obscure Suede b-sides all night when what you really need is a bit of Chesney Hawkes to groove to. A bit of S-Club.'

Colin – a tall, bald feller with a ponytail and an n-shaped moustache like Lemmy from Motorhead – chooses that particular moment to wander over to them. He throws his keys and his fags down on the table before slumping forwards, his face resting directly on the grimy table.

'Y'alright Col?' ventures Spadge.

The bulk of Colin doesn't stir.

'Col?' says Spadge again, poking his inert colleague with a random spoon. He doesn't give a shit about rousing Colin; all Spadge is bothered about is amusing Aley.

It seems to be working.

This time, the bulk of Colin drags himself up from the table. 'Oh, sorry dude. Heavy one last night. I really can't be arsed today.'

'I wouldn't worry about it mate, I never can be arsed, working in this place!'

At this, Aley laughs. It isn't an amused laugh; it's more of a nervous why-does-everyone-moan-so-much-surely-it-can't-be-that-bad-hope-it-isn't-like-that-last-place sort of laugh.

She notices Jimmy B wander over, and she isn't encouraged when both Spadge and Colin roll their eyes. 'Alright gents,' he ejaculates. 'How many quotes we got today, then?'

'Enough, Jables, enough,' says Colin, smirking. 'I'm on for a six quid a deal bonus this month. With my bonus I'll be taking home more than you, dude!'

'Ah, you wish mate; you wish. What about you, Spadge?'

'I've been training 'ant I? I've only got a couple.'

Jimmy B turns to Aley. 'Aley... Aley... Aley G. You enjoying it?'

'Yeah,' she lies. 'I really like it.'

'I liked it for the first couple of days,' Spadge scoffs.

'Yer and me! Look at us now,' Colin adds.

'Gents! Gents! Don't go putting her off before she's even got started. Anyway, you're due back on the phones. Your ten minutes are up.'

'Course they are,' Spadge smiles at Aley. 'They always are.'

As they begin to move back towards their desks, Colin elbows Spadge in the ribs. 'Did I miss owt in *Big Bruvva* last night?'

Aley opens her mouth as if to answer in his place, but Spadge gets in there first. 'I don't watch it, Col. It's a load of shite... I can't stand it. I've got better things to do than sit around watching ponces sit around.'

In his bedroom in his mum's house, Spadge sits in front of his PC. On the one hand, he knows he should be rewriting his CV. In his actual hand, however, he holds a padded jiffy bag bearing the customs stamp of Jersey. *Optical Media. £28.99.* It could only be the new *Simulife* game that he'd pre-ordered.

He'd been reading all the rave reviews about it on the internet. It sounded amazing. You get to control one of four characters - each a fairly average middle-class person. The object of the game is to live their lives vicariously. You can get them up in a morning and give them their virtual breakfast before packing them off to work for nine hours or so. In the evening you navigate them towards the pub, or if you're feeling lazy just plonk them down in an armchair on 'snooze' mode while you go off and do your own thing. *Brilliant. And to think losers like Col waste their evenings watching reality TV!*

But, and it is a big but, that CV really needs doing. Urgently. The longer he puts it off, the longer he has to wait for another job – simple as.

With a sigh of resignation, Spadge opens up his old cupboard – still full of childhood relics – and digs out his old 'Record of Achievement' folder from school. Dusting it down, he can't help but laugh at the title spelt out in fancy gold-embossed letters. Every single person in school got one of these, and how many of them will have gone on to achieve anything of any worth? Even he, top of the class in just about everything – except Science; he was shit at Science. *Set Five* shit – finds himself trapped in a circle of torment.

Good job, good pay. Stressed out. Breakdown.

Easy job, rubbish pay. Dickheads bossing him out. Superiority complex sets in. Must escape.

Good job, good pay. Stressed out. Breakdown.

Easy job, rubbish pay. Dickheads bossing him out. Superiority complex sets in. Must escape…

It doesn't help that he can actually see the circle. He's Prometheus; forever trapped by the failings of his own character; forever destined to push that boulder up his own personal mountain. Unless he gets his finger out, it will be a life in sales or customer service.

He'd take the boulder any day.

With the still shrink-wrapped *Simulife* CD-ROM in one hand, and his 'Record of Achievement' in the other, Spadge reluctantly makes his choice and pulls out a slightly crumpled copy of his CV. He cringes as his eyes scan over his personal statement:

```
Despite the fact that I did not complete my
course I feel that the knowledge that I
acquired whilst studying, combined with the
customer-facing experience that I have
gained over the last few years, will enable
me to perform exceptionally well in any
commercial environment.

In addition to the skills that I have
developed throughout my career (please see
'Employment History', below), I have also
picked up some generic skills that are vital
in almost every type of job. Namely:

    - I am an extremely proficient touch-
    typist. Whilst I do not possess any
    formal qualification, when the Old
    Cleveland Street Agency last tested me
    I was averaging 70 words per minute.

    - I am fully versed in every aspect of
    I.T. and computing. I have an excellent
    working knowledge of Office and e-mail
    packages, not only in their day-to-day
    use but also in their installation and
    maintenance.

    - I have outstanding organisation
    skills and an obsessive attention to
    detail.
```

>   - Cumulatively, I have well over a
>   year's proven customer service
>   experience.

My hobbies include watching Swindon Town
lose, eating out, watching films and the
designing / building of websites.

Absolutely un-em-ploy-able. The employment history is even worse. Spadge can feel the palpitations coming on. He'll never escape Happyloans…

Job Title: Personal Loans Sales Advisor
Salary: £15,250 p/a + commission

My current role is centred around the sale
of financial products, primarily unsecured
personal loans and optional payment
protection and life assurance packages. To
be able to serve in this capacity, I have
had to gain an 'Advanced' qualification from
the Financial Services Regulatory Committee.

My core duty is to take customers through
personal loan applications on the telephone.
To be more precise, this involves:
>   i) going through the Data Protection
>   Act 1998 with them
>   ii) performing capacity checks
>   (weighing their income against their
>   expenditure to calculate their
>   disposable income)
>   iii) performing credit checks
>   iv) advising the customer which
>   financial product(s) best suit their
>   needs and budget
>   v) sensitively informing the customer
>   of our decision, and if necessary
>   referring applications where I suspect
>   fraud or money laundering to the
>   relevant fraud prevention agency

       vi) sending out the appropriate paperwork to the customer.

The position also involves obtaining and verifying legal agreements and documentary evidence, as well as meticulous record keeping. I am also required to provide a high level of service to both customers and loan brokers when dealing with queries, and I pride myself on the fast and efficient service that I deliver.

In the seven weeks that I have been with the company, my performance for the company has always been exemplary. I regularly exceed my sales targets, generating revenue for the company and also earning commission for myself. Last month I was extremely proud to finish third (out of over eighty sales advisors) in the league table, having quoted over three hundred customers in a single month and having one of the best customer-to-quote conversion rates in the whole company.

In the past I have also been allowed to chair our weekly team meetings and on occasion, deliver our morning 'huddle.' Our huddle is arguably the most important part of the day as a team because we are given our daily targets, and together we have to get ourselves into the frame of mind where we want to beat them.

Finally, I have responsibility for training new members of staff. I am very proud to say that each and every one of the individuals that I have trained thus far have gone on to excel in their new roles. I am pleased that the weeklong formative training-

-weeklong. That's all. And then she'll be off on her own.

Spadge thumps his fists down on the desk, spilling his tea and scattering biscuit crumbs all over the floor. He can feel a strong misogynistic streak developing within himself, ironically *because* of his intense love for the female of the species. He hates feeling like this. A woman on his brain. Bending over backwards to make her notice him. And in the end…

In the end they all leave him.

He doesn't mind when it ends because of something *they* do wrong – he can play the wounded soldier like the best of them. He just can't bear it when it's all *his* fault. *His* drinking. Like with Becky-Lee.

But she's forgotten now.

All Spadge has on his fickle old brain is Aley G.

```
Job Title: Social Researcher
Salary: £4.50 p/h

Upon returning to Swindon I took a temporary
assignment as a Social Researcher,
conducting telephone interviews with victims
of crime in Scotland on behalf of the
Scottish Executive. This role taught me a
lot about tactfully handling delicate (and
potentially traumatic) subject matter when
speaking to-
```

As he reviews his pitiful montage of work experience, images of Aley float around in his head. Her curves. Her jet-black hair. Her gorgeous smile…

'How long have you been here then?' she'd asked him at lunch.

'Just a couple of months. I'm in between careers, sort of thing.'

She'd nodded with understanding. 'Me too. I graduated a couple of years ago and got on one of those graduate training schemes with-'

Bitch! He'd thought. *Does she even know how hard them things are to get onto?* But then she'd smiled, and all the wonder of the world unfurled.

'-but it didn't work out. Same sort of thing, day in, day out. And I felt a lot of resentment from the longer-serving members of staff.'

'So what do you fancy doing next then? You gonna go for the management scheme here?'

'Are you?'

'If nothing better comes along,' he replied. He neglected to add, *which it won't*.

'I might. I dunno. I spilt up with my boyfriend recently-'

YES! YES! FANTASTIC! MINE'S A PINT!!!

'-but we've been speaking a bit on the phone the last few days and-'

OH NO NO NO…

'-I might go back up to see him. He lives in Hull; he's training to be a solicitor. He's got a training contract with White Walker Sewell. If we get back together I might move up there…'

Those nasty words had twisted around and around in Spadge's mind. The world was so unfair. A sensation – it may have been sadness, or rage, or even both – had surged through him. Why weren't there birds like her in Hull when he was living there?

```
Job Title: Duty Officer / Cloakroom
Attendant
Salary: £4.25 p/h

In late 2003 I worked part-time as a Duty
Officer for my local student union. The role
mainly involved front of house duties - I
```

```
was responsible for checking students'
N.U.S. cards, signing guests into the
building, looking after the cloakroom in the
campus nightclub and also dealing with any
lost property claims. Whilst the role was
not particularly challenging, I found it
extremely rewarding as I like to deal with
people on a face-to-face basis. I enjoyed
providing and pleasant and efficient service
and serving as an effective first point of
contact for all-
```

Spadge slumps down into his chair and slips off his soaking wet jacket. His watch beeps. It's nine o'clock.

'Can we all be on *available* please!' comes the inevitable battle cry from Jimmy B.

Spadge pulls on the headset and sacrifices himself to the machine before him. Before the first call comes through, he has just enough time to notice that Aley's seat is empty.

She didn't last long.

'*Happyloans*, how can I help?'

Eight hours of hell are now just that little bit less bearable.

LOVE'S JUST A COMPETITION (AND I'M WINNING)

ONE MINUTE SHE WAS SPINNING AROUND AND around on the roundabout, her mother smiling happily and chatting away to her latest bloke. Her mother kept meaning to tell her just how proud she was of her swimming certificate, and just how much she loved her, but she'd just had so much else on her mind recently, *what with having to repay those overpaid benefits and sorting out that bloody gas meter and...*

The next minute she was downing sambuca with him off the cricket team from A Block. He'd fancied her ever since he first laid eyes on her. *Talk about a stunner!* She was totally out of his league like, but *nothing ventured...*

She'd felt a bit ill after that.

She'd felt that instinctive impulse to get herself home.

Not to the 'Halls of Residence' Home. Home Home. To her mam.

But she couldn't.

She staggered; she wobbled... she wandered aimlessly through the streets of Hull.

Drunk and lost.

She was slaughtered.

And that's when she got slaughtered.

And people being people, they cried bloody murder; locked up their daughters and threatened their sons. And all the while she walked amongst them, lost and invisible; suddenly and terribly imbued with an excruciating sort of wisdom.

In a sense, it was a mercy that she was beyond the sight of the living. If any mortal eye could have looked upon her, they would have found themselves staring into her hollow, impassive eyes and questioning what force could rip the soul straight out of an innocent young woman. They could never understand, you see. It was all a matter of perspective.

This wasn't just death.

There was something very wrong with the universe.

In his own private hell, Galileo prostrated himself before the man who had sailed off the edge of the world, and returned with the head of a dragon.

Right next door to hell, Einstein wept as the laws of physics leapt up before his very eyes, painted themselves cream and danced before him in a pint pot, singing protest songs. After a while they transformed themselves into rather repugnant-looking telephone boxes, and in the end, defeated, Einstein joined them in their new state.

Next door but one, Stephen Hawking rose to his feet, gobsmacked, as the Truth – *capital T* – hit him. It had all been based on false premises and flawed assumptions. His whole life. The whole world! He knew he should have been a Priest...

And further down the road at number 146, two men of the world discuss the things that make the world turn: money, football, and shagging.

In that order.

'NO!'

'Please! You don't need it. Ah'd lend it yer, if it was t'other way round!' Will begs.

'No!'

'But it's a dead cert,' the hardened gambler whines. 'Please! Ah need to pay 'er back all o' money she lent me for me 'olidee.'

'What 'olidee?'

'Exactly! She'll rip me balls off!'

'Well… you shouldn't 'ave bet it on another one of yer stupid three-legged nags!' snaps Tom, sick of Will's incessant scrounging. He turns his attention away from his rather annoying friend and picks his team. He clicks *proceed to match* on the screen and then sits back and allows the hurried flashes of text to conjure up the image of a football match in his head. And they say that people don't read anymore.

Will sulks as Tom's Rotherham side romp to another victory, taking them nine points clear of his second-placed Sheff U in the 2017-2018 Premiership. He wishes he spent as much time rutting slags as he did sat with Tom playing on this unfathomably addictive game. Come to think of it, the blame for failing two of his modules last semester can be placed squarely on the doorstep of the vendors of this narcotic software.

Will rises to swap seats with Tom as his side prepare for their third round cup tie away at Maltby Main. The virtual media are bigging up the game as something of a local derby.

Tom picks up a piece a colourful piece of paper which, at a first glance, looks uncannily like a small child's drawing. He scratches his head and stares out of the bedroom window, as if balancing a great truth. Eventually he speaks: ''ow many points is it if you go down on 'em, but they don't suck yer off? Do yer get the full five?' he asks, his 'tally' in one hand, a red crayon in the other.

Will rubs his stubbly, perfectly formed diamond-jaw thoughtfully. 'Yeah, ah reckon' he eventually answers. 'As long as either you go down on them, or they go down on you, yer gets yer five points oral bonus.'

'Nice one,' Tom smiles as he adds five points to his tally. He briefly glances up to grab the green felt tip, chuckling to himself as the pathetic non-league side take the lead against Will's Premiership giants. 'What 'ave yer called yer pros?'

'Me prozzies?' Wills looks over at his gigantic A3 tally that is spread over two textbooks on Tom's bed. 'Ah was gonna give 'em joke names, like Brandy and Shirley an' that, but in th'end ah just called 'em Pro 1, Pro 2 etc.'

Tom nods curtly in a stern, business-like fashion. 'Imaginative,' he quips. "ow many points yer got then mush?' he asks, reaching for his friend's tally.

'Gerrofff!!!' Will yells, snatching his tally out of Tom's thieving hands.

'Come on Will! Show us yours an' ah'll show yer mine! Yours will be 'igher anyways, won't it? Two in two nites, ah believe sir?'

Will pulls a smug face, and then slaps his tally down for Tom to see. He glances through the list of names with a raised eyebrow and stops part of the way down. 'Will,' he asks. 'Who's *The Flabster*? That 'un from last Sat?'

'Aye. Can't remember 'er name. That fat 'istory lass what come round 'ere an' 'ad a pop at us – fek knows wot she was on. Didn't even do owt that bad to 'er!'

'Mad,' Tom says, shaking his head. 'Still, brilliant comedy value. Especially for the new guy, that Jamalie.'

'Aye. Ne'ermind anyways. Ah got this feelin' ah'm on for the 'at trick tonite! Ah'll 'ave owt ta get to number forty-eight. Ah reet want to knob a black, if ah can. Ah sit next to this one on me course, she's well 'ot. Ah coul-'

Tom throws his crayon at him. 'Yer daft racist!'

Sheff U equalise in the last minute. Will tenses his right fist and punches the air.

'Yer jammy bastard!' Tom moans. 'Ey, what was that fat bird like anyways, any good?'

'Nah. Just the usual, like. Bit frigid.'

'D'yer get yer brown wings?'

'Not really. Ah tried poking it up at one point, but she wock up and made us teck it out,' Will says, his voice satiated with genuine regret.

'Ne'ermind mate. Guess who ah finally did last week?'

'Not…'

'Yep: 'annah.'

'Well that's quick work mate,' says Will sarcastically. 'Only took thee, what, six, seven month? Ah 'ope this means ah don't 'ave to 'ear any more on that dreary saga now. If ah 'ave to 'ear another word abart it ah think ah'll chuck up.'

'Like after a meal, ey?' Tom says, instantly regretting the slur.

Will turns to look at the monitor, completely ignoring his friend's cruel jibe. He needed to keep trim for the ladies, didn't he? What was he supposed to do – go to the gym? *As if.*

'Fine - if that's gonna be yer attitude, ah'll keep the details to mesen.'

And with that, Tom rolls himself a spliff, takes a slice of dead tree and a pen, and begins to write up his latest adventure.

Tom's top-secret super bumper action packed uni Diary of ~~adventure~~ epic adventures, Wednesday 21st April 2004.

I did it!! Finally! The girl who's kept me hanging on a string for six months has finally put out. It was well worth the wait, but it's only strengthened my already worryingly intense feelings for her. The last few nights I've lain awake having horrible nightmares about her going missing like that lass the other week. The states Hannah gets herself into, well . . . I worry don't I? For all her faults I do love her. Prob too much.

Anyway, it was last Sunday aft. Hannah just came round, totally out of the blue. I'd had loads of filthy messages off her all week, but by now I've learned not to expect owt from her. She came in, marched straight up to my bedroom, drew the curtains and pushed me down onto my bed. I'd been waiting months for this, I hadn't even been as nervous when I lost my virginity in those dingy nightclub bogs. What if I wasn't good enough for her? What if it didn't live up to months of fantasising? Fortunately, she didn't leave me much time to be nervous as Hannah seemed suspiciously expert at what she was doing for someone who hadn't been laid 'in ages.' It was weird —I just wanted to tell her how much I loved her, but . . . I don't know. It was all wrong. She was too aggressive. I thought the first time it would be, you know, nice. Well, love is nice, and love is good, but love isn't what Hannah was thinking of as she tore off my clothes and started sucking me off.

I have never, ever, heard a girl make that much noise. It was almost embarrassing. I remember thinking it was all a bit... embellished. After a couple more minutes my suspicions were all but confirmed when she squealed at the top of her voice and then pushed me off her.

'Got what I wanted,' she smirked as I laid there naked, still a few minutes away from what I wanted.

'What...?'

'I should go... I have to meet Winston down in town soon...' she began. Winston is this huge black dude who she reckons is just her 'best friend.' I wish I believed her. I want to.

'Oh no. Not like that girl,' I said half-laughing, praying that she was joking. 'Not after all the shite I've been through with yer, I've gotta finish the business.'

She laughed and began picking up her clothes off the floor. The way in which she casually picked them up while laughing to herself made me love her and hate her all at once. Even so, it was time to put nice guy, doormat Tommo to one side and bring back the heartbreak kid to put right and put down this situation.

I pushed her back down on the bed as she struggled pathetically. 'You ain't going nowhere,' I said with a smile on my face as I kissed around her neck and pushed her back down. She once told me she loved it rough, that she loved being dominated. Maybe with a girl like this you just have to show her who's boss.

She closed her eyes and we went at it again even louder this time. This time though I just stopped, got up and started to get dressed.

'WHAT THE FUCK ARE YOU DOING?' she shouted in genuine anger.

'I thought you had to meet Winston in town. I'm getting dressed so I can walk yer to the bus stop, then go for a few bevies with Will,' I said, cool as a cucumber. Prob cooler, actually.

'I WANT YOU TO FUCK ME NOW!!!' she shouted, standing up on my bed with my covers wrapped around her body. By this time, my boxers and T-shirt were on.

'I've lost interest now babe, come on, let's go,' I said as I pulled up my jeans and began to look around for my watch.

'NO-ONE REFUSES ME!! NO-ONE TELLS ME NO!!!' I could almost see the steam coming out of her ears. I raised an eyebrow.

'First time for everything,' said I, putting my hat on as I opened my bedroom door. 'I'll wait for yer downstairs.' I was walking out of that door feeling like the king of the world... then she got to me. The bitch got to me.

'I could always go somewhere else for sex...' she said calmly, reaching for her clothes. She had me. She had me over a barrel. I closed my bedroom door in front of me, and with that I stripped naked, got back into bed, and finished what I'd started. I didn't enjoy it half as much after that.

Afterwards, we were both laid there naked and I turned to her, just so I could hold her in my arms. I wanted to kiss her and tell her I loved her — yes Will, if you've nicked this again I am a great big poof — I wanted just to lay there for a little while with her in my arms, but she rolled away and wrapped herself up in my covers leaving me cold and naked to her right, and leaving my bed covers even crustier than usual.

'Rules,' she said, pointing a gaunt finger at me.

'Rules?' I exclaimed. What was she on with? Rules?

'You can't keep pestering me for sex. We only have sex when I want to.'

'Whoa whoa whoa princess,' I held up my hand. 'What if I don't want to?'

She laughed out loud. 'Please!! Like you can refuse me. Next rule, if I get a boyfriend, you aren't allowed to cry and make a fuss and stuff.'

I just laid there with my mouth wide open not believing what I was hearing. I couldn't even speak. This, I thought, was a girl who was in love with me, who was just too afraid to admit it. This, I thought, was a girl who wanted to be with me as badly as I wanted to be with her. She had told me she 'didn't think she'd survive' if I hurt her. She was just too scared to take a chance on me. Nevertheless, here we were in bed together after having our first shag. We'd taken what I considered to be a huge step towards a relationship. Apparently, she didn't agree.

'Boyfriend?' I shouted.

'Don't you dare get angry?' she shouted back. 'You scare me. You know how Cookie treated me. You remind me of him.'

I bit my lip and held my breath. 'Ah'm sorry.' I thought for a moment. 'If you don't wanna take the big step and go out with me, why don't we just see each other, casual like?'

'Sort of like fuck buddies,' she nodded. 'I suppose . . . But only when I want to. And you can't get upset when I pull.'

'WHAT?' I shouted again. She glared at me again.

'Ah'm sorry. What ah mean is if we're seeing each other we can't pull other people.'

'Then it's a relationship, dickhead!' She shook her head. 'I knew you'd be all possessive if I slept with you.'

I stood up and started to get dressed. 'Yeah, well...' I didn't finish my sentence. It would have gone something like 'Yeah, well, I'd hardly call not wanting you to bang other men possessive'. Instead I just looked at her, and I saw the same skinny, ugly, manipulative bitch that all my friends saw and warned me about. But I also saw her other side, and that's why I loved her. Ninety-nine per cent of the time I saw the cold heartless bitch in her, but sometimes, just sometimes, I saw her weak side. I saw her tender side. I saw the good in her. I looked at her and I saw a deep, caring, intelligent girl who hid behind the visage of a selfish bitch because she was terrified of being hurt again, and I think I loved her for those moments when she would let her guard down just for a second.

There was no sensation to compare with it. But this wasn't one of those times.

I turned to back to look at a fully-clothed, messy-haired Hannah. 'Come and stay here with us tonight,' I asked her with puppy-dog eyes. She opened her mouth to speak but I cut her off. 'I don't care if you don't want to have sex again. I just want to wake up next to you. Please. It'd mean a lot to me.'

She put her hair brush in her bag. 'I'm busy tonight. Walk me to the bus.'

'Oi! Shakespeare,' Will yells across at Tom who is lost in catharsis. He is pointing at the portable TV on top of the chest of drawers. 'Check it out.'

'*…a twenty-year old Sports Science student was reported missing this morning by her concerned…*'

Tom shakes his head. 'Puts stuff in perspective, dunnit? An' ah thought ah 'ad problems.'

'Yer,' Will replies, his attention once again focused on his team. 'Ey, ah 'ope it don't put birds off goin' out. It was already a bit of a sausage fest last nite, thinkin' on. It better not get no worse!'

'We were steamin' last nite, weren't we?' Tom reflects. 'It would 'ave been well easy for us ta get done in. Ah can't even remember getting 'ome.'

53

'Aye. We'll 'ave ta be careful. Meck sure we allus teck Gristle out wi' us from now on!'

'Yeah reet,' Tom scoffs. 'It's probably 'im what killed 'em both!'

The two friends laugh together.

Then they stop laughing, and hold each other in a cold stare, just for a heartbeat.

And then they laugh again, and all is well with their little world.

THE DELICATE SOUND OF CHUNDER

AH RECKON ONCE YOU'VE BEEN TO UNI – *if yer do it reet, that is – yer can't go back to the real world. Look at Spadge. 'e's provin' it. It's like… it's like 'eroin. Even those junkies who sort themsens out, write books an' meck movies an' 'ave millions in the bank still know it's theer. They know that the pleasure is theer to be 'ad, but they can't touch it. An' that's what's 'appenin' wi' the old Spadgewalker. 'e's grievin' for a life that 'e can never have again.*

For me it will be even worse; ah know it will. Ah can't even bear ta think about leavin' it all behind. Ah just can't. Ah know it seems a long way off for us now – the first year not even ovva – but it's just flown an' time's gettin' quicker every day.

Sometimes ah wonder what it would be like to look at me life through different eyes. Ah'm not talkin' about some weird out o' body experience - ah'd just like to see mesen through, say, 'is eyes. 'im. That lanky streak o' piss stood over by the drinks machine, thinkin' 'e's somethin' in 'is Loughborough vest. Ah'd love ta know what 'e mecks o' us. Theer 'e is, sippin' 'is mineral water like a fag, doin' 'is little warm-up stretches. It's a pint o' diesel what yer need in yer before a big race. Everyone knows that. Tradition, innit.

'What d'yer meck o' these lot then, Will?' ah ask.

Will turns to me an' quietly voices 'is concerns about them all bein' ravin' 'omos an' them needin' to be taught a lesson about runnin'. Yes – runnin'. Will an' me. We're both on the runnin' team. Ah know it sounds rubbish, but it tecks far less effort than proper sport - it requires no skill; it keeps your gut down (especially if, like Will, you regularly partake in a bit o' the ol' barfing); and, most important o' all, it 'as all the fittest women. Well, apart from the Netball team. Oh, an' Gristle 'as a big thing for the Women's Rugby team, but ah can safely say 'e's alone on that one.

Ah nod very slightly before neckin' the last few dregs o' me pint. 'Agreed mate,' ah say to Will. 'Thing is though,' ah pause, uncertain as to whether or not ah should show weakness. Ah fuck it. 'Lookin' at them lot, an' then lookin' at us lot... thing is... well... they'll piss all o'er us, wayn't they?'

Will laughs, not wi'out concern. 'e knows ah speak the truth.

'They're theer suppin' their mineral waters, warmin' up in all their matchin' vests an' that. We're 'ere in Garlic Bread *t-shirts gettin' leathered! Ah mean, look at Martin. Just look at him. 'e's a joke. 'e doesn't even 'ave any proper trainers.'*

'Stop worryin',' Will says dismissively. 'We'll 'ammer 'em.'

Ah get the distinct impression that it isn't me that 'e's tryin' to convince... Eyup. That one wi' the fringe is givin' Mel the eye. Will won't like that.

Suddenly an' aggressively, Will leaps to his feet. Ah smell ructions. 'e struts straight over to 'im wi' the fringe.

'Reet then,' Will says. 'You lot ready?'

'Yes, almost,' says fringe-boy. 'e sounds well 'aughty – like a posh bird, but a bloke.

'Did... um... Your lot's coach tell yer about our special rules, like?'

Fringe-boy is brickin' it now. Absolutely brickin' it.

'Special rules? I didn't hear mention of any special rules.'

'Ah best run through 'em now then.'

Fringe-boy 'olds out 'is 'and in a sorta "stop" sign. It doesn't touch Will's chest, but it's too close for comfort. Fringey turns 'is 'ead back towards the rest o' 'is team. 'Does anyone else know anyhing about these special rules?'

Silence.

'There you have it. If you don't mind, we'll crack on with the eight hundred metres then-'

'Ah fek off,' says Will, pushin' Fringe-boy so 'ard 'e falls over onto his public-school-silver-spoon arse. Ah teck a step closer just in case, but immediately it's pretty clear that this guy isn't gonna retaliate. 'e looks on the edge o' tears. Poof.

'You're on our turf now, sunshine. An' we 'ave our own rules 'ere what date back to when… um… William Willyforce-'

'Wilberforce?' ejaculates Fringe-boy, somewhat bravely.

'Yep, 'im an all. Ever since they was on the runnin' team, back in the day, they allus 'ad it where yer 'ad to run two 'undred metres, then neck a pint o' diesel, then run another two 'undred metres, an' then neck another pint o' diesel, an' so on until you've done an whole mile. A chunder *mile!'*

'But that's impossible!' Fringe-boy almost squeals. Mel does not *look impressed; 'e's blown that one.*

'Bollocks it is,' says I, confident in me drinkin' abilities. 'Me an' you. Chunder mile. Now.'

'Now Mr…. um…?'

'Just call me Spadge.'

'Spadge?'

Spadge shrugs his shoulders. 'That's me.'

'*Indeed.* I notice in your CV that it says you enjoy providing a 'pleasant and effective' service. In what ways do you think that you do this?'

Who would ever have thought that an interview for *Skyline Holiday Camp* would be this hard? Spadge inhales deeply.

'I think it's important to meet the customer's expectations which in this job… er… would be getting their meals to them quickly and efficiently, for example… whilst, um… maintaining a pleasant… exterior.'

Spadge recalls his old mate from school, Greg #2, who got into working for a local radio station. Greg now spends half his days 'de-umming' interviews – cutting out all the 'ers' and 'ums' from pre-recorded interviews. If only Greg #2 was here now with his digital scissors.

'Very good. We also noticed that you've had some experience dealing with sensitive matters… oh…' the interviewer glances back at the piece of paper on his desk.

'Oh… well, a *fortnight*'s experience at any rate, speaking to people about being the victims of crime. Is that right?'

'Yeah, yeah.'

'How would you react, say, if you were bringing out somebody's evening meal, and… you noticed that they were being… erm… the victim of a crime?'

'I don't… really… follow. How do you mean? A victim in what way?'

The interviewer holds out his big fat hands theatrically. 'Oh I don't know. They are being… er… *assaulted* by another patron.'

'Does that happen a lot at *Skyline*, then?' Spadge asks, wanting to retire.

'Ah feel a bit bad now, see. We was only playin' wi' 'im.'

Ah nod solemnly. Against all known laws o' medical science, ah feel fine. Better than fine. Certainly better than four-'undred metre Fringe-boy!

Ah'm absolutely buzzin', man. Ah feel like King o' the World. If it wasn't for fear o' chuckin' up purple sick all over 'em all, ah'd be all for gettin' 'oisted up on the team's shoulders an' all that. Ah can tell Mel is impressed an' all. She keeps givin' us the eye.

Fringe-boy's stretcher is loaded up onto the Ambulance. Under any other circumstances, this would be well funny. It took them about an 'our to get the Ambulance up over them Tellytubby 'ills behind the 'alls o' Residence.

All the Loughborough team are gathered round the Ambulance givin' us all some reet evils. If yer ain't up to the game, yer don't step in the ring mush. Simple as. Still. Poor bastard. Collapsed lung at his age. Don't bear thinkin' about.

'I can't believe you did it in eleven minutes!' says Mel, 'er eyes all big an' 'er tits all wobbly. 'That's a pretty respectable running time for a mile, never mind with drinking eight pints of snakey b too!'

Ah shrug me shoulders arrogantly. It's well weird gettin' more attention than Will. 'Well, y'know. Cocky bastards, wont they? Needed learnin''.

'I can't believe you haven't been sick!' she says, passin' me another pint.

'All man,' says I, thumpin' me chest. She's gettin' it tonite!

Will sneers.

Wednesdays are like the best nites ever. Ah love 'em. Ah live for 'em. Yer just can't beat 'em, man.

Ah'm a bit worse for wear now though if truth be known, but ah've proper slowed-up the drinkin' an' ah'm concentratin' on Mel. Ah know ah should be focusin' on 'annah, but well... Mel's well up for it an' ah 'ate waste. On the dance floor earlier she was grindin' on me, an' now stood in the crush at the bar she's deliberately got her right tit pushin' into me left side. Gaggin' for it. Ah know she's not the best lookin' lass in the world, but she's gorra crackin' body an' she's even done 'er 'air nice tonight.

Will's got the reet face on. Don't know what's up wi' 'im... No - ah do. It's 'cos 'e 'asn't pulled yet. 'e's allus like this when 'e 'asn't got a woman; it does me nut in.

'Who wor that?' asks Gristle as Will hangs up his mobile.

'It was Spadge. Ah cun't 'ear him reet well, though. 'e was banging on about gettin' a job at *Skyline* or somet in Skeggy.'

Gristle laughs his cartoon-dog laugh. He then takes a large swig of his pint and salutes with it towards Tom who is getting off with Mel at the bar. 'Go on mah son! Ah'm surprised you 'ant 'ad 'er yet. Well tidy.'

Will mutters curses under his breath. 'Ah'm goin' bar.' And with that, he storms off.

Between what is now now, and will be now shortly, devilish thoughts enter Will's selfish mind. A cunning plan begins to form. *Tom's already pretty vegged, ain't 'e? It can't teck all that much more to get 'im proper fucked. Well, not proper proper fucked. That's wheer ah come in…*

Half one in the morning and the lights start to raise. Tired bar staff half-heartedly rove through the Union's various rooms collecting glasses, cleaning and moaning. Bouncers clear out the last few punters; punters like Gristle, who is sat at a table in the corner supping his pint, *inviting them* to try and remove him; punters like Tom, who is sparked out in a pool of purple puke and orange piss under that same table.

He will really, really regret wearing that cream suit when he wakes up.

'Ah you tool-' moans Gristle as he drags Tom's stinking, inert carcass across the concrete floor of the university car park by his hair. He can't resist putting the boot in a bit. He's got the responsibility of having to take him home, so it's his right, surely?

Pissed-up lightweight can't 'andle 'is fuckin' drink. 'e would 'ave 'ad that fit Mel an' all if 'e wouldn't 'ave got caned. 'is loss. Will took her 'ome! Tommo missed out on a reet shag theer.

Over by the Wilberforce building Gristle suddenly hears a horrendous, guttural squeal. As soon as he hears it he freezes. If he had time to think about it, he'd inevitably come to the conclusion that someone else is getting done-in. Unfortunately – or fortunately, depending on how you look at these things – for Gristle's mind to run through a train of thought that complex, a full ninety-minutes is normally required, if not extra time and penalties. As it is, he unfreezes just as quickly and races off towards the building, leaving Tom stinking, bleeding and unconscious on the ground.

Cats fating! After all that it was just fuckin' cats fatin'. The little fat ginger one is taking a right hiding, though. It won't last much longer under that onslaught. *That big black 'un is a reet nasty fucker.*

Gristle: eighteen-stone death machine. Strikes fear into the hearts of even those closest to him. Bites off the ears of erstwhile loved ones. Cuts off the fingers of people who owe him money, and then uses them as props in the most perverse of drinking games.

Gristle: cradling an overweight and injured ginger kitten.

Gristle: leaving his friend to either die of exposure, choke to death on his own sick (rock 'n' roll), or be murdered.

Gristle: taking his little baby pusscat home.

Little baby… *Rocky.*

TREACHERY IN THE PURSUIT OF BEAVER

THE PARTING OF WAYS AFTER THE EXAMS
at the end of June had been hard. It wasn't so much the people that it was hard to say goodbye to; after all, Spadge was long gone now and there's only so much of Will that you can take. It was the things they represented that Tom missed the most - the uni lifestyle, the booze, the women. The spring had brought with it an onslaught of barbeques, alcohol and even the odd fling here and there, and although Tom's body was enjoying a break from the bombardment of toxins, his heart and his mind missed the uni life.

Spending his nights alone in that (currently surprisingly tidy) house would have made for a refreshing change, though. After the hectic second semester he could have used the solitude to get back into running, grow a colossal beard, or perhaps even just catch up on nearly nine months' worth of sleep. Unfortunately, Gristle had elected to stay and 'keep 'im company' for the rest of the summer holiday; his precious few months of privacy torn from him as painfully as a scab from a wound.

Strangely, little Rocky was making the summer just that little bit more bearable though. Tom hadn't had a pet since childhood, and so he'd found that he was completely unprepared for the intense emotional bond that he now shares with his new feline friend.

The cat has even made him grow up a little bit - he's got a routine going now and everything. He comes in from work and opens the back door, and in trundles Rocky; more often than not with the bloody spoils of war hanging from its mouth. As soon as some wet food is put out though, Rocky soon forgets the kill and, in true feline style, takes the easy option.

After eating, Tom usually puts a ball of string in his back pocket, but in doing so ensures that just enough string is unravelled to drag along the ground behind him. This way he can cook his tea and potter about a bit while Rocky just chases him around. Following his mad half-hour, Rocky invariably curls up inside the airing cupboard and has a bit of a nap before buggering off again come dark. Buggering off home, perhaps, Tom finds himself wondering.

Home. Were he speaking rather than thinking, the word would have stuck in his throat. It was impossible for Tom to contemplate returning home for the summer as the majority of students do; such a simple concept is beyond him. Whereas most students, through poverty, are forced to return to their parental home every summer to live rent-free and work shite jobs just to pay off a fraction of their insurmountable overdrafts, he no longer has the option. For him, the very notion of home is one buried under a mountain of hurt; a mountain so large that it eclipses almost everything else. The mountain has become so familiar to Tom that he no longer notices its presence. He never looks back.

Except in his dreams.

Inside his head, Tom is walking home from work. He isn't in Hull; he's back in the village where he grew up. Everything is softer and brighter, and nothing seems to exist beyond the boundaries of his perception. For some reason, the whole place feels strangely artificial, and even though his conscious mind knows that it isn't real, right now it is real, and it is everything.

He is walking past a small playing field on the new estate, just five minutes' walk from the home where he lived with his mother, father and little brother. There are no children having a kickabout on the field though; in fact not a single blade of grass moves. Dead calm. Every single atom is frozen. Tom glances in slow motion over his shoulder to see a passenger jet falling from the sky. No smoke or flames; just an eerie silence.

Tom wrinkles his brow, almost annoyed that the plane isn't hurtling towards ground in an epic blaze of glory. Instead it drops silently, gracefully. Tom, almost lucid, takes the conscious decision not to move. He's going to stand his ground this time. He's had this dream a hundred times before and there is little left in it for him to fear.

He focuses on the front of the aircraft as it gets bigger and bigger, increasing in size exponentially. Tom's resolve begins to weaken. It's not getting bigger and bigger; *it's perspective!* The sheer enormity of the craft bears down on him. This is when you're supposed to wake up.

But he can't. He's awake, and the nightmare is unfolding yet again in front of his waking eyes like a song on repeat. He's thankful that his death doesn't seem to hurt. Or maybe it does; maybe he's just become used to it. He feels like he's been hit hard, and then he's overcome by a strange dizziness that eventually succumbs to nausea. He envisages himself as a swatted fly, buzzing around insanely and about to die. His last thoughts before oblivion are of Rocky. *Who'll feed him now?*

One more time the world falls away in a bath of flames and two burning eyes pierce Tom's very soul; the last thing that he'll ever see…

''ello? 'ello? Can you 'ear me?' the voice cuts through his twisted vision and within seconds Tom feels his heartbeat beginning to slow. He wipes the sweat from his brow. 'I'm sorry about that, sir. You're through to the *East Riding Power Services* Contact Centre. *My* name is Tom. *How* can ah *H*elp you today?'

Fuck. It 'appened again.

* * *

'I'm not sure I really like leaving you here on your own, princess,' Anna's father tells her as he dumps the last of her many, many bags down in the middle of the living room. 'Are you sure you won't come back and stay with me and your mum for a bit longer? I can't see there being any more jobs up here than there are back home.'

Anna smiles at her father and wraps her sylphlike arms around him. 'Don't be daft, Dad. We live on a farm in the middle of nowhere. No offence, but I don't fancy shovelling shit for the summer.'

The old man looks down at her warmly.

'I know what's really bothering you and it needn't,' Anna tells him with quiet authority. 'Those girls vanished months ago and there hasn't been so much as a single assault round here since – student crime has actually *gone down*, if anything.'

'Don't you think that's because students have all been too scared to go out? Or maybe because even the yobbos who're usually trying to mug all you students are running scared? There's a killer still out there.'

'Dad!' snaps Anna. 'You don't know that. No bodies have been found.'

Her father frowns.

Anna holds her hands up to pacify him. 'Look. I promise I won't venture out at night. I'll get a job – day shift – and every night I'll be locked up safe in here.'

The old dishevelled farmer smiles and waves an accusatory figure at his daughter. 'Just like your old mum! You just be careful then, dear.'

Within moments, a much lighter people carrier is turning off Worthington Street and disappearing over the brow of Black Hill.

Anna slumps down onto one of her many, many bags.

Suddenly she's afraid.

'Yer gonna 'ave ta ring us back, ah'm on me mobile fern,' the voice hisses.

'Ah'm afraid ah can't do that, sir' replies Tom's impassive voice. 'We're inbound-only.'

'Ah'll *inbound* you in a minute! Tha' can bloody well tell us why ah got a bill in fronta me for seven 'undred and twenny free parnd, forty-eight pee! Ah'm an old aged pensioner; ah have me telly and me radio and there's no way tha's tellin' me that...' the voice goes on and on.

Tom begins to apologise vacantly. Only seconds have passed since he was bathed in flames, but already the harsh radiance of reality is beginning to render his waking nightmare just a silly little episode, something to be forgotten about; just something else for the chlozapine to sort out. 'Does your bill *h*ave a big '*E*' next to the amount of units used?'

'Yer what?' asks the voice of the elderly man... or elderly lady. It's hard to be sure. Tom really hates this job. I mean, *he really hates it*. From half eight until five to five he spends all day every day apologising for a company that, at best, has its head up its arse; at worst, despicably sets out to rob its customers. Tom suspects that the truth lies somewhere in the middle, but probably closer to the latter.

'In the top right*h*and corner of your bill there should be a breakdown of charges. If any of the readings are followed by a capital '*E*', then your bill *h*as been estimated by the computer. If you can provide me with a meter reading, ah can generate you a new bill.'

'Ooh aye. It 'as. Why 'av they done that, then? Th'man 'asn't been for months ta read it... Oooh. Me fern battery's goowin on me...'

'I'm afraid *East Riding Power* no longer *h*ave every meter read each quarter. The computer now estimates customers' readings and the onus is on them to provide us with an accurate reading.' The words came out of his mouth but they weren't his. They were quoted verbatim from the handbook, complete with aitches and free from inflection. Free from personality. He was employed to be a talking chimp; a verbal punch bag; a faceless drone upon which customers could unleash their pent-up fury.

'That's bloody ridiculous. Ah've been a customer of 'em for over fifty years and ah've never 'eard the like o' this. Does tha' computer always estimate a bill wot should be about eighty quid at seven 'undred and twenny free parnd, forty-eight pee?'

Silence.

'Ah say, does tha' computer always estimate a bill wot should be about eighty quid at seven 'undred and twenny free parnd, forty-eight pee? Seven 'undred and twenny free parnd, forty-eight pee? Ah'm a pensioner tha' knows!'

Silence.

''ello? 'ello? Can tha 'ear me, thee? Where's tha gone lad?'

'Yeah; alreet. The computer allus churns out estimate bills about a thousand per cent 'igher than what they should be – you know why? Because most people don't read 'em. They just pay 'em. Some daft sods even go on direct debit an' don't know what's 'it 'em when they check their bank balances. It's a conscious policy to screw money out of customers... *Why?* Because they can! Know what else? AH 'ATE 'EM TOO. An' ah 'ate gettin' abuse from people like you, because no matter 'ow much you gi' me stick, ah still feel fuckin' sorry for yer!'

Silence. Tom honestly doesn't know if he's actually said these things, but a nagging feeling inside tells him that the customer heard him regardless.

'ello? 'ello? Can tha 'ear me? Yer there lad?' yells Tom's earpiece, and he allows himself the luxury of breathing once again. Part of him wishes that he did have the guts to actually say what he thinks, but that particular brand of courage eludes him presently, save in his head. *Best just to think it, but even then...*

'Can I take your meter reading please, ma'am?' says Tom, his heart being slowly dragged down to the bottom of the Humber.

This really has to be the most depressing job ever. He gets all this shite, and no bloody thanks. He has to sit through briefings about how in about fifty years' time there'll be an energy crisis the like of which the world has never seen because even so-called 'green' organisations protest about the government's proposals to build wind farms to save the world. They'd spoil 'natural beauty', see. Tom feels himself sinking deeper and deeper...

It's worse than that, though. As the temp, all the rest of the staff think that they're better than him. *Sinking...*

He spends his days under the command of fat, balding, talentless Nazis who are made team leaders when they reach a certain weight. *Sinking...*

...and their lackeys who think that they can throw their weight around just because they are 'assistant team leaders' or 'coaches', purely down them having worked for the company since leaving school at sixteen. *Sinking...*

... and, just to finish him off, the Inland Revenue bend him over and take him to brown town every Friday night at midnight, taking him for a quarter of his pitiful wage just to line the pockets of the likes of *'cash in 'and'* Gristle and *'ah'm not at uni, 'onest guv'nor'* Will as their fraudulently-claimed Jobseekers' Allowance. *Sinking...*

'I'm just generating your new bill now ma'am. Bear with me...'

Sinking…

'There we go. It'll be sixty-nine pounds and thirteen pence. I'll get that in the post for you this afternoon.'

His finger clicks print, and suddenly he's under. His lungs fill with liquid fury and for the briefest of moments he is consumed by guilt. Were he born ninety years earlier, he would have ended up spending four years in the trenches. He could be paralysed, have cancer, be an arm or a leg short, or be bound by love to nurse a moribund spouse. He could have spent twelve hours every day in darkness down the pit for sixty years like his old grandfather. Did his grandfather ever complain? His guilt only fuels his anger at *East Riding Power*, at the world, and at himself. Tom needs a reason to be able to justify his depression, but like just about everything else important in his life, it evades him.

Behind his consciousness his illness sits, festering. He can feel its effects, but he can't get at the heart of it. He's safely locked it away behind a chemical wall constructed around his pre-frontal cortex. There it must remain.

Tom sits on the lavatory in *East Riding Power*'s clinically modern toilet. This could mean that it's either his eleven o'clock shitbreak, or his two forty-five shitbreak. Tom is thankful that it's the latter, as every second that he spends spouting the company's scripted rhetoric is further eroding any semblance of self-respect that he once had. A little over an hour to go, that's all; if he's lucky he might be away by five to five.

The first few bars of a blockbuster sci-fi movie's theme ring out in all their polyphonic glory, just as they do in lectures when he deliberately leaves his phone turned on so that should anyone ring him, everybody will know just how cool his tastes are. 'Y'alright Spadge, 'ows *Skyline*? Is Will alreet?'

Tom idly pulls as much toilet roll out of the holder as he can feasibly fit in his pockets as he speaks. *Well, times is 'ard!* 'You're jokin' me. 'e never! 'e's a fuckin' filthy chuff.'

Content that his pockets are now full (but not *too* full) he moves on to the wiping of his arse – a delicate enough operation whilst holding a mobile phone; doubly so when his nasty case of *Farmer Giles* is taken into account. 'Ne'er mind, mush. *Aaaah…* Sorry mate, just wipin' mesen… Fuck off! Look, if you were getting abused all day long by psychotic grannies you wouldn't wanna put the phone down on a pleasant conversion just while you wipe up a bit of Brad Pitt. Wait on mate, ah think someone's comin in…'

It'll be Matty, me team leader, come to sack me! he thinks.

Tom puts his hand over the speaker grille and tries to listen. This is all he needs. If he gets sacked, he won't even be able to afford September's rent. He'll be out on the streets; no-one to turn to. Only one thing for it. Tom squeezes for all his life is worth.

'Oh my,' squeals a slightly effeminate voice from outside the cubicle. 'Who fathered that?'

Tom coughs inside the cubicle. 'Better out than in, Davey Boy! Thank fuck for that! It's alreet, Spadge, it's just *Dave Straight but Camp*.'

'*Just* Straight Camp Dave! Wooooooooooo. Cheeky sod! Is it a bird?' Dave begins to gyrate against the toilet door, making what he believes to be sex noises. They're not.

'Sorry Spadge,' says Tom, laughing. 'No it's not a bird! It's just Spadge! Sorry mate, go on…. Yeah…. I said fuck off, Straight Camp! Dickhead.'

Just for emphasis, Tom bangs on the toilet door. Hard.

Deflated, the gayest straight man that ever there was shuffles quietly towards a urinal.

'Anyways Spadge... Oh man! Ah forget to tell yer. Ah've gorra cat! It's all man! We called him Rock- oh did 'e? Oh reet. Ah didn't know.'

Tom spends about four minutes pacing back and forth within the cubicle - very small paces, obviously - and nodding whilst he listens to Spadge rabbit on about shite.

And then Spadge piques his interest with an unusual request.

'Yeah... no probs. Is she fit...? Okay. 'ave you told 'er ah'll be droppin' round? An' she wants us to? Fantastic! Weird, like, but fantastic!'

Tom presses *End Call, Menu,* * on his mobile and then smiles to himself. 'Good ol' Spadge. Another Anna for me tally!'

Tom checks his bleach-stained hair via the reflection in the window. It's getting disgracefully long now, his burgeoning locks held in place only by a girly alice band. He'd noticed people staring at his hair in the street; he reckoned he even saw one woman smirk at it. Mindful of such things, he quickly removes the hair band, tucks his lengthy fringe behind his ear and then carefully constructs his pulling face. *Positivity, baby. Positivity.*

In the last split second before the door is opened, Tom looks away and adjusts his skinny tie. As this new Anna opens the door, Tom turns to face her with a look of feigned surprise on his face that soon gives way to an easy smile. 'Alreet. Anna, innit?'

'Ah! Spadge's friend,' she says, sounding genuinely pleased. 'I bet you think I'm a right weirdo! Come in...'

Ah might be gettin' a double-name bonus on me tally... Tom thinks to himself as he crosses the threshold.

Anna stands in her new seventies' terracotta kitchen and waits for her new eighties' kettle to boil. To tell the truth, she feels a bit stupid. Jobless, poor, lonely and bored to tears she'd phoned around all her friends until one finally answered – Spadge, one of her friends from her course who'd dropped out just after Christmas. His mates still lived two doors down and she'd asked him if he was living up here for summer, but it turns out he's working as a waiter for *Skyline* or something with his mate, that tosser Will Surewood. *Christ, that was a mistake and a half.* Spadge was a nice bloke though, and he offered to send his two old housemates who are still up here round with a cup of sugar to welcome her to the street – a nice enough offer, but she can't help feeling like a Billy-no-mates charity case.

Thinking about it, she remembered this Tom guy from a night out near the beginning of the year, back in Freshers' Week. She'd quite fancied him at the time, but he'd ended up getting off with that Hannah from E Block. She was a filthy slapper – apparently Phil the Greek from D Block did her up the bum and she shat all over him.

'I hope you don't take sugar,' Anna says, smiling as she passes him his steaming hot cuppa. 'I was expecting a delivery.'

'Cheers,' says Tom, oblivious to the joke, and no wonder – Spadge hadn't said anything to him about sugar.

'Sorry 'bout all the mess, I haven't had chance to unpack anything,' Anna apologises. There are two boxes neatly placed in the right-hand corner of the living room just beneath the large bay window, and one small bag next to her on the sofa.

'Don't worry 'bout it,' says Tom, looking curiously at his tea rather than drinking it. 'Looks like a decent 'ouse. They've done it up better than ourn. Is it as nice as 'alls?'

'Oh yeah, I forgot. You weren't in Halls last year, were you? You lived with Spadge and Will and that lot.'

Tom smirks and raises an eyebrow at the mention of Will's name. *So that dickhead Will did tell all his mates!* Anna rages, silently.

Anna kicks Tom playfully spilling tea on his one clean work shirt. He's genuinely aggrieved, but after a month of just Gristle and a cat for company, a bit of female flirtation certainly doesn't go amiss. 'I didn't think you'd know about that. I'm not like that normally,' she lies, 'he took advantage!'

'Sounds like Will,' says Tom, staring down his tea-stained shirt. He's sure that tea doesn't leave a stain that colour – what the hell has she put in this brew? What if she's trying to poison him? Concentrating hard, he puts the vision of himself vomiting blood on the carpet out of his mind – at least for now – replacing the image of a slow and painful death with a mental picture of this new Anna bird in the niff. It does have a certain poetry to it.

'Will tells me everything yer see,' he ventures. 'Ah think you were number thirty-six.'

Anna learns forward with mock indignation on her face, mouth wide open. 'BASTARD! I can't believe he counts us!'

''e 'as this tally thing wi' you all on,' Tom continues, ruthlessly betraying his *'bestest friend'* in the hope of getting a go on his new neighbour. 'It's sick if yer ask me.'

Ironically, Will would praise such treachery in the pursuit of beaver. 'You all 'ave marks out o' five in different categories. You, for example,' he says, looking up as if he's taxing his memory (but in reality is just carrying out his own summary assessment), 'got five for tits, but your arse let you down. You did good on 'x-factor' though – 'e's normally real tight wi' marks on that one. Still, arse looks alreet to me. You done a bit o' weight since then or somet?'

Tom smiles to himself. *Still got the ol' magic.*

Anna now looks genuinely upset, and Tom realises that perhaps he's gone a bit too far. Rather than shag him, she'll probably never shag anybody ever again.

'Well…' he goes on, desperately trying to salvage the situation. 'It's only 'cos 'e's insecure. Tiny cock, ah reckon.' That should do it. *Oh shit! No it won't - she's seen it.*

'…and floppy!' she chimes in, much to Tom's surprise and delight. At that, he casually shifts her bag off the sofa with a flick of the wrist and plants himself in its place beside her.

'Really?'

'No,' she says matter of factly. Tom's face drops.

'It is little though… yeah?' Tom asks almost pleadingly.

'Not really. About seven inches, if I remember right.'

'That is little!' he taunts. Anna raises an eyebrow.

'Yours bigger then, is it?'

'Twelve-incher,' lies Tom.

'How big is it really?' she asks mockingly.

'About twelve inches' he replies, straight-faced. 'Maybe even twelve an' 'afe.'

'It's not. No chance,' laughs Anna.

'Believe what you like,' says Tom, quite proud of his spontaneous display of guile. Well, he had learned from the best. 'Ah 'ave the truth on me side.' The girl that he had met just ten minutes ago looks back at him expectantly.

'Prove it then,' she challenges, folding her arms.

Bugger, thinks Tom.

SNAKES & LADDERS

GRISTLE NECKS THE REMNANTS OF HIS FIRST pint, and then moves onto his second. With his Chav hair, oily denim dungarees, and torn lumberjack shirt he looks like the kind of stranger that mothers tell their children to be wary of. He looks eagerly across at his friend. His entertainer. His own private storyteller.

Entertain me or ah might get bored an' 'ave ta bust some 'eads.

'So reet, ah'm sat theer in 'er living room, literally about ten minutes after ah'd arrived, an' ah've got this fifteen-inch ruler in me 'and an' this Anna bird is-'

''er from E Block?' Gristle interrupts.

'No, that's 'annah. This is Anna,' snaps Tom, annoyed.

Gristle looks very, very confused.

'Ah'd really done it this time – me an' me bloody stories! In the end, ah just thought fuck it, an' pulled me kegs down – all man! *'e who dares wins*, ah thought.'

'Wot she do?' grunts Gristle, his second pint already half empty.

'Well… Me cock didn't quite stretch to the twelve-inch finish line,' Tom confesses, laughing. 'But ah reckon she was still well impressed.'

Gristle leans so far forward that Tom can see the gaps in his teeth and smell the alcohol and gasoline on his breath. 'She suck you off?' he leers, letting out just a little bit of a burp as he does so.

'Well, that's between me an' 'er innit!' Tom snaps defensively.

'So nowt 'appenned then?'

'Nah,' Tom smiles. 'She looked well shocked, laughed a bit, then asked me for me mobile; said we should go for a drink in the week or somet. Still, better than nowt ah reckon.'

Gristle just laughs. Not at Tom; not with Tom. Not at anything. He just laughs, and drinks, and then starts a fight with a ginger bloke at the bar. That's Gristle.

Anna wakes up parched. She fumbles around for her bedside clock to see what time it is, before suddenly getting her bearings and remembering that she's back at uni and nothing has been unpacked. She reaches down onto the floor beside the bed and turns her mobile on. A shot of adrenaline races through her body as she reads the welcome note on its screen.

Somebody has altered it.

You're going to die tonight, it tells her.

She's wide awake.

Tom sits bolt upright in his bed. Gradually his breathing begins to slow again. He takes several deep breaths then lays back down, closing his eyes and rolling onto his side. He feels a sharp pain in his chest and his hands begin to shake uncontrollably. Maybe he ingested something at work, or at that Anna's house? Or even at the pub? Automatically he rules out the last option – *alcohol kills all germs, dunnit? There was that dodgy tea, though... Poison! Poisoned!*

His heart begins to beat faster again.

Every time he tries to close his eyes and go back to sleep, he thinks that he can feel himself rising from his mattress; several cold and clammy hands beneath him, gently forcing him to rise.

The poet Edward Young once said that *"by night, an atheist half-believes in God,"* or words to that effect. Right now Tom believes in anything and everything.

Rise.

It is dark and the frozen, dank hands of the dead are lifting him.

They are there. It is not his imagination. It is fact. Reality. He cannot deny their presence.

One hundred and ten percent kosher.

Shouldn't 'ave drank tonite…

He pulls the drawstring light switch down (the type you might typically find in a bathroom) and looks around his small, clinically and thriftily-decorated bedroom. Overwhelmed by the non-committal neutral shades and terrorised by something that can't quite exist, a voice that he can't quite hear whispers to him.

Ah'm not 'ere. This isn't 'appening.

Pulling himself out of his bed and wiping the sweat from his brow, he picks up his new mobile (one of these fancy new Bluetooth ones) and turns it on. He just needs to chill for a bit. *It's just stress from work, aggravatin' stuff.*

Games, games, games. *Tetris*, nah; *Bounce*, nah; *Snake* – yep. *That sounds alreet.* Tom presses the button to display the instructions.

"Make the snake grow longer by directing it to the food. Use the keys 2, 4, 6 and 8. You cannot stop the snake or make it go backwards. Try not to hit the walls or the tail, or the snake will…"

Tom pauses.

'Or the snake will… *die.*'

As he stares into his phone… through his phone… beyond his phone… the two burning eyes that plague his nightmares become almost visible. Without realising it, Tom is quietly muttering instructions to himself as a monk might mutter the word of God. Sometimes his speech is so quiet that it's almost inaudible, yet his lips do form the words and his larynx does move to produce the softest of sounds. The words just flow right out of him and he can't stop them. He isn't even aware that he's speaking them.

'… and every memory, every experience will die with it. All its life it has searched for food, and more food, and more food; a never-ending quest. If navigated successfully towards every possible piece of food, in the end, ironically, the snake will die anyway because it will become so large that it cannot move without touching its tail or the wall. But if you martyr yourself to caution and avoid the food, you will simply navigate the snake around in circles. Forever.'

All the colour has drained from his eyes, which both stare expressionlessly into his brand new phone. His mouth moves slowly and precisely - these words are not his.

'Unless you can get the highest score, nothing will remain of the snake post-mortem. It will be as if it never existed. Even the highest scoring snake's life is only preserved as a score – a mere number; not nearly enough to capture the essence of the snake that once was. Eventually its skin will flake away as its form slowly decomposes and the worms will feast on its serpentine body.'

Whilst the vessel of his body, locked in some sort of autopilot, speaks about the mortality of snakes, Tom is once again a prisoner of his nightmares. The aeroplane is getting bigger and bigger; his resolve at breaking point. The sheer enormity of the craft bears down on him. This is when he's supposed to wake up.

'You're just like the snake. It's all about the game. Some score 1,013. Most want to score high. Some score just 9, some score 81. Some don't score at all. Some like…' Tom's empty eyes suddenly show a glimmer that somebody may be behind the wheel again.

Tom is hit hard and a strange dizziness takes hold, eventually succumbing to nausea. He's just a swatted fly, buzzing around insanely and about to die.

'Like me ba… like me baby… *Some don't score at all*… like me baby…'

The world is scorched away by flame and two burning eyes dance before Tom's hazy perception.

'…brother.'

Tom is sat breathing heavily and sweating. Tomorrow would be another world - people bustling around the call centre going about their business; angry customers shouting their mouths off, oblivious to the horrors. Tomorrow Tom would be another person, immersed in the daily grind and bureaucracy of 'real life'; possessed by it. *Consumed* by it. And *enslaved* by it.

This night would hardly be given a second thought; it would simply be shrugged off and buried deep down inside him alongside all the other nightmares; all the other demons. It's just night that makes it real. Tom closes his eyes, the fear wrapped tightly around him like a hitch-hiker's towel.

And at that exact moment, Tom knows that sleep will come, which is odd in itself as people usually, upon searching their memory, struggle to pinpoint the exact moment of falling asleep. One's memory of the time approaching sleep tends to blur into dreams, and dreams into waking.

And that's just what had happened to his memories.

But not just with sleep.

With everything.

Will must be pissed or stoned.

Yeah, that must be it; that's the only explanation for this unexpected bout of amnesia. His last memory is of driving his dad's car down a winding country lane, but the recollection is all disjointed and blurry... a doubtful tapestry of light, sound and colour.

Perhaps he's crashed, and this is what brain damage is like, from the inside.

He finds himself climbing up what must be a ladder, though it's so dark he can't make anything out. All that he can do is climb, and with each rung a voice in his head cries *'all man!'*

He comes across a hatch on the side of the tunnel. For some reason, despite the darkness he knows that this is the escape hatch. The voice in his head yells at him to keep on climbing.

'But ah'm so tired,' Will protests, forcing the hatch open.

He finds himself in what appears to be a clothes shop. He reckons it to be a clothes shop because of its changing rooms. *Not just a pretty face, eh?* Curiously, everything is in sepia. *What 'av ah been suppin'?*

In the corner of his eye he sees them. He sees *her*.

It must have been two years since he'd last spoken to Laura. And as for Holly, not a single word had passed between them since she told him to fuck off out of her life.

''olly,' Will says, his feigned Irish drawl sated with regret.

'Hi,' says Holly, her anger understated but its hatred plain.

Will has this horrible feeling, just like he had a couple of years ago, that these two words may be the last that they'll share. Here she is, after all this time, stood before him in a mysterious clothes store with dodgy lighting somewhere in Skeggy. Her hair is down, and the harsh contrast of the cream light and the brown room illuminate every curve on her magnificent figure.

They stand face to face for a macroscopic eternity, until her mate Laura wields her axe to break the ice. She speaks.

Will is temporarily afflicted with dysphasia; Laura's words are absorbed correctly by his ear only to be turned by his brain into incoherent gibberish.

Before long, Holly enters their 'conversation'… not that Will can follow it. His heart skips a beat every two seconds - a sure sign of his proximity to *her*.

The wonderful summer of '99 will be forever etched into his memory, synonymous with the soundtrack of that irregular heartbeat. He didn't ever want that beat to end; he even *enjoyed* the feeling of dread because it reminded him of just what he had to lose and of just how lucky he was to be with such a girl.

Now, however, his heart is beginning to dance to a different tune; a tune analogous to a song of praise with its strong and affecting cadence. Could this be it? Has he now served his penance? Is it finally over?

The walls of purgatory crumble like the Walls of Jericho, and Will's thoughts turn to the future: to how he'd somehow pull a degree out of his hat and get a job; buy a house; get a gerbil (Holly always loved gerbils); get married; and have 2.37 children.

Against all hope he pulls Holly into his embrace and soon they are both apologising profusely and speaking of memories past. And in this one blazing moment of transparency, this unique and blinding shot of interstellar light, Will Surewood is at peace. He's happy. A single tear of joy runs down his left cheek.

However, life is such that these heaven-sent moments expire all too quickly, and this one is destroyed by the machinations of Beelzebub himself and his mischievous suggestions.

'Laura ain't looking bad these days,' Satan whispers to Will. 'In fact, I have it on good authority that she takes it up the shitter.'

Will strokes his chin thoughtfully before turning to face the horned one and mustering a reply. 'You reckon? Says who?' Will asks, all the time wondering how he can be so calm when face to face with the Fallen Angel.

'That Greek kid from D Block. Big lad. Bushy beard,' Lucifer says, gesturing towards his own gut and then his own pointy goatee.

'Or! It's Phil the Greek you're on abart!'

'That's it!' says the red one with the devilish smile. 'So,' he adds, turning back to business, 'one up the bum-'

'No 'arm done!' Will finishes.

Laura and Holly, and indeed the entire shop, are frozen in time as Will and *Shaitan* partake in their little tête á tête. Now fair dues - Will does find this apparent temporal anomaly curious but, on reflection, not quite as odd as having a chat with the dreaded Beast about Phil the Greek's brown wings.

Putting such trivial thoughts out of his mind for the time being, Will walks right up to Holly and holds out his right hand, as if to touch her breasts. *Time should freeze more often*, he thinks. But the Devil had sewn his seed well. *No jubblies in the world are worth losin' yer ten-point brown-pottin' bonus for!*

Will circles behind the two girls and positions himself directly behind Laura. There is no way in hell that Will could defend finding such a creature as Laura attractive, but even so he can't stop himself. It's nothing to do with attraction. Hell; Laura's not even remotely human - a laugh stolen from the farmyard, a face that makes her arse look good, bum cheeks comparable in size to twin moons... yet he still wants to get between them. *Again...*

'AH'M SORRY!!!' Will screams as he tears through the fabric of his own personal hell and finds himself back in the waking world. Beside him is a naked woman – mid-forties, bleach blonde, overweight. Since he'd started work at *Skyline*, he'd been seeing this sixteen year-old who just wouldn't put out, so naturally he gave up on her. Luckily her mother was well up for it.

Fumbling around on the floor, Will picks up his pack of fags and his lighter. Sparking up, he is possessed by the desire to headbutt the wall, but out of consideration for his colleagues in the 'shed' next-door trying to have a bit of a lie in, instead he silently puts the cigarette out on his arm.

Will is getting tired of the game.

Dog tired.

Time for a change.

Will puts down the clippers with a giddy sense of satisfaction and admires himself in the mirror. 'Ah look a reet chuff!'

The essential 2004 'Becks bonehead' has replaced his floppy, highlighted Lion's Mane.

''ad to be done, like, 'ad to be done!' he says to Spadge, who is laid on the narrow bed in their 'shed' chuckling to himself. 'Shed' was a term that the staff at *Skyline* used to describe their patently horrid housing. Most of the staff there not being over furnished on the old imagination front, these sheds were thusly named because they actually *were* sheds. Each shed is split down the middle with two tiny beds squeezed inside, cold running water, one plug and one bog shared between ten - hardly worth the fifty pence an hour that *Skyline* deduct from their three pound an hour wage, Spadge reckons. Still, anything's better than *Happyloans*.

Will doesn't think that Spadge's tame chuckling qualifies as paying him enough attention. 'Ah cut off me mane what ah've 'ad for about two year an' you don't even gi' a shit!'

Will runs his fingers over his head. 'It's like when we woz at school an' ah'd have a number two all ovvers. Ah'd run me fingers o'er it, an' get all the bitches to do it 'an all! Can't beat the feelin' man!'

Spadge looks up at Will with a face that most people would have a hard time believing is only twenty-four years old. Spadge's middle-aged appearance isn't so much the result of having an old-looking face - it's his farcically receded hairline. He is bald almost as far back as his scalp, but for the thin Mohawk-like line of hair than runs down the middle. Spadge's eyebrows are raised as if to say, *seriously?*

'Yeah bollocks! Ah mean like, course you *can* beat the feelin' *– fallin' in love wi' a lass…*'

The Spadge that most people find difficult to prevent from talking is for once lost for words. *Will? Fall in love?* He looks at Will with a puppy-dog's eyes, completely and utterly confused. First his girlfriend chucks him for pissing on her, and then he finds himself living in a shed with a flawed imitation of one of his closest friends. *Life's shit.*

Will realises that he's committed the cardinal sin of breaking character in front of a mate, and so he quickly tries to remedy the situation. He waves a dismissive hand.

'Yeah reet! 'ad yer theer. Point ah'm tryin' ta meck is that runnin' your fingers o'er yer shaven 'ed is quality!'

Will once again admires his reflection in the mirror. His opinions on the aesthetics of his outside and his inside differ greatly, and the disparity is slowly beginning to eat away at him.

* * *

Gristle wakes up as he usually does on a Saturday, bright and early, just in time for the football results coming in so that he can check his coupon. The year before he moved up here to live with Will and the lads, he'd had an unbelievable run of luck at the bookies. He'd just banged a tenner on eight results that won him the best part of ten grand. A bit of reckless re-investment then began to reap its rewards shortly afterwards, and soon enough he'd got nearly thirty K in the bank.

Things had gone a bit downhill though since. So downhill, in fact, that if he didn't get a result today his illegally-obtained 'student' overdraft would be maxxed out and he'd be left trying to scrape a living from his eighty-nine squid dole every fortnight. *Ah'll just 'ave to rely on other sources o' income, wayn't ah?* he thinks to himself, smiling at his chest of drawers. Of course, his thoughts have none of the linguistic fluency of *Ah'll just 'ave to rely on other sources o' income, wayn't ah?;* they are more akin to a series of mental grunts. Nevertheless, *Ah'll just 'ave to rely on other sources o' income, wayn't ah?* is what he's struggling to think to himself.

The report comes in from Anfield. The closest Gristle's beloved reds got to scoring was *'eskey* hitting the crossbar. *Donkey!* The last of his money gone; just like that. Gristle says nothing, he just laughs a slightly tapered version of his dreadful cartoon-dog laugh. After all, it all means nothing to him. Like everything. Life's little more than a mild diversion when you have a brain the size of a lentil.

Gristle begins to rummage around in his bedcovers, looking for ammo - a bit of cheerful shooting always cheers him up. It doesn't take him long to load and cock the 4.5 millimetre weapon with military proficiency.

Fear is an emotional response that Gristle rarely experiences, yet today as he pulls open the mid-seventies' curtains he is *scared shitless*. He pulls back from view and violently pulls the curtains together, ripping the right-hand curtain down the middle as he does so. He looks at his chest of drawers again, this time without a smile. This time in fear. *They'll throw away the bloody key this time. There's a fuckin' cop car parked outside me fuckin' 'ouse!*

Gristle is going down.

Anna shows the two officers out. Still quite shaken, she feels much better after having spoken to the police, and in truth, maybe even a little bit silly for reporting it. She closes the door behind her, making sure that she locks it tightly.

Tom is waiting for her in the living room. Bless him; he'd been round like a shot at three in the morning when she'd rang him, and he didn't laugh at her or try it on with her or anything. He just held her close to him until morning. That's like *a million points* in her book. She can't remember ever feeling as safe as when she was wrapped up in his arms.

When she first read the altered welcome note on her mobile, she'd assumed that it was Tom playing a sick joke on her, but when she thought about it her phone had been upstairs in her bedroom the whole time that he was round. He didn't ever leave her living room, so it couldn't have been him. In a way though, she wished that it would have been Tom playing a sick joke. At least she'd have known who it was.

She walks up to Tom, no doubt looking a state in her PJs and slippers, and rests her head on his chest. He doesn't say anything - he just looks at her with those big, brown eyes of his and kisses her forehead. It's weird how comfortable she feels with him after, like, *a day*, and she hasn't even snogged him yet. She's seen his penis, though.

Nice.

THE JIHAD DROP

'...**WE FIRST SAW THIS THREE HUNDRED POUND** *behemoth make his debut three weeks ago, and ever since then he has completely decimated all compet-'*

Jamal shakes his head at the bar's gargantuan TV screen and then returns his attention to his infinitely more interesting glass of mineral water. He gently kicks at his suitcase with his right foot. *Still there.*

In spite of himself, his attention is drawn back towards the big screen.

'*...definitely! Last week in the triple-threat match, we saw him single-handedly tear apart the Tag Team Champions, Trippie the Trampler and Willie Mac. What impresses me most is that for a man of his size he's incredibly quick; he's one of very few athletes I've seen that can actually walk the top rope, and as for that Jihad Drop finisher of his: wow.*'

On the screen, a vaguely Eastern-looking - but nonetheless clearly American - wrestler is slowly waddling down the aisle towards the ring. Gesticulating passionately at the booing crowd to each side of him, he walks up the three metal steps that lead into the 'squared circle'. When he reaches the top step, his deafening entrance music reaches its crescendo and pyrotechnic flames shoot out from all four ring posts. The wrestler then places his right hand on the top rope, and in an impressive display of both strength and agility, uses it to propel his hulking frame into the ring. It all looks effortless.

A bald, odd-looking fellow in a tuxedo then speaks into a microphone which is almost as big as his apparently pregnant head.

'*Ladies and gentlemen, the following contest is scheduled for one fall. In the ring, from Afgan-ee-stan, weighing two hundred and ninety-seven pounds: the Muslim Monk!*'

The Monk's music suddenly stops and he snatches the microphone from the purportedly petrified ring announcer. The Monk speaketh.

'Killer Klotschkow! Before I am forced to destroy your infidel body, I shall first give you the opportunity to convert. You have until the count of five to get out here and prostrate yourself before me!'

Jamal finds himself staring slack-jawed at the screen; he's never been so offended in his entire life. Now he understands why his father never let him watch wrestling back in the eighties.

'The Ram-ee-dam Slam! Oh my god, this is it. He's gonna finish him off! Why didn't he just convert...?'

'Do you mind! Killer Klotschkow isn't one of these unpatriotic sell outs! He'd rather take the Jihad Drop than... than... submit to that oppressive SOB!'

'I think it's academic now. Klotschkow can't take much more of this kind of punishment. If I were Earl, I'd just stop the damned match.'

'Damn right. Klotschkow can't defend himself. It's a massacre. Good God! No... What's that fanatic doing out here? It's Al!'

'He's saying something to the Monk. Oh no. I think they're gonna go for the Five Pillars!'

A bell sounds as 'Al' – the mirror image of the Monk - slides under the ring's bottom rope with a fold-up steel chair. From a safe distance, the ring announcer calls the referee's decision.

'...the winner of this bout, as a result of a disqualification: Killer Klotschkow!'

A cheer goes up around the arena. Fans stand on their chairs chanting the Killer's name. But it's all for nought.

Al holds the steel chair against each ring post in turn as the Monk slams Klotschkow's head into them, one after the other. Finally, Al places the chair in the middle of the ring for the Monk to piledrive the Killer onto.

'They'll break his damn neck! Put the women and children to bed!'

The 'Jihad Drop' - the last and without doubt the most brutal limb of the Monk's 'Five Pillaz' finishing manoeuvre – absolves the soul of another non-believer.

'There you have it. One of the most heinous and devastating manoeuvres that you'll see in sports entertainment today – the Five Pillaz. The Monk may have lost on a technicality, but he and his partner Al Qaeda have certainly sent a message out to Willie and the Trampler ahead of next month's Tag Team Championship Steel Cage Mat-'

Jamal is so affronted that he doesn't even know where to begin. With kids watching rubbish like this he's certainly going to have his work cut out for him teaching them anything in Hull.

'...and remember folks, we'll be visiting the UK next month with shows in London, Birmingham, Manchester, Sheffield and Hull. Bring the whole family along for what promises to be an electrifying afternoon of sports ent-'

Jamal's head slumps forward into his hands. Dragged from the guttural depths of the commentator's Oklahoman throat, the word 'Hull' echoes around his head, mocking him.

Downing his mineral water and hammering the bottom of his glass down on the bar, Jamal decides he's going to need something a bit stronger.

He calls the barmaid over.

'Red Bull. *Hold the ice.*'

Sometimes he surprises himself at just how damn cool he can be.

* * *

Anna collapses forward and Tom slumps onto her back. She needed that fuck.

They both roll apart briefly so that they can disentangle their bodies and clean up all the consequent fluids. Anna reaches across onto the bedside table and pulls out a wad of tissue, while Tom ties a knot in the used slimy condom and then just lobs it on the floor. Before Anna he had never used a johnny before in his life; not even the very first time. The very idea of them turns him off. Still, not hell bent on dying young with AIDS or something, he'd thought that with Anna, he'd better use protection. *Ah know where she's been,* after all.

After the oh-so romantic process of waste disposal, Tom lays on his back and Anna snuggles up to him. He had been surprised how slim she was when they had first made love; there wasn't an ounce of fat on her body. It had actually made him feel quite insecure as he'd been piling on the weight recently. Her arse was an absolute peach - far nicer than he'd imagined from Will's description - but her tits weren't anywhere near as big as Will had made out. Oddly, her arms put him off. They were each covered in deep lacerations, and some of the scars seemed fairly new. Fresh.

'Why did you act like a dickhead when I first met you?' Anna asks, rubbing the hair on Tom's chest.

'Back at the start of first year? Ah didn't, did ah?' he replies, furrowing his brow.

'Yeah. I bet you can't even remember. You always do it when you're with your mates. You're like a different person.'

'Ah don't…' Tom whines, quite lost for words. 'It's just, like, ah 'ave a laugh wi' the lads. It's different to when ah'm wi' you.'

'It's not you though, is it, Tom?'

Tom shrugs her away and stands up. Anna finds it difficult to take him seriously whilst his cock is swinging free, not unlike the pendulum of a great grandfather clock. Nonetheless, he looks angry. Defensive.

''ow the fuck would you know who ah am? Ah've know you about seven week!'

'Seven weeks…' Anna corrects. *'Plural,'* she adds, smiling. 'Seven fantastic weeks.'

'Whatever…' he trails off before looking up at her, composed. 'No; they've been sound… ah suppose. But you don't know me. Ah don't even know me. When ah'm wi' me mates ah'm just as much me as ah am when ah'm wi' you; *more so,* 'cos ah'm wi' them more often!'

'You haven't been recently, though, have you?'

Tom pulls on his jeans. 'No, but…' he pauses, looking straight at her. 'No, but they 'aven't bin 'ere. It won't be like this when they're back in a couple o' days.'

Now its Anna's turn to frown. 'So you don't want to be with me… *properly?*'

Tom looks at her awkwardly, just like all those summer placement arseholes did when they each said 'if it was up to me, love…'

Anna wraps the sheet around herself, suddenly protective of her nudity. 'I've invested a lot in you. I like you. I… I mean, yeah. I like you. I thought I was falling in love with you. And I thought you felt the same.'

Tom is now fully dressed. He is wearing a plain, yellow t-shirt from *Top Man*; stonewash jeans with the knees torn out, again from *Top Man*; and brown *French Connection* trainers… from *Top Man*. Tom likes *Top Man*. He is certain of this and it is crystal clear in his mind. However, he is far from certain about what he feels anymore. This is neither crystal clear in his mind nor in his heart. As much as he enjoys the security that Anna gives to him, she is far too clingy for his liking, and that isn't even the half of it. She never eats, she rarely sleeps, she's weird about when and how they have sex, and what really clinches it for him is his inability to go down on her. Every time he tries to make himself venture south, he has a vision of Will's diseased protuberance...

He simply cannot bring himself to 'officially' be with a girl whom Will has soiled. He knows it's a shite reason to chuck someone, *but theer yer go*. He'd sleep around and have fun, but when it came down to it there was only girl that he'd ever seriously consider being with, and it wasn't this Anna. It wasn't this cheap, rip-off version with slashed up arms and a broken brain. *She didn't even 'ave all the letters!* What's a Hannah without both its silent aitches? Nowt.

'So where's this leave us?' she asks pleadingly.

'Dunno. Just shaggin', ah reckon. If that's alreet.'

'Oh. I see.'

'Inabit,' says Tom nonchalantly, showing himself out. Time he had some time alone. If he was lucky, he might be able to squeeze in a bit of 'Tommy time' before Freshers' Week.

Anna bites her bottom lip and finds herself looking around her bedroom, holding back the tears. Was it something she said?

Not again!

Tom looks up at the sky and curses. He only had it five minutes ago! No matter how many that he has cut, why is he forever destined to lose his keys? *It's a conspiracy!* Somebody must be stealing them, plotting to either rob him or set up a key-cutting shop. Or just maybe he's just left them on Anna's bedside table. Upon reflection, he finds the latter more likely. *Still...*

Rather than go through all the exertion of ringing the doorbell, Tom just leans his shoulder slightly into the door, about three quarters of the way up, and it opens without effort. Only the finest the security in a *Studicom* student home!

After checking to see if he's received any post, Tom takes a right turn at the radiator and walks straight into the living room to be greeted by Gristle, naked and unconscious on the sofa with two empty bottles of sparkling white wine beside him and Rocky curled up asleep in a ball on his chest. This isn't what surprises him, though - this is routine. What really knocks him for six is the sight of both Will and Spadge stood before him, rubbing each other's freshly shaven-heads.

Tom runs his fingers through his flowing locks and smiles a fretful smile. They're back from *Skyline*, then.

'Mad twats!' he says. 'Ah can't believe it. You was obsessed wi' your manes or whatever you called 'em... Well, you were any'ow Will! You look surprisingly better though, Spadge! *Younger.*'

'It's the future! Long 'air's outta fashion again, innit. *Bloody Becks!* 'ad to be done, like' Will roars, charging straight into Tom and trying to lift him up.

Either Will has got weaker or Tom has got fatter, but either way Will ends up collapsing under Tom's weight and being pinned to the ground by his mushrooming gut. 'Yer gret fat chuff! What yer been doin' all summer, pie-munchin'?'

Tom feels quite hurt but hides it well, restraining his retaliation to a well-placed knee in Will's crotch. 'That skin'ead is gonna teck some gettin' used ta!' Tom remarks as he gets to his feet, laughing.

Will, still laid on the floor nursing his genitalia, points an accusatory finger at his best friend. 'Tha better not be tecking the piss outta me new *hairodynamic* 'airstyle!'

Tom just shakes his head, a huge grin covering his face. Will, meanwhile, clambers slowly to his feet, nursing his balls. 'Ah can't believe 'ow fekin' fat you've got. It'll 'ave ta go – yer wayn't get any woman lookin' like that.'

Once Will has finished destroying his friend's self-confidence, he looks at his floppy blonde hair, as if he's just noticed it for the first time. 'That'll 'av to go an' all.'

An iniquitous smile covers Will Surewood's face.

Balancing on his tip-toes (so as to avoid the minging, probably dog-shit ridden kitchen floor) and wearing nothing but a towel to hide his modesty (which, he reckons, needs hiding) Tom examines himself in the kitchen window. Through the light's reflection he sees a terrible, twisted image of himself and two rather nasty words begin worming their way into his brain: *cancer victim*. Waves of lament pass over him as he gazes sorrowfully towards the bin containing his shaven locks. He stares deeper into the reflection. *Cancer victim wi' tits. Tommy five bellies.*

His mood instantly brightens though as the water in the bathroom audibly ceases to flow, and after a few seconds of cloth rubbing against skin; zips zipping; and belts buckling, Gristle's muscular frame arrogantly waddles past. The façade of his Herculean countenance is quickly destroyed, however, as he looks at himself in the kitchen window - just as Tom had done a moment earlier - and commits the cardinal sin of flattening his one-inch-long fringe down over his face. *The scally,* Tom thinks, wincing in case Gristle somehow knows what he's thinking. Gristle pulls a mean, ugly face in the window that is exacerbated by his grotesque, toothless smirk. Tom would love to see Will and Spadge try to take Gristle's hair!

Gristle suddenly turns and screams as loud as he can in Tom's face – 'AH'M FOOOOKIN' GORGEOUS!' - and gives Tom a hard poke in his flaccid stomach, just for good measure. Gristle then trots away, shadow-boxing as he takes his leave.

Without warning, suddenly Gristle spins around and yells 'OI!', nearly making Tom drop his towel. "n' tell vat Anna bird o' yours ta think on before she brings th'old bill sniffin' round again! Ah ended up flushin' all me gear last time… ah fought they'd finally come ta teck us away! Gristle don't wanna end up doin' time again! Wot the fuck am ah gonna do for brass now, ey? Tha can sub us twenny squid as it's your lass's fault!'

The desire for self-cleansing now even stronger, Tom makes a move to race for the bathroom door, though the absurd notion that someone can come out of *that* bathroom 'cleansed' holds him back rather. Tom would come out of there feeling dirtier than when he went in, as always. Nevertheless, duty calls. It's Saturday night, and the first Saturday night of the year no less - *Freshers' Night!* Hundreds upon hundreds of loose, battered first years looking for no-strings sex. And if he's really lucky Anna might not be there. If he's even luckier still, the proper Hannah might well be.

'I've got a bad feeling about this,' says the voice of a dashing space pirate, ringing out around the room in glorious 7.1 surround. Almost instantaneously a noise erupts from the drunken mouths of Tom, Will, Gristle and Spadge. The noise is half way between 'yay' and 'way,' but it's the follow-up that counts:

'Down in one, yer twats!' Gristle yells, relishing his role as games master with as much zeal as the Dark Lord relishes cruelly choking those under his command. The difference between Gristle and Vader is that Gristle is not as forgiving. He ain't called Gristle for nothin'.

Jamal looks on in distaste, having opted out of the outlandishly intriguing 'drinking game'. He is making the effort though, just like his fiancée had told him to. He has a six-pack of premium lager all to himself, and he is venturing out with his new housemates – *it's going to be a wild night, and no mistake!*

In marked contrast to Jamal's pitiable collection of cans, Will, Spadge, and Tom each have one litre measuring jugs in front of them. Each jug is full to the brim with the cheapest sparkling white wine known to man. This is the kind of stuff that makes you retch just by smelling it; three bottles for a fiver from the offy. And the way Gristle is barking orders at the three of them (each member of the trio as bald as the day they were born, if not more so) makes Tom feels like he is in a concentration camp, with Gristle cast as the remorseless commandant dolling out the torture.

With the exchange of a brief, determined glance they all take the plunge together.

Jamal has got to guiltily admit to being a little bit amused.

The trick is not to breathe and to down the wine in as few large gulps as possible. Tom is finding it really hard; harder than usual. Perhaps it's the three months of relative sobriety taking its toll. Or maybe it's because, for some reason, his plonk reeks of rotting bacon. He finds himself wondering just what he's putting into his body...

As usual, Spadge finishes way ahead of both Tom and Will. Spadge can literally despatch a litre of the shittiest wine in about twelve seconds, and Will ain't too far behind him. Spadge is doing what he usually does, celebrating his victory for about ten seconds by mimicking the trademark postures of American wrestling Tag Team Champion, *Trippie the Trampler*.

Tom can feel the cheap vino swishing about in his gut, but it is Spadge who looks like death incarnate. A necking race takes its toll, and this outer-space drinking game can be especially excruciating. Once (or sometimes more) per movie, when one of the characters says *'I've got a bad feeling about this,'* everybody has to down a litre of wine. There are other rules for other eventualities too – for example, when the droids have one of their camp little arguments, everybody has to neck half a pint; and when the Dark Lord indulges his capriciousness by executing his own men they have to neck a full pint. A cool Vader saying is two fingers, a limb or appendage being hacked off is four fingers, and so on and so forth.

Spadge is now doing his usual trick of going very quiet and breathing very deeply for a few minutes. He stands with a look of grim determination on his face before eventually nodding sullenly to signify that he's not going to be sick and that the game can continue.

'Ah find your lack o' faith disturbing,' Tom says in the deepest voice that he can muster as Will sticks a bucket in front of him. Will's face then lights up, his face contorting into what look like kissy-lips.

'Wooooooo. That's fating talk, youth!' he says, jabbing Tom gently but precisely in the stomach with his fist – payback for this aft's knee in the crotch. And just like Luke's superbly timed shot down a certain exhaust port, Will's precise hit does its job. Tom pukes into the bucket, meaning that the first round is on him.

ESCAPE TO DANGER

SAT ON PEWS IN THE CORNER OF A CHURCH that has been turned (arguably sacrilegiously) into a pre-club bar, two young attractive women enjoy a quiet drink and reflect on the finer things in life.

One of them, a curvaceous and pretty student of criminology by the name of Bethany Hunt, slams her empty shot glass down onto the table in front of her and sucks on a lemon.

…ullllllrh! Anything to thin the blood. It certainly beats listening to Katie bang on and on and on about this fit guy on the train back up to Hull. Apparently, he recognised her from when she showed someone round his house. She was trying to make some notes from her textbook or something, and he kept writing her flirtatious messages in the margins of her paper. Sounds like a right obnoxious twat. I'd have slapped him.

I ask her; I say 'If he was so fit, why didn't you do anything?'

'I know what his lot are like,' she replies, smiling to herself like she's above it all. 'They only wanna have me. Once he's done that he'd lose all interest!'

You must be shit in bed then, *I think. Rather than destroy her confidence though, for some reason I temper myself, meekly opting to say that she's being a bit harsh on men in general. She leans over to me as if she's about to murmur some heresy that the church walls might somehow pick up.*

'Tell you what though, Beth,' she says, 'I would be happy with a fucking dog-ugly bloke as long as he loved me.'

That's Katie's problem. She's beautiful inside – and beautiful out. I fucking hate the cow.

I look across to the bar and see this group of lads – right mingers. I point out the ugliest, baldest one. He looks like a right Chav. 'What about him, pet?'

'Not that fucking ugly,' she laughs. 'Gotta have some standards!'

'Ah've queued for afe an 'our to get served,' Will whinges to the lads, foolishly thinking that they may actually care.

Handing out the second round of drinks (the first were gone in the blink of an eye; *'strawpedoed'* within just seconds), Will takes a good look around him for the first time since their arrival.

...twenny minute piss-take ah've just ad tryin' to get a round in! Still, there's some well-fit fanny out tonite, not like these sad twats ah'm wiv will do owt about it. Tom's got the reet face on. Fek knows what's up wiv 'im. Ah bet 'e's still pinin' about that slag 'e's obsessed wi' – not the Anna 'e's bangin' (ah've had her); t'other one from E Block. All 'e does all fekin' nite long is just stand theer, lookin' mardy an' gettin' bladdered. We allus lose 'im, then find 'im later on in a puddle ov 'is own puke an' piss. No respect for 'imsen. 'ow's 'e expect to get a woman if 'e's got no respect for 'imsen, ey? Still, gotta love the lad, 'e's a good 'un – me bestest mate. Spadge reckons Tom's on somet for depression; mecks sense ah reckon after that shite wi' 'is brother an' their old man. Ah best keep an eye on 'im tonite. Just in case.

Come to mention it, ah'm a bit worried 'bout me old man an' all – 'e keeps tryin' ta ring us at stupid times in the nite, but ah've missed all 'is calls. 'e never rings; ah can't even remember the last time ah spoke to 'im. Random, innit. Ah 'ope nowts up.

Oh... this is shite. Ah'd rather be playin' on me career than this. Sheff U are on for the double his season, meck no mistake! Ah think ah'm gonna sign that Petrov on a Bosman when ah gets in... unless ah get a screw, like.

Where 'as Gristle feked off to? Sometimes ah think 'e doesn't ever even wanna get shagged; all 'e goes on about is fating. Ah just can't work out, like, wot goes on inside some sad people's eds, even me own mates!

Some people are just fekin' weird.

* * *

Gristle nods his head ever so nearly in synch with each beat of the pulsating dance track. He loves all that rubbish. Every few seconds he takes a mammoth gulp of his pint.

Dum-dum-dum-dum. Ner-ner-ner-ner. Dum-dum-dum-dum. Ner-ner-ner-ner. Ah wannanuvver fuckin pint, where've them lot fucked off to? Dum-dum-dum-dum. Ner-ner-ner-ner. Dum-dum-dum-dum. Ner-ner-ner-ner. Who's that fuckin' tosser? What'chu lookin' at? Dum-dum-dum-dum. Ner-ner-ner-ner. Dum-dum-dum-dum. Ner-ner-ner-ner. Chin you, dickhead. Dum-dum-dum-dum. Ner-ner-ner-ner. Dum-dum-dum-dum. Ner-ner-ner-ner. Phwooar! Ah'd gee 'er one! Dum-dum-dum-dum. Ner-ner-ner-ner. Dum-dum-dum-dum. Ner-ner-ner-ner. What'chu lookin' at? Dum-dum-dum-dum. Ner-ner-ner-ner. Dum-dum-dum-dum. Ner-ner-ner-ner. Ah'll chin thee, knobhead.

'Alreet love…' ah says to these two lasses comin' outta the gents. 'ow come bitches get away wi' that, but every time ah go in ta women's ah get into fuckin' shit wi' bouncers!

'Tosser,' the fat one says to us. Unprovoked. An' ah barely touched 'er arse!

'Yeah? Fuck you then, fuckin' slag.'

Dum-dum-dum-dum. Ner-ner-ner-ner. Dum-dum-dum-dum. Ner-ner-ner-ner. Where've them lot fucked off to? Ah wannanuvver fuckin pint! Dum-dum-dum-dum. Ner-ner-ner-ner. Dum-dum-dum-dum. Ner-ner-ner-ner. What they lookin' at? Want some do they… Oh man! Love this 'un. It's quality.

Dum-dum-dum-dum-Everybody…

Jamal steadies himself against a huge column and examines the orange-flavoured alchopop that has been thrust into his hand. As soon as they got into this place he was forced to pour one of these fetid things straight down his throat with a straw and it had nearly made him sick. And that was after six cans of lager before they'd even left the house! Jamal burps…

…in public! What's happening to me? I've only been living in this hostel of the damned for six accursed hours, and already I'm a drinking, belching yobbo. I'll be covered in tattoos and wearing baseball caps next. I'm sure that would go down well on my first teaching practice.

To be fair though, Tom and Will, despite looking like a pair of right roughnecks, have actually been very welcoming and made an effort to assimilate me into their little group. Spadge also seems quite pleasant - when I can get a word in edge-ways, that is - but I'm not very keen on this 'Gristle' at all. The others might shout, swear, drink, and have no respect for either themselves or anyone else, but I do get the impression that their hearts are at least in the vicinity of the right places. It doesn't seem that this Gristle even has a heart though. Or a brain, for that matter. I noticed a civil court summons in the mountain of newspapers, flyers, and post addressed to Ben somebody, which I assume is his real name. That reminds me, I do keep meaning to ask why they call him 'Gristle', though I don't think I really want to know…

Katie runs gracefully up the steps from the dance floor, picking her drink up from the floor beside Bethany's bag. The whole action – right from leaving the dance floor to putting the bottle to her lips – is one beautiful and delicate manoeuvre, the sort of set-piece that one might see in a margarine advert, played in slow motion.

And then she opens her gob: 'Check out the arse on that!' she says, pointing at a guy who is walking down the steps onto the dance floor. As she points, the guy, who obviously has heard her, spins round and there is a look of tentative recognition between them - more on his part than on hers, peculiarly.

'You know him or something?' Bethany asks. The guy has now wandered over to a group of lads who are pathetically struggling to dance. Clustered tightly together with their imitative skinheads, the three of them look like a bit of a freak show. *Look at that little one with the ginger stubble!*

Bethany feels a pang of guilt – she normally has to pay good money to see something as funny as this. Still, even she has to admit, Mr Arse does move better than the rest of them.

'That's him!' Katie shouts, after two blessed minutes of silence. 'It's him off the train today! Him who lives in that shithole I told you about! I didn't recognise him without his cap on; he must have cut all his hair off since last semester! Ooooh. Suits him better than that blonde, floppy do that he had,' she says girlishly. 'Mind you, his mate's alright as well. I think they live together if I remember right.'

This arseman certainly has balls – though in Bethany's experience, men like him don't usually have the cock to match – he's just staring a hole straight through Katie. Bethany's gotta admit, there's certainly something in those big blue eyes. If she didn't know better...

Katie is smiling back at him, obviously flattered, though at a loss for what to do...

...she looks so cute just stood there with her VK bottle, writhing uncomfortably. She's so perfect that if I was a guy I'd want to fuck her. Oh my god, what a tit! He's only beckoning her over with his forefinger! How does he expect a woman to respond to behaviour like- oh. *She's going over to him. Here's to the power of positive suggestion!*

And here's to big, blue eyes.

It isn't long before Katie has her coat and is leaving with Mr Surewood. Bethany and Tom share the taxi with them, both having had enough of being packed liked sardines into a hot and confined space with an average forty-minute waiting time on drink. *Freshers' Week* – rubbish! First they can't get in the *'Freshers Only 'til Twelve'* disco and now, thanks to an uncompromising taxi driver, all four passengers end up back at the girls' house.

Katie was actually quite chuffed with the cantankerous taxi driver – having Will dropped right at her door means that she can get laid without having to look too desperate. She also rather enjoyed being sandwiched between Will and Tom; fawning over the pair of the them, stroking their legs, kissing Tom on the cheek, not very slyly massaging Will's groin...

In contrast, Bethany seems pleased to be out of the taxi and back in her own kitchen.

'Politics,' Tom responds to Bethany's enquiry...

...and then she gives me this funny look, like 'you study politics? Bollocks! Ah can really see you as Prime Minister!' Ah get that a lot. Ah suppose it's me tattoo addiction, an' the new skinhead 'airdo can't be 'elpin' matters.

After stickin' 'er bottom lip out an' noddin' wi' this amused sorta look, she pulls 'er tea bag out o' the cup an' 'ands me me cuppa. Ah saw 'er meck it so it should be alreet.

'I'm doing criminology,' she tells me. 'But I'm doing a free elective in international politics.'

'Cool,' ah says, wishin' for once that ah'd been to more lectures, an' paid more attention to the ones that ah had been to, so that in situations such as these ah could impress women wi' me mountain o' political knowledge.

'Well, you'll be alreet wi' that. World's full o' criminals,' ah say, sittin' down in the livin' room - 'er on the sofa, me in one o' the armchairs. Ah'm a coward deep down! We don't have to wait long before bein' given somet to talk about. At first it's the tell-tale squeaky mattress that we can 'ear through the ceiling, then it's 'er fit 'ouse-mate's whimpering... then moaning... then screaming. Soon afterwards we 'ear an Irish accent yell 'Backa tha' fekin' net!!!' in a broad Yorkshire dialect. Even durin' shaggin', Will maintains 'is pretend Irish voice.

Ah feel an 'eartstring break as once again the weight o' the world crushes me already weak spirit. It's so easy for Will, an' there is nobody in this world who deserves to be God's gift less. Ah 'ave to work for me women, put the graft in, and even then 'afe the time ah end up gettin' 'opelessly attached to 'em, screwin' things up good an' proper.

Bethany is wearin' this tight black dress. Barely covers her arse. Tits look fantastic. Body an' 'afe on her. 'igh 'eels too - bit o' class don't go amiss. 'igh 'eels an' no knickers, ah wonder…

NO!

Self-hate an' disgust teck their firm 'old o' me. AH'M IN LOVE WI' 'ANNAH. AH'M IN LOVE WITH 'ANNAH. SHE'S THE ONE. WE'RE IN LOVE. Ah've convinced mesen o' this fact, but ah'm 'avin' more difficulty bringin' 'er round to me particular way o' thinking.

The self-loathin' 'as now begun in earnest, because at this specific moment in time there is nowt ah wanna do more than go to bed wi' this angel who 'as just made me a cuppa…

While languishin' in me self-'atred ah notice that mein 'ost *is nowhere to be seen. Ah'm more disturbed by the fact that ah actually care. Ah shouldn't care. Ah should only care about 'annah. That's the way it should be.*

A guilty relief washes over me as she sits 'erself on the arm o' me chair. Ah can see up 'er skirt from this angle an' her legs are absolutely amazing. She 'as got a pair o' knicks on, sadly. Black an' a bit see through though; lil' bit on show. Can't argue wi' that.

When she smiles cutely an' tucks her flame red 'air behind her ear, ah realise ah'm not so sure o' me feelings for 'annah as ah was about three minutes ago. Under any other circumstances, this girl would be me dream woman. Fantastic legs, good arse on 'er, the faintest 'int o' a tummy, an' fantastic breasts – just the way ah like 'em. Best o' all though, she 'as the most beautiful face an' the deepest, darkest eyes. It looks like there's another universe behind them; another wondrous world. Preoccupied by me sexual evaluation ah fail to notice that she's clutchin' a bottle o' JD. The first thought to enter me 'ead is girls don't drink whisky.

* * *

'Ah'm not walkin' all the way 'om!' yells Gristle, hurling his glass bottle into the grubby waters that flow beneath the city's incongruously transparent shopping centre.

Spadge is being sick.

Jamal is petrified...

... I suppose the queues for taxis down by the waterfront is quite ghastly, but surely that's to be expected considering the mass of humanity in the vicinity this evening. I get the feeling that Tom and Will leaving with those two lovely young ladies did not improve Gristle's mood. Nor mine, to be quite frank. I've made a huge effort with those two tonight only to be left babysitting their pet psychopath. Still, I shall have thirty like this come November. I had better get used to it.

By jove, what is he doing now? Gristle is grabbing at the handle of a taxi door before it's even stopped, yanking it open and leaping out of it, dragging Spadge behind him. I suppose I'd better join them.

'Worthington Street please driver, it's a right at Black Hill-' I say to the cabbie but am quite rudely cut off by him telling me in no uncertain terms that he knows his own turf.

Spadge is nervously rummaging around in his pocket looking for money, giving Gristle a strange look as he does so. They are so drunk that they think I've not noticed. If they think I'm paying for them, they have got another thing coming!

Ten minutes later, Jamal and Spadge are legging it as fast as their legs will carry them up Black Hill. In spite of himself, Jamal is laughing; exhilarated by the thrill of the chase. Spadge glances behind him expecting to be overtaken by Gristle as per usual, but alarmingly, Gristle is just stood there at the brow of the hill; squaring up to the taxi driver and shouting profanities at him. For his part, the driver is swearing back at Gristle in Arabic; Kosovan; or possibly even Welsh. *Most unwise.*

Spadge stops running and then tugs on Jamal's arm, halting him too. Together they stand frozen; two rabbits in bright headlights. The urge to run almost overwhelms them, but is defeated by a stronger, masochistic predilection. After he regains his senses, Jamal thinks that he should go over there and offer the driver double fare for 'the inconvenience.' Spadge disagrees vociferously.

Inside himself, Jamal vows never to drink again – *he's going to be a teacher for heaven's sake! Drinking and running away from a taxi without paying! Whatever is next? Stealing traffic cones? Flirting with young girls?* Heroin? *It's a slippery slope...*

Jamal looks on in horror at what unfurls before his eyes.

EDUCATED & TRAINED

TOM WIPES HIS MOUTH WITH HIS RIGHT HAND and passes the bottle of whisky to Bethany with his left. She accepts it and takes an impressively large swig, controlling her facial expressions carefully so that she betrays only the slightest discomfort. She then passes the bottle back to Tom and looks deep into his eyes. They're the most bonnie pair that she's ever seen, she reckons; two dark oceans of reddy-brown. Eyes that have seen it all, and done it all. Tom has the eyes of a kindly old grandfather, so warm and wise. So loving. Bethany almost believes that they could swallow her whole.

'Don't talk to strangers,' her mother would warn her as a child. It's ironic, then, that she would never dare to discuss her thoughts and her problems with either a friend or relation, yet here she was wading through the story of her life; this stranger lapping up every word with as much zeal as he laps up her whisky. He just sits. And he listens. And he waits. He waits not for the chance to speak, as so many people (particularly obnoxious and opinionated student types) often do. He waits not for the chance to jump her bones, as so many people (particularly the old beggars down at that old train carriage place and the underage scallies in the Welly) do. What he's waiting for she doesn't know. Maybe he's been waiting for her.

'What about you, pet?' she asks.

'Oh no…' Tom protests. 'You *do not* wanna know,' he says slowly.

'C'mon, pet. It can't be that bad,' she says, attempting to force their strange competition forwards. Surely if he didn't want to be probed about whatever was so bad, he wouldn't have created so much intrigue about it?

He'd have just said that he had no problems and left it at that.

'Come on, Tom. I told you, so you can tell me. What are the three worst things that have ever happened to you?'

Tom puts the whisky bottle to his mouth and he drinks. And he drinks. And he drinks. He drinks until there is nothing left in the bottle but dregs. His eyes well up with tears and Bethany can't decide whether this is a result of the quantity and strength of liquor that he's just sunk… or something else.

'Ah… ah lost…' Tom fights back the tears and blows air into his cheeks, releasing it slowly to calm himself. 'S'alreet.'

Beth looks at him. She feels a sense of overpowering attraction; not necessarily sexual, platonic or even maternal – she can't explain it. All she knows is that those big red whisky-sore eyes are sucking her in.

Tom cocks his head to the side, avoiding Beth's deep gaze. He opens his mouth and speaks. The words that form the story of his loss drip from his mouth like blood from the dead.

'Remember September 11th?'

'Course,' Beth replies, uneasy about what would follow.

'Ah was working at an outsourcing company at the time, manning an IT 'elpdesk for this BACS software. Ah remember the news sorta leaking in, gradual. All the drama queens were latchin' onto it; end o' the world an' all that. Ah never paid much notice.

'It got to abart four o'clock, our time. Ah was sat at me desk on the phone, 'afe-way through re-installing some guy's software when suddenly ah remembered.

'Ah… ah… 'ad to end the call abruptly, ah me-an… ah was almost in tears wi' shock. Ah still managed to maintain me impeccable telephone manner though,' Tom continues, smiling at Beth through his tears.

She smiles back at him with warmth.

'Ah then went on to breck two o' the company's most sacred rules in under a minute: turning me 'andset onto *not ready* an' then turning me mobile on an' runnin' into the bogs.

'It was me mam what answered. She was in a reet state, obviously. Ah mean, yer would be, wouldn't yer? Ah asked her where *they* were…'

Beth's mouth begins to move to ask 'whom?', but she thinks better of it. She walks over to the threadbare armchair that is cradling Tom's weak and defenceless mortal remains and kneels before him, gently taking his right hand and clasping it in hers. Somehow, this wasn't how she expected her *Freshers' Week* to go. She'd been banking on more tequila slammers and free groceries from the bazaar.

'All… all they knew was that they were due into New York that morning. Poor sods. They knew no more than ah did. As for me, ah was numb. We'd just gotten word that the Pentagon had been attacked too. Ah kept thinking, what if they were on a tour in the Twin Towers or somet? What if they were in there when them planes crashed into 'em?'

Bethany squeezes Tom's hand. Inside she feels a heartstring silently break.

'Who was it?'

Tom laughs. 'That's the thing. They were fine. Me bruvver, that is, an' his bird. Took 'em abart a day to get word to us, but they were fine. They'd toured the towers the day before. Mental.'

Bethany looks confused.

'Two days later, they were both killed in a coach accident. One o' those big eighteen-wheelers jack-knifed on Route 66. They were burned alive.'

Silence.

Bethany puts her hand gently on Tom's leg, just above a nasty purple diesel stain.

Tom jerks forward in his chair and rubs his eyes. 'Ah'm sorry. Ah'm so sorry.'

Bethany looks into those eyes again. Where only a few moments ago she saw a dark and peaceful reddy-brown ocean that she could happily call home, now she sees nothing but red. She recoils slightly, as if this damaged young man's twisted emotions are infecting her like disease; a sickness jumping from his soul into hers. *Rage. Hate. Fear.*

But especially *fear*.

Tom's jaw begins to wobble as his comparatively calm storytelling gives way to a full-blown rant. His voice isn't loud; there's no need to worry about waking up the neighbours. Quite the opposite, in fact. The volume of his voice is disturbingly controlled, as if excessive decibels would merely serve as a conduit for the emotion to escape, and something tells Bethany that he doesn't want that. He's used to his pain. It brings him comfort.

Tom looks at Bethany straight in the eyes and she can't bring herself to match his gaze. There's a disturbing ambiguity about him now, and it frightens her.

His voice lowers to an undertone.

'...'is 'eart. 'is 'eart stopped pumping blood around 'is body. 'is lungs stopped inhaling air an' oxygenating 'is blood. 'e was just gone. Ah 'adn't... ah didn't even.... ah never 'ad time for 'im. It was like 'is life was just spent, while ah was too busy pissing about on t'internet an' playin' stupid football manager games.'

Silence descends once more, marking out Tom's territory in the same way that Rocky's spray does his. Tom becomes deathly quiet. In fact, he becomes so quiet and so still that when he does open his mouth again, Bethany visibly jumps.

'On a long enough timeline, everyone's survival rate drops to zero.'

Bethany doesn't know what to say to that.

'Who wrote that?' he snaps, his voice brash and aggressive.

Beth opens her mouth but no words follow. She just shrugs her shoulders. 'Freud?'

Tom laughs, and it's not a nice laugh.

'Palahniuk. What 'appens when people die?'

'Is this one a rhetorical question?' Bethany smiles, anxiously trying to lighten the mood.

'Not quite,' Tom replies coldly. 'See, not unlike a GCSE exam paper, the answer's in the question. *They die.*'

Beth can't help but cry. She's had enough. It's all too much; especially after a night's worth of alchopops and about a third of a bottle of whisky.

Another long and tense hush ensues.

Bethany is starting to get sick of this. She's been moved enough for one night. She's bored now. And she needs the toilet.

'Yeah, but…' Bethany says softly. In twenty-seven years she'd never really thought about it. 'Death only… I mean… You just have to treasure every last moment 'cos, as a very annoying and persistent holiday rep once told me, life isn't a dress rehearsal; these moments will never come again. No second chances. Sometimes it's harsh… sometimes it just reminds us what we've got.'

Beth gives herself a pat on the back. She should write that down.

Tom looks up, nodding but still not smiling. 'D-'yer know what ah did, a few days later, when ah found out abart the accident?'

Beth shakes her head.

'Ah went to the cinema. Ah saw *Scary Movie 2*. Ah didn't laugh once.'

'I suppose that's got to be expected, pet,' Bethany says gently.

'Yeah,' Tom sighs, rubbing his hands down his red face. *'It was shite.'*

He's back. He's Tom again.

Beth smiles and takes him by the hand. He smiles at her, more powerfully now.

Wow. Finally opened up to someone. But why this girl? Why not Hannah? Or even Anna, for that matter? Why not Will, who helped him through it all?

Tom smiles. 'Reet then, that's number one. Reckon you can 'andle another two?'

Bethany looks at him as if to say *you're taking the piss, pet,* but somehow she knows that he isn't. She tries so hard to be a considerate and attentive listener, but she really, really needs a poo.

Tom's voice has become hoarse and dry. Too many tears. Too many diaphoretics.

'...well. Can you imagine what losing a son did to me dad?'

Beth looks to the ground. She's genuinely touched by his tragic tales, and more than that, she's flattered that he'd tell them to her... but she *really* needs to take a dump. She's touching cloth.

'They found 'im mangled wi' 'is motorbike underneath a bush; no evidence of a collision. It must've been too much... me brother's death, like... it just got to 'im. An' nuffin' used to get ta 'im.'

Bethany hoists herself up and kisses Tom on the forehead. 'I need a drink of water. You want one?'

Tom grins. 'Inabit.'

Bethany is gone for a period that feels like forever. Tom finds himself out in the stars, and he doesn't like what he sees. The only constant that he can see in all the vastness of the universe is death, and the very idea of it both frightens him and turns him on; makes him feel like the animal that he is.

And he can't stop thinking about Beth's bits; that brief glance up her skirt has really started something. It shouldn't be anything to get excited about. It's just reproductive organ. A means to propagation. But what would Beth be to him if she didn't have one? If she didn't have a body, for that matter? What if she was just the loose construct of a personality... sort of floating about? Would he still be feeling this way? Or is he only feeling these strong emotions because her personality is all wrapped up inside legs and arse and breasts?

Bethany's trapped in there. Chained to an animal. Enslaved to instinct.

And, as an animal, that beautiful personality could be lost. *As could mine...*

Fancy that...

You could die like him.

Educated and trained for all those years, just to be burned alive in the wreck of a bus.

Game over.

No extra lives.

You do not know why this is so, whether it is fair or not, or just how this life that passes before your gawping eyes even exists. Why does it even matter? You're just another no-one. What makes you better than a fly, an ant or a fish? They live, in comparison to you, for a feeble amount of time. Achieving nothing. Understanding less.

Perhaps your limited though greater knowledge does make you somehow better; after all, the might and wisdom of the human race puts you on another plain, surely? You may be just mere animals - mortal as fuck - but you understand science, nature and astronomy.

But who is to say that your vast intellect is not dwarfed by superior beings? Are you to them as the insects are to you? Are you even further removed? After all, you didn't make the insects…

… but something made you.

What would your God make of you now?

THE ANTS ARE KILLING EACH OTHER! *They have primitive flying machines and they are dropping rudimentary explosive devices on one another! They are burning each other! Gassing each other!* Torture! Rape! Kill! *They are exterminating themselves and polluting their world. They are slowly killing themselves with tobacco, alcohol, cholesterol, cars, bullets, chimneys, reality TV, wrestling and t'internet.*

Look – they have fired up their ovens. Another 'final' solution. They are poisoning them. They are destroying them. They are fighting and dying for causes not even their own. They are dying for the rich, dying for the powerful; dying, Dying, DYING whILsT the elEphanTs mOUrn anD tHe PIGS CONTEMPLATE deAtH.

Take the gun. Put it to her head. 'You're going to die, right here, right now. This is the end. The final curtain. I CAN MAKE YOU DIE, BETHANY. Are you scared?'

Everything you are. Everything you could be.

No more fanny-fun for you.

Bang-bang-a-boom!

It can all be extinguished.

That is the only true POWER you have.

It is all in your head, waiting to pass into nothingness. The people you loved. Family. Friends. Lovers. The girls that you have loved in vain. Hannah – the girl you are so stupidly, utterly and unselfishly in love with.

AH CAN MECK A DIFFERENCE!

At least to one person.

To one girl.

Perhaps your head is out in the stars.

Perhaps ah am the stars. Ah just wanted… ah just want-

You just wanted Hannah. Love across the stars.

Or maybe you just love the idea *of you and her. The sensationalism. After all you have been through... the miraculous coming together! You just want it to payoff like a wrestling angle. You just want her... and now-*

Ah just still want her. Still.

You still just want Anna. Still, too.

No... ah just want Beth. Now. Too.

You do not want any of them. Never have.

Ah just want Beth. Still. Now. Too.

YOU DON'T CARE ABOUT ANYONE ELSE BUT YOU

then now *forever*

AH DON'T CARE ABART ANYONE ELSE BUT ME

bUt aH mUSt!

Before ah die ah 'ave to... Wi' every day that passes by it's one day less that ah 'ave to spend wi' 'er.

But what if ah'm wrong?

What if ah pick the wrong one?

Beth? Anna? 'annah?

No... ah can do it.

It's just...

There's a problem.

Ah'm not sure that the fire in these eyes is mine. Ah think ah may be suffering from the stigma of a curse that ah inflicted on mesen long ago. And it's getting bigger and bigger.

It's perspective.

Time to die again now, Tommo.

Okay. Fair play.

Fair enough.

Furry muff-

'Aaah!' Tom jumps as Bethany strokes his short, short hair.

'Nodded off did yer?' she asks, handing him a glass of water. 'I'm off to bed, pet.' She pauses, looks him in the eye and then bites her bottom lip. 'You're welcome to... er... go head to toe with me if you want.'

Tom feels like he's been hit hard, and he is overcome by a strange dizziness that eventually succumbs to nausea. He pictures himself as a swatted fly, buzzing around insanely and about to die.

'Ah'd love to,' he smiles, his vision a blur of beauty and terror. There's a rogue idea gestating in his head about taking something so beautiful and turning it into something ugly and disgraceful.

Or, at least, there was. That particular voice has suddenly fallen silent.

Will can't sleep. He tosses and he turns. He takes countless sips of water - all of which only contribute to his discomfort, rather than alleviate it.

Minutes turn into hours.

He shouldn't have had that pizza on the way home. It's made his mouth dry and his stomach bloated. He can feel it in there swimming about. *All them greasy calories.* He'll be fat and then he'll never get any stunners like this Katie ever again.

He opens his mouth wide and swallows a massive lungful of air. He then closes his mouth, and gulps the air down as quickly as he can. He repeats this action several times until there is a very lumpy, very smelly pile of sick on Katie's bedroom floor.

Not his problem.

Will lays back, relaxes, and lets the Sandman's grip tighten around his throat.

But as soon as he begins to dream, Will longs for consciousness. Lucid dreams are the worst; a life of drink, drugs and women brings only grim, uneasy dreamscapes. Nightmarish wraiths. Fat, deformed visions of his future.

His hand clasps the piece of paper in his hand. He will never surrender it. Not like this.

'I will give you to the count of three Mr Surewood,' hisses the hooded figure looming in the shadows of his mind. 'And if you do not give me your little tally, then I will shoot you in the face.'

'Bring it,' whispers Will's sleeping mouth. 'Just bring it.'

Bethany strips naked and cuddles up to Tom, who is already in the buff beneath the sheets of the comfiest bed that he can ever remember being in. *So much for going 'ead to toe.* The touch of her skin against his body warms him both inside and out. There's no blatant sexuality to it; at least, not right now. It just feels warm. And good. And natural. *Animal to animal.*

Bethany closes her eyes and falls asleep instantly. She dreams sweet dreams. She dreams about a bridge over a river. She dreams about Tom.

So this is death! It feels... ah dunno. Weird. Ah expected more angels an' choirs an' that.

Less darkness.

Fewer ladders.

At least, ah suppose this is a ladder – it feels like one.

Will finds himself climbing up what must surely be a ladder. A voice in his head tells him to keep on climbing and so that's exactly what he does.

Crawling through a conveniently-placed hatch and appearing in a curiously familiar clothes shop, the first thing that he sees is her. A memory hits him like a sledgehammer.

''olly,' he says, his voice trembling with emotion.
'Hi,' Holly replies.

Will pulls Holly close to him and holds her ever so tightly; ever so lovingly. He's breathing their past.

A single tear of joy runs down his left cheek.

In the corner of his eye he notices Holly's friend, Laura, and more memories come flooding back – these not so stirring.

'Laura is looking very nice these days,' Satan whispers.

Arse checks with more meat on them than a battery-farmed elephant... but Will wants to slip his cock between them all the same. *Again...*

'AH'M SORRY!!!!!!' he screams. Once more his cries trigger the transition from one world into another; more of a rip than a segue.

He clutches Katie's sheets as a cold sweat envelops him.

It must be a sad life when its most outstanding moment is standing on an old stone bridge in the pale moonlight. The tall and polished trees cast shadows over the river below, and you're kissing a beautiful young man. You're sharing a bottle of whisky.

Tom looks into Bethany's eyes and he tells her that he loves her. And he means it.

They've fallen in love in just one night.

Maybe it's more romance than love *per se*, but in Bethany's drunken heart it feels as real as real can be.

Bethany feels so cold and so drunk, but she's glowing with a sense of contentment and hope. Tom holds her tight as the river ebbs and flows beneath them, and as he says 'Ah love you' everything suddenly makes sense to her. Her whole life seemed to have been building to this moment. Her whole life had always been geared towards the bridge.

She stares down at their reflection in the water.

In the undertow she sees a hand that will not let her go.

Never before has Bethany Hunt felt so joyful. Her eyelids flutter ever so slightly as her sleeping mind embellishes and romanticises the evening. And in another world – a world almost free of embroidery and romance – Tom rolls over, looks at her face and smiles softly.

Almost.

He leans forward and gently brushes a few strands of red hair out of her face, then he kisses her gently on her lips. She seems to feel it despite the gulf in reality between them; her smile widens, and she lets out a long, contented sigh.

Tom lays awake for a few minutes staring into the darkness, considering. The night, especially the drunken night, seems about as far removed from reality as you can get. How would he feel tomorrow? How would Bethany feel? Would he even remember the baring of his soul? Would h-

-rld falls away in a bath of flames and two burning eyes pierce Tom's very soul; the last thing that he'll ever see…

THE PERFECT CRIME

AWAKE.
Tasting the alcohol in the back of his throat, Tom's first instinct is to run his fingers over his eyebrows. Standard procedure. He's thankful to feel their presence beneath his fingertips.

Tom's second instinct is to open his eyes, but as he does so the brightness very nearly blinds him, and so he skips straight ahead to step three – touch. He is lying in a bed. A very comfortable bed, it seems. He is wearing his boxers, which tells him very little beyond the fact that he probably hasn't pissed the bed.

Wincing, he attempts step two once again, and this time manages to keep his eyes open long enough for them to adjust to the light. Looking around the room, he sees posters of Kurt Cobain and Bob Marley on the wall. He finds the combination a little bizarre, but even so the former poster impresses.

Mentally, Tom is in as much anguish as he is physically. This is blatantly a girl's bedroom, which begs the obvious question - what has he done? He should have been somewhere else last night. He should have been with *someone* else. With Hannah. His unfathomable obsession with her now infects his every thought, bringing both magnificence and terror to his insect life.

Wistfully he recalls the first time that they ever made love – the *only* time that they've ever made love. As he holds that thought, the bedroom door opens and a strikingly beautiful Geordie redhead in a very skimpy silk dressing gown walks in with some spaghetti on toast and a cup of what looks like tea. Without even realising it, while he'd been reminiscing about Hannah he'd been rubbing himself. Again, wanking himself sober was standard procedure when he felt rough in the morning; always did the trick. This redhead notices him making a tent of the sheets as she awkwardly – and very probably *deliberately* - tries to place the breakfast try right on his lap. Tom is lost for words, and so he quickly grabs the mug of tea and drinks a hefty gulp. *That's weird,* he thinks as he puts the mug down. He never even considered that she might have put something toxic in it. The after-taste makes him wish that she had, though.

'What this?' he grumbles, having found the words which were eluding him just moments since.

'It's *green*,' says the redhead, smiling. As she sits herself down on the edge of the bed, her dressing gown parts ever so slightly. Tom can almost see her right breast. No bra.

'Riiigght...' Tom says slowly. 'Green.'

'It's good for hangovers. Anti-oxidants. Flushes out your system.'

'Thanks.... um... 'annah?' *Well... it's as good a guess as any.*

Bethany sighs as she stands and begins to tidy up the room around him. 'It's Beth, remember?' *So much for the bridge.* 'Bethany?'

Tom looks at her intensely, sifting through the haze to try and place the memory.

Bethany stops her tidying up and points an accusatory finger at him, far too close to his face for comfort. 'Look, Tom. Last night really meant a lot to me,' she begins, Tom beginning to panic.

Ah'm scum. Ah'm scum. Ah'm scum ah thought ah loved 'annah. Ah thought ah loved 'annah... Ah'm no better than Will.

'Do you even remember what we were talking about?'

A thousand memories hit him like bullets in the head; rapid-fire.

Slack-jawed, he can't do anything but smile up at her.

With a sigh, Bethany throws down her mucky washing and wanders back over to the bed. She climbs up on to it, knocking Tom's breakfast all over her carpet. Well... *Studicom*'s carpet, strictly speaking.

Tom glances down at the mess on the floor, but Bethany's gaze is unflinching. She's looking him square in the eyes. Steaming hot, Bethany learns forward and gives Tom the biggest, dirtiest and sexiest snog of his entire life and as she pulls away, smiling tenderly, Tom feels the impact of the softest bullet ever shot.

Tom gets dressed and says an awkward goodbye to Beth. Strangely enough, she asks him to go out for a drink and he accepts, albeit guiltily, unsure of whether he'll actually go through with it. He pulls open Beth's bedroom door and walks straight into Will in the hallway; his tongue rammed down that Katie bird's throat. It's all coming back to him now.

'Morning sexay,' Katie says. *To him? To Will? To thin air?* Tom can't be sure.

Will frowns. So it was to Tom. *Nice one.*

'You off 'ome, mush?' Will asks him, slapping Katie's posterior quite savagely. She pretends to be annoyed about it. She's not.

'Umm... aye mate. One sec.' Tom turns around and shouts another goodbye to Beth. She smiles at him with that Bethany smile again and he's lost in an effervescence of conflicting emotion. Katie shakes him out of it.

'And tell your mate here that I only ever want to see one bodily fluid from him next time - and it ain't puke.'

Will smiles sheepishly. 'Few too many jars, wannit. Ah 'ad ta get wrecked to be able to go 'ome wiv you!'

This time Katie really does look angry. 'Funny,' she says over her shoulder as she ascends the stairs. 'I had to get trolleyed to be able to go home with you, *sick boy*.'

Tom can't help but chuckle to himself. A few too many jars, indeed. *A likely story.*

'Bye Tom,' Katie shouts downstairs as Will and Tom both leave.

'Inabit.'

The two friends walk to the end of the road in silence. Will is seething not only because of his new bird being so flighty with his best mate, but also because she treated him with as little respect as... well, with as little respect as he did her.

Tom's mind is gurning away. Painfully. Trying to make sense of it all. It can't.

Will stops suddenly.

'What's up, mate?' asks Tom.

Will is staring intently at an old tramp who's going through some bins at the end of the road.

'Nowt mate. Nuffin'. It's just... for a minute, ah thought ah saw...'

'Who? That mystery murderer?' Tom jests.

'Yeah reet,' Will scoffs, resuming his walk home. 'Ah thought someone 'ad got arrested for that anyways? Ah'm sure that Katie said somet about 'em tecking some woman in for questionin'.'

'*A woman?* Seriously?' Tom sounds appalled. 'Women can't be serial killers. That's just wrong. It just don't 'appen.'

'Aye. Oh ah dunno, ah was vegged. Mebbe ah didn't 'ear her reet. Anyways, Ah'm starvin. Fancy gettin' some scran before we go 'ome?'

'Ah'm not that fussed mate, watchin' the gut and all that. Not all of us can be like thee and just chuck it all back up!'

'Fek off! It's good for yer. Better than bein' a gret fat chuff like thee! Ah don't see thee gettin' birds the standard of me Katie. It wor the bestest, muckiest shag o' me whole life last night, by the way. Number sixty-three! No condom bonus too.'

'Good for you, mate,' Tom couldn't be less interested.

'You do that weird un'?'

After a brief internal deliberation Tom mumbles 'number twenty-one', wondering whether he's lying or not as he says the words.

Will smiles at him. It's the sort of smile that one often sees a father give to a son that he's proud of, not that Will would know much about that. Will throws his right arm around Tom's shoulders and thumps him lovingly in the chest.

'Nice one, mush. Told yer all tha needed was another bit o' fluff to forget about that 'annah slag.'

Tom glares at him, momentarily incensed. *No-one says owt about 'is 'annah.* Although... is that who Will meant, or did he mean Anna, who Will himself had porked? *Ah fuck it. Ain't worth arguin' about.*

''annah slag*s*,' Tom says with a grin. Will looks dumfounded. *'Plural.'*

Will shakes his head. 'Come on, soft lad,' he says. 'Let's go an' get a sausage sandwich an' a milkshake from the twenny-four 'our supermarket.'

Tom looks at his watch. 'Won't be oppen yet, mate. It's only 'afe seven.'

'It's twenny-four 'our! There's a comically-over-sized flashing red sign on the front of the building sayin' "24 HOURS". Course it'll be oppen.'

'Ah know it does, but it still don't oppen till 'afe eight on a Sunday. Shuts at ten 'an all.'

'This country! Come on then, let's risk a fry-up down t'old railway carriage instead. We'll fill our tallies in an' all. Ah'm quite impressed wi' the weird 'un by the way; fit as, cut above your normal crap like…'

Will's last comment prompts Tom to stop and reflect for a moment on Will's relentless pursuit of women. He doesn't seem to care about anything else anymore. He wasn't always like that, not back in the old days. Not when Holly was about.

Even for a while after she chucked him, he wasn't anything like this. There was a time not so long ago when Will was always there for him. He'd helped him through just about every atrocity that life had thrown at him, but now he did little else beside shagging and talking about shagging – unless of course you count a bit of gambling with Gristle. Thinking about it though, even that's probably just because he wants a cool vice to impress the ladies with and add a little more depth to his colourless character.

And it saddens Tom. He feels sadness not only for Will, but also for himself. Somehow along the way, he's become infused with Will's hopes and dreams. Will's doctrines have become his own.

Tom casts his mind back to just before they moved up to Hull; to just after Gristle came out of the young offenders' place. Both he and Will were sat in his living room with crayons, colouring in their tallies. It was then - sat crayoning his colourful, innocent-looking chart - that Tom realised he couldn't do it anymore. He couldn't keep chasing Will and the tallies. There would be no end to it.

He saw them as old men in a Bingo Hall, tallies neck and neck, shagging grannies in an attempt to knob one more than the other one before death. Chances are that the 'winner' would simply be the last man alive in any event. It was then that Tom realised he wanted more from life, and soon afterwards Hannah came along. Unfortunately though, she's left him feeling every bit as empty as he did being Will's reluctant apprentice.

    And so Tom presses on with his tally.

    Tom presses on with his pursuit of Hannah.

There's nowt else to do.

Tom and Will walk up Black Hill looking like the living dead, hungover as hell and extremely disappointed that they couldn't get their usual greasy fry-up from the old railway carriage place thanks to some nonsense about environmental health. As they turn into Worthington Street and draw closer to their house, even in their zombified state it's evident that the front door is noticeably ajar. Enraged, Tom pulls out his mobile phone and begins to compose an angry text. It goes something like this:

```
Spadge  u  chimp.  Uve  left  door  open  again.
Just  cos  u  dont  live  here  no  more  dont  mean
u can take piss and let us get robbed. Cock.
```

As Tom is thrashing away at his phone, Will is examining the door closely with an uncharacteristic look of concern on his face. 'It's not been left oppen, mush – it's been *forced.*'

    The two young men look at each other. 'Gristle? 'ome?' begins Tom.

    '…on a Sunday? Wi' the bookies *an'* the pubs open? No–' continues Will.

    '…chance in 'ell. Jamallio? Surely 'e wouldn't, an' probably couldn't, force–' Tom carries on.

    '…a door if 'is life depended on it, an' ah doubt very much Spadge would breck in.'

The two perturbed students look beyond the door that is swinging in the wind and into their vestibule. Making as little noise as possible, they tip-toe inside.

First off they check the downstairs. Jamal's room is locked, and the living room, bathroom and kitchen are all as they left them – looking like a bomb had hit. So far, so good.

Treading carefully so as not to make a sound, Tom ascends the narrow staircase. Will is right behind him. Narrowing his eyes in concentration, Tom is sure that he can hear a noise coming from his bedroom, and so he silently looks at Will who nods in acknowledgment – *'e 'ears it too!*

Almost at the top of the stairs now, Tom reaches for the handle of his bedroom door...

'Wait!' Will says in that whispering-voice-but-still-loud-anyway sort of way, making Tom jump and nearly fall back down the stairs. 'What if it's that murderer? Murderess. Whatever. The one who... yer know... took them two lasses? They still ain't found no bodies. Mebbe she's put the corpses in your room?'

Tom lets out a deep breath and waves an accusatory finger. 'Why would she do that?' he scoffs.

Both men almost jump out of their skins again as Tom's pocket begins to vibrate and play some polyphonic sci-fi, which at the moment seems even louder than it does when it goes off in lectures.

Tom answers it and hopes for the best. Somehow he thinks that whoever was in his room might have done one out of the window by now anyway. 'Yeah, course ah am!' he yells at Spadge down the phone. 'Oh... ah know. Sorry mate,' he apologises, his voice going quieter again. 'Well some fucker 'as brocken in! What... Gristle... not again! The mad twat. Oh you're not! What about Jumanji?'

Tom doesn't know whether to laugh or cry. Spadge, Jamal and Gristle have all been banged up for the night! He waves a dismissive hand at Will. 'Ah'll tell yer in a minute, bud,' he whispers, before saying 'alreet Spadge, ah'll see thee in a couple a week. 'ope you an' Becks can gerrit sorted.'

Tom slides his mobile into his back pocket and then pushes open his bedroom door cautiously.

Jamal sees Spadge off at the train station, reminding his new friend that he is lucky not to be returning to Swindon with a criminal caution.

Jamal stinks. He hasn't shaved and he can taste decaying proteins on his breath. One night – just one night – out with these yobbos was all that it took for him to spend his first night in jail. Thank the lord he has been let off with a verbal warning – even a caution would have had the potential to destroy his teaching career.

GRISTLE.

So now he knows, and his initial assessment was correct – *he didn't want to know.* Jamal had learned that Ben 'Gristle' Davis was so-called because of his perverted propensity to bite people's ears off.

His thoughts running off on a tangent, Jamal wonders if he can somehow use this revelation to get out of his housing contract – surely *Studicom* are under some statutory duty to disclose such matters about a property's co-tenants?

'I'm living with a monster!' Jamal mutters to himself. 'What would Mother say? What would Uncle Indra say? What would the people on the PGCE think of me if they ever found out?'

Outside the station Jamal instinctively moves to flag down a cab, but then, remembering the previous night's misadventures, he thinks better of it. Instead he zips up his cardigan and braves the late September winds. He's sure that there's the odour of rotting fish in the air today.

Looking inside himself, Jamal feels deeply ashamed. In spite of his fear, he enjoyed running away from that taxi.

But it was theft and it was wrong.

But it was also *extremely* liberating.

Glancing around the squalor of his bedroom (as long as his PC and CDs are okay, Tom doesn't much care for the rest of the room) he is first struck by the female clothing scattered across his floor. His eyes move from the clothing and onto the bed. Somebody is asleep in it.

Tom fights the desire to quote Daddy Bear, instead looking nervously over at Will, who smiles and suddenly yanks the covers away to reveal the scrawny, naked figure of Anna.

'She's done a bit of weight since ah 'ad her,' Will observes.

'Shhhh!' Tom says, rounding on him. 'If she wecks up an' finds out ah slept someweer else last nite ah'm in for it good and proper!'

Tom forces Will from the room, who for his part is chuckling to himself, repeating 'Ah can't believe the mad bitch brock in!'

Tom closes the door behind him and puts it on the Yale. He quietly strips to his boxers and snuggles up to Anna, pulling the sheets over them both. He has to admit to being a bit relieved; he might not have wanted to come home to Anna in his bed, but she's better than Jack the bloody Ripper. *Or should that be Jackie?* He'd have to pick up a paper later.

For the first time in a good ten minutes, Tom allows himself the luxury of breathing easily. Anna must have been hammered if she broke in, so chances are she won't remember his not being there when she fell asleep.

He's gotten away with it.

The perfect crime.

Bow to the master.

A few short hours later the sun begins to go down over Black Hill. Well, not in reality of course – it's Black Hill that's moving, not the sun. But from the perspective of the students asleep on Worthington Street, the sun is vanishing beneath the horizon in a stunning wake of light blue and soft magenta.

Half awake, Tom feels a soft, female hand stroking his stubbly face and he hears a husky, female voice. 'How hammered were we?'

Tom smiles as he opens his eyes. Every muscle in his body contorts as Anna's world-weary visage comes into focus, so close to him that she obscures everything else in his field of vision. His insides cry out in confusion and pain. *'ere comes that awful feelin' again.* His mouth just says 'Spadge', flatly.

His skin crawls under Anna's delicate caresses as he wishes that it was Hannah laying beside him naked – his *real* Hannah. He wants so badly to shout and swear and rage and throw Anna out of his house; to tell her that he never wants to see her again, but how could he without revealing his own transgression? For all his loathing, he can't bear to have her think of him as being like Will. He needs the high ground, always.

Maybe he should end it for good. He certainly wants to. The trouble is he's never been any good at chucking women, especially when they cry. He's always been a slave to the guilt-trip. Besides, he's never had to chuck a neurotic and potentially dangerous lover… it could end up being the death of him. You never know.

An indignant mewing gradually gets louder and louder as Rocky trundles into the room. As the cat notices Tom in bed, it looks up at its adopted master and mews silently in the way that cats do when they want something. The mouth opens, but no sound follows.

Daddy, I'm so hungry that I don't even have the strength to make the noise commensurate with begging.

It feels wrong. It's as if someone has just pressed *mute*.

'Eyup little sausage!' Tom says chirpily, scooping up the cat and plonking it down ungraciously on his lap. It often amazes Tom just how much capacity this little creature has for improving his mood.

Rocky purrs as Tom tickles around its ears, under its chin and around the sides of its belly. 'You is getting reet fat, isn't you Rocky feller? We is gonna 'ave to watch them treaties aren't we then? Yeah we are.'

Anna shakes her head. 'You are so gay.'

'*Jealous*,' Tom snaps back in a playful tone, thinly veiling the intense anger that he is feeling towards her presntly.

The doorbell rings, and for once the cheap and gloriously inappropriate *Star Spangled Banner* is the most beautiful sound that Tom could wish to hear – the perfect excuse to escape Anna's clutches, if only for a few blessed minutes.

He rises to his feet and moves towards the staircase. Anticipating Tom's next move, Rocky runs down the stairs first and positions itself directly ahead of the front door.

'Meow', Rocky says, which is cat for *am I not a clever cat? Please give me some milk.*

Rocky looks quite dejected when Tom doesn't respond. Instead, Tom pulls open the door to reveal what looks very much like a tramp.

'Meow,' Rocky adds, which is cat for *I refuse to associate myself with a stinking, fetid creature such as the one that has presented itself at my door. Be sure he leaves quickly, Thomas.* And with that, Rocky trundles away in search of the airing cupboard.

'Yeah?' says Tom aggressively. He can't stand scroungers. Jehovah's witnesses. Do-gooders. Double glazing salesmen. Gas men. People who knock at the door, generally. Dickheads all.

This guy couldn't even pass for a do-gooder, though. He isn't even trendy-scruffy - *the rips in them jeans are genuine*, Tom observes, hoping that this tramp (which, to him, translates as potentially murderous rapist) can't hear his thoughts. This guy's homish-like beard is hardly all the rage either, not unless you're of the Jewish persuasion or early-noughties Brad Pitt.

'Zwilltheer?' asks the tramp, the beard making it difficult to make out his mouth, let alone have a stab at guessing his age.

Tom begins to shut the door. 'Sorry, not today mate.'

The tramp puts his boot in the door, making Tom wonder if the Gods really do have something personal against him. Sometimes it seems like his life is just one great manipulation; a master plan to ensure that whatever happens, he loses. 'No, no...' the tramp says, his size twelves keeping the door firmly open. 'Duz Willzurwud live 'ere?'

Will! Tom's big brown eyes suddenly open wide and he relaxes slightly. *At least it won't be me gettin' bummed*, he thinks to himself, and then immediately wishes he hadn't. He's going to have to get better at not thinking. His thoughts are not secure; people are always listening.

'Ye... urm... actually, who's asking?'
'Sizfavver.'
'Come again?'
'Sizfavver!' the tramp repeats angrily.

And for those English speakers among us? Tom thinks, but manages to limit his actual response to 'What?'

'Tizjimzurwud, hisfavver!' the tramp replies with slightly less menace, probably because of the huge slurp of special brew he's just taken from his can.

Tom gives up. 'WILL!' he shouts, turning to the tramp and adding 'one sec, *mate*'. The word 'mate' is uttered with complete distain.

After an eternal moment, at the top of the stairs two hairy legs covered in fake tan hone into view, followed by some blue and red *Playboy* boxers; a flat but flaccid and equally tantastic stomach; wide shoulders; a stubbly, good-looking jaw; and a closely-shaven head.

Will utters a single word from beneath his furrowed brow.

'Dad?'

THE FAST TRACK TO FAME

TOM LOOKS AT HIMSELF IN HIS FULL-LENGTH mirror. He is wearing some machine-torn black boot-cut jeans from *Top Man*; a baggy, forgiving black t-shirt emblazoned with the legend *Jesus is My Homeboy* (whatever that means); and he has several brown leather bands tied slackly around his wrists. He still isn't used to the skinhead. He may have to let it grow out, at least a little bit. Still, he didn't look too bad. Much better than some. Much worse than others. *Average*.

Tom thinks about all the faces that he's seen and all the people that he's known and cared for. It saddens him to think that one day, when he's long gone, nobody will remember just another face in the crowd. Indeed, his poor old mam and his friends may all remember him until they too die, but after seventy years, or a hundred… then who would remember? He'd just be a name in a census for a historian to glance over. He'd be a stat. A number.

He moves closer to the mirror, looking so deep into his own eyes that he can see the small red veins that bind the white together. Veins carrying the blood around his body to make him function. He is a machine. *A machine so easily broken.*

Goosebumps suddenly spring up on his arm. Somebody is dancing on his grave again; *some presence*. He thinks about the two girls who, with no explanation, just ceased to be. Did they just pack their bags and go? Or is someone, or something, taking them away and-

What if he's the next victim? What if he dies tonight, without having set things right with Hannah; without having resolved within himself his own feelings towards Bethany?

And what if he killed the killer? Would he be a hero? Or would they lock him away? Either way, he'd be more than just another no-one. He'd be a newspaper clipping. Perhaps even a bit of TV footage; a documentary, even. Better than a statistic, surely?

And then it hits him: *it would be so easy.*

It would be so easy to make himself famous; to carve his own dark and bloody niche deep into the annals of time. A killing here, a killing there. So much easier than a peace prize here, a cancer cure there. And in the end, who's more of a man? The killer? The man who knows what he wants to do, and has the conviction to sate his blood lust, or the hero who dedicates his entire life - all that he is - to making the world a better place? Is the hero not the weaker man, letting the wills of other men break him and mould him into a shape imposed by society?

Tom looks once more into his brown and red eyes. He has the power to have an effect on so many lives in so many ways. He could make them so much better. Or so much worse. He could even take them away.

He could buy a cheap machete, run down Worthington Street and lop off some young hottie's leg. And she'd be left like that, forever; hobbling around, blue-badged. That action could never be undone, and it would be she who would have to live with the consequences. He could take something fit and sexy and gorgeous and turn it into something that reeks of imperfection. He has the power to do that, if he chooses. A brief lapse of sanity on his part could ruin a life. It could even *end* a life.

But people don't seem to appreciate this when he looks them in the eye. They don't recognise the power that he has over them; the power to shape and to bend and to mutilate, or even extinguish, their dismal little lives.

All he'd have to do is to loosen his grip that little bit more, and he could end up being very, very famous indeed. Then Hannah would be sorry-

But who's he kidding? He doesn't have the balls to do anything at all. He can barely step outside his digs, he's so afraid of the world and who he'll meet; who his heart will use to torture him next.

His thoughts turn to his father.

Tom remembers the dad who taught him to read, write and ride a bike. And then he went and killed himself on one.

But what happened that day?

Who cast the final stone?

What was the final straw?

Tom stops and wonders what his final straw could be.

Hopefully he'll never find out. But everyone says that.

Looking at his watch, he sees that he has time for at least one more glass of liquid paraffin (or whatever it is that he's supping) before Gristle will be ready. He takes a sip - pulling a hideous, disgusted face as he does so - and then tries to imagine Daddy's final day.

His ever-enlarging cat sits underneath the radiator, selfishly soaking up all the warmth. It opens its eyes just a tiny little bit and then yawns, exposing a fierce arsenal of teeth.

Everyone's a killer.

Tom sits down on the bed and has a bit of a cry.

Time and experience had taken the looks of a young Jimmy Dean and forged the face of an older, troubled man. The youthful, clean-shaven face had given way to a grey, unkempt beard and his hair had receded so far back that he was practically bald. However, the biggest change between the boy that he was years ago and the man that he had become was the permanent worry-line etched across his forehead.

His grief was only to be expected. He was stood in a cold hospital room looking down on his dying niece, Gemma. He was hoping against hope that he wouldn't lose his favourite niece, but he also knew that his hopes and prayers meant nothing. It wasn't a matter of how much he hoped or how often he prayed; it was a matter of whether the treatments would prove effective.

'Uncle Matty,' came a voice. The man looked down at his niece, in his heart knowing that at seven years old, her story was all but over. The voice continued fearfully, yet brave and resigned. 'What's it like to be dead?'

These words almost broke the man. 'Ah don't know, lovey,' he lied. But he knew, and that knowledge was slowly eating him up inside. He wanted to believe that a girl who knew nothing of wickedness or evil would go to a better place. He wanted to believe that his son wasn't lost forever. He *wanted* to believe.

He needed to believe that it didn't just go black.

A few hours later Gemma died, and when she did, she took the last vestiges of Matty Briggs with her.

DESTINY'S CRUEL HAND

IT'S WEIRD FOR TOM AND GRISTLE TO BE at a party without Will. Growing up, Will had the strength of character to mediate between these two diametrically-opposed youths, serving as the conduit for their unlikely friendship. In his absence, however, they have little to say to each another. Tommo can't help but remember Gristle throwing eggs at him, stealing his shoes and taking his dinner money. Gristle's mind, on the other hand, won't allow to him access to any memories prior to his release from the young offenders' institution. It just doesn't go back that far. Not enough storage space.

Gristle takes a huge swig of his sulphuric acid (or whatever it is that he's drinking) and then crouches down and pokes at his ankle fiercely. Unwisely, a number of the student party-goers begin to stare at him, but fortunately most of them are more enthralled by their host - Doctor Shabba - and his amusing diversions. He is pulling out all the old party games – *Spin the Bottle, The Tractor Game, Truth or Dare,* and even his own creation, *The Room.*

Tom doesn't spend long pondering on just how a law student ended up with the handle 'Doctor Shabba'. He just accepts it as he accepts 'Spadge' and 'Gristle.' Besides, he has more on his mind. The nightmares are now worse than ever before, affecting him to the point where they open out right in front of his waking eyes. These are no longer short and intense dreams but prolonged and painful tortures. He can no longer brush them aside - they have to be faced and conquered.

As if dealing with the grief of a family lost wasn't enough, his fragile pubescent emotions won't give him a moment's respite. He can't get Bethany out of his mind; it's as if she'd summed up his whole existence in just one drunken night, and he doesn't know whether he likes that or not. Perhaps he does.

On top of that, he is teeming with feelings of guilt, remorse and fear for what he would eventually have to do – and soon – to Anna. If she weren't so unhinged, she'd have been chucked long back, but it's getting to the stage now where he can't put up with her any longer. She has to go, no matter what she does to herself.

And just to cap it all off, floating like an oil slick on top of the water is the dark and poisonous, yet insufferably seductive, presence of Hannah. Whatever issues he faces at the bottom of the Humber, whenever he looks up all he can see is her slimy soul obscuring all the world's light.

'Your turn geezer,' chirps the East End accent of Doctor Shabba, the stout law student DJ who looks like a young Colin Baker – garish *Doctor Who* trousers and all.

Tom is shaken out of his waking nightmare. 'Wh-at?'

'*The Room*, me old china; here we go. Pick a card. Any card.'

Tom moves to take a card with the lumbering reflexes of someone totally pissed-up, but he is beaten to it by Gristle who violently snatches a card, only to crouch straight back down and ram it into the side of the electronic tracking device securely attached to his ankle.

''scuse us, mate,' protests Shabba, but fortunately for him Gristle is too busy trying to escape the bondage of his already-broken curfew to traumatically sever his ear with his teeth.

'Don't ask, mate,' says Tom, grabbing the twenty-stone DJ by the arm and dragging him away from Gristle speedily and with surprising strength. Safely away from Gristle, Tom forces a smile and looks Shabba in the eye. 'Reet then! Pick a card, wozzit?'

'Er… yeah,' says Shabba, looking back over his shoulder and scowling at Gristle who is now poking at his anklet with the indoor TV aerial. 'Who are you two anyways? I don't recognise yer.'

'Ah…' Tom began. 'Ah'm a mate of Spadge's. That youth over there is Ben. Gristle, we call 'im. One of me 'ousemates. 'e's no trouble… really.'

Shabba reluctantly holds out the incomplete pack of cards.

'Pick a card. Any card.'

Katie pulls the chain to flush the toilet and looks over at the bath with concern. She hears the water leave the lavatory, travel underneath the floorboards, up through the pipes behind her, turn right and then reappear in a gurgling fountain of faeces just above the bath's plughole. Sometimes she wishes that she would disappear.

Before moving away to wash her hands, she makes sure that she puts the toilet seat up. *'Leave that chuffin' thing down one more time an' ah'll teck it off!'* Will had already warned her. Times like these make her glad that she won't have to try and let these properties to unsuspecting students anymore come this May.

She jumps back from the sink and almost falls into the shit-ridden bath – a knee-jerk reaction to the freezing cold water coming out of the taps. *Why won't Will just stay at mine?*

Katie wraps Will's red silk hooded dressing gown (the sort that boxers wear) tightly around her, double checking in the mirror that, barring a bit of leg, none of the more provocative parts of her body are exposed. She can't stand that filthy old man leering at her.

She tip-toes out of the bathroom and through the kitchen, careful as always not to touch the filthy floor whenever possible, then she takes a deep breath to prepare herself for the crossing of the living room. Opening the stiff wooden door, she looks across the lounge and sees a glimpse of her possible future.

Sprawled cataleptic across the two-seater sofa is the stomach-churning form of James Surewood, her new boyfriend's father. At one end of the sofa lies a pizza box with a slice or two of *Mexicana* left festering in it. At the other, six empty cans of special brew have been laid to rest. Some of them have been crushed and are laid on their sides haemorrhaging fag ash and flat lager, just beside a few leaves of encrusted toilet roll. *So that's where all the loo roll went.* On the TV one of Tom's (at least, Will says that they're Tom's) pornos has been left playing on repeat and worst of all, Katie is sure that she can see more *Mexicana* living in that man's beard than she can in the pizza box.

Is this what she'll be letting herself in for twenty years down the line?

In her heart, Anna knows that the best month of her life is over. She's sat cross-legged on the patio in the rain, soaked through and sobbing her heart out. Some specky-four-eyed geek from the Chess Club is the only person willing to give her the time of day. That bastard Tom has the cheek to interrupt her essay-writing, drag her out with that animal he calls a friend (who's on a curfew anyway, and won't even keep his filthy talons off her), then fuck off to play *Spin the Bottle* or whatever it is just because he wants to get off with that slag Hannah from E Block.

Anna rises to her feet defiantly. *She isn't going to take this shit no more.* 'Thanks for listening Norm,' she smiles at the apparently anthropomorphised mole. 'But I think I'll do this my way. *I'll learn the tosser.*'

With that, she storms back into the house.

'*Teach!*' yells Norman after her, and then takes her Bishop.

* * *

Katie pushes Will's bedroom door open and is surprised to see that he is nowhere in sight. The same can't be said about his cat.

Rocky – now roughly equal in size to a small pig – is frantically clawing underneath the bed. To the cat's left is a large collection of mauled sweet wrappers and crisp packets. Sensing her approach, Rocky sits up on its ample hindquarters, casually licking some chocolate off its paw as it does so.

'Meow,' Rocky says as it rubs itself around the bottom of her bare legs. In this context, 'meow' roughly translates as: *Katie, you may want to sit down. I have unearthed concrete evidence that proves that Will is suffering from at least two discrete eating disorders.*

For Rocky, it is fortunate that twenty-first century human beings have yet to master the art of cat communication. For if Katie had understood the cat's true meaning, she would have no doubt replied: *says you, fatty.*

Katie kneels down to stroke Rocky as Will enters the room, his cheeks red and his breath tainted with the unnaturally fresh odour of half a tube of super-strength toothpaste. As he sees the evidence of his binging all over the floor, his eyes momentarily betray his fear of exposure.

'Y'alright babe,' an Essex voice croons in the darkness.

'It can't be...' Tom says, his alcohol-blunt mind trying to calculate the odds. Even in his stupor though, it doesn't take him long to figure out that something is up.

The female pushes him onto the bed and climbs on top of him. Tom makes no move to resist. 'This has got to be a set up,' she says to him, teasingly.

'My line,' Tom quips, wishing that the rules of this game were in his favour. A bloke picks a card; a bird does the same. They both go into the eponymous *Room*. The bloke has to do anything the bird wants him to. A simple and popular game - *usually*.

'Somebody's gotta girlfriend...' Hannah taunts. Tom tenses immediately. He'd almost forgotten about *other* Anna.

Hannah rests all her weight on him and plants a passionate kiss on his lips. She can feel him getting harder. *Good.* She's toyed with her little plaything for long enough; if she doesn't act now she's gonna lose him to someone else. She might not want him, but no-one else can have him either.

'Pity,' she says, casually unfastening her bra.

Tom's heart begins to beat with both anticipation and fear. Anticipation of what may follow. Fear of her pulling away at the last minute as usual, leaving him high and dry. Fear of Anna. Fear *for* Anna.

Hannah maintains eye contact with Tom as she rips at his flies, almost cutting him to shreds with his zip, such is her zeal. It's just like in porn.

Tom's soul twists. He is aware of her manipulation but unable to really quite believe it, let alone fight it. Tom's body writhes. He aches as she tenderly teases him. *Mebbe this time she's real... mebbe this time she means it...*

... but no. There's allus somet. Allus somet goin' wrong, this time it isn't 'er though...

Pieces of wooden shrapnel spray from the door, quickly followed by an almighty crash. In the now-empty door frame stands the silhouette of two figures.

Gristle and Anna.

You've done it now, Tommo.

* * *

Night.

Katie lies naked, Will's head buried in her bosom like that of a child. She has to admit, having an arrogant stroke sexy flash boy break down in tears to you after gorging and purging isn't the biggest turn-on in the world - nor is it the best way to get to some kip - but it has given her hope for the future of their relationship. She's never felt closer to a bloke.

''e's 'aunting me int 'e,' Will whispers without moving a muscle. The Irish burr is gone. ''e's a warning… 'e's me in the future.'

Katie strokes Will's closely shaven head. It feels good. 'You're nothing like him,' she says comfortingly, hoping that she has sufficiently disguised her own nagging doubts on the issue. 'Why would you even say that?' she says, testing Will. *Now we'll find out how serious he really is about me.*

Will wriggles free of Katie's embrace and makes a move towards his bedroom window. He softly peels open one of the curtains and stares up into the night sky. And in that moment, every hope; every dream; and every fear seem to flow concurrently through his mind. He looks back at Katie, who has now sat up in the bed, the moonlight gently illuminating her perfect breasts and stunningly attractive face.

Perhaps it's time.
Time to be a new man.

Tom stands on the patio and casts his eyes up to the heavens above him. On just a handful of occasions in his short and catastrophic life he's had this 'crisis' feeling - a sense of the overwhelming significance of one specific moment; an urge to act decisively. Before today, he could count those times on one hand. Today he needs two.

Hysterical female voices are screeching all around him. He can feel his world tearing apart. He should be fighting back the tears. He should be begging the stars for forgiveness. He should feel fear. He should feel sorrow. He should *feel*.

But something inside him has changed. All he can feel is quiet disassociation from the events unfurling around him, as if the world that once span around him is now no more than chimera. An invisible force field surrounds the man who feels nothing; its invincibility protecting him from sticks, stones and words sharper than knives as he makes his way back home - leaving Hannah, Anna and Gristle to face whatever destiny's cruel hand may throw at them.

Time ah had some time alone.

Will sits himself down on the edge of the bed with aberrant nervousness. It's as if he's an unwelcome guest, not the host. Katie moves to touch him but he pulls back. He stares forward blankly, straight into his wardrobe door. He wants to tell her the whole story but he doesn't know where to begin. He wants to confess all of his sins - all his shagging, gambling and cheating… and he wants Katie to be the one to offer him absolution. Every fibre of his being is crying out for him to change, and just to make sure that there are no more half-arsed attempts at self-improvement, fate has placed the living embodiment of his future slap-bang on his living room sofa. *Do what must be done,* he thinks to himself.

Without saying a word, Will opens his wardrobe and tears away a colourful chart comprised of childish scrawl from the inside of the door. He places it in Katie's hands, and then turns on the light.

And he waits.

***

Ah can't separate what's real an' what's fake... It's all too real. Laughter. Gristle, tears. Tom, 'annas... plural. One crocodile, one real. Tears eaten by the crocodile.

She was with him and she should be yours! Can you not see it? ARE YOU TOO STUPID to see it? She wants him. She does not even want you; so why are you so scared? Why do you fear?

Ah don't fear...

LIAR! You think that you are hard but you are the weakest person in the world; the weakest person that ever there was. Have the courage of your convictions. Do what must be done.

Ah can't... Ah couldn't... It's not reet...

She is laughing at you, sunshine. They are all laughing at you. That is what you are for. That is why you were made.

- A heart that burns like a furnace -

Break her! Bend her to your will. Show her who is boss! Kill her laughter. Cut off its oxygen.

She's bleedin'... It's not reet. This isn't me.

She can hear you. She can hear inside! She can hear <u>me</u>. She will tell everybody about me!

Sex then blood. She can't even...

She uses her power over you; twists you and manipulates your feelings.

She won't remember this... Too much cider... She's just 'ad a lickle fall...

It is her own fault! She started all this...

... ah didn't start this...

... you brought a lot of pain...

... ah couldn't 'ave...

... and now she has brought a lot of BLOOD...

NO! Time for sleepy sleepy sleep-sleep.

For you, or for this one?

151

Ah... ah... can't stop it. Ah'm not strong enough.

And what of him...? I suppose that drink will rob him of his memory, and if it does not, then that is just too bad. His life is shit anyway, but why-

-won't yer just let me be?

Never forget that it was you who brought me forth. I am yours, as you, my dear, stupid, coward, are mine.

Forever.

αποκαταστασις

WITH NEITHER THOUGHT NOR FEELING, THE old man kicked off his sandals and waded into the gently receding tide. Distantly, he half-remembered his irrational fear of the creatures that once lurked in the murky depths of the ocean.

He found himself trying to evoke that same feeling of dread within himself. He wanted to feel the goosebumps as the fish swam by his toes. He *needed* to feel his blood turn cold.

But there were no fish.

There was no fear.

There was nothing.

Defeated, he stared down at his reflection in the water. Years upon years' worth of silver beard and long, unkempt hair masked all but his dark grey eyes. He must have stared for a day at his wizard-like reflection. Perhaps even for years.

He had lost faith in appearances long, long ago. No matter how far he had travelled, or however many millions of people he had met, their faces all looked the same to him. They all congealed into one great mass of humanity. Oh yes, there was the odd nuance of difference here and there, but effectively there were a finite number of facial and bodily templates that humanity had been carved from. Each and every template had been replicated trillions of times. Duplicated. Distorted. Copied and pasted. Dished out along with birth certificates and National Insurance numbers.

Humans, he thought. *Humanity*. Two words that he had neither spoke nor even thought in a long, long time. Two concepts that he could no longer truly grasp.

He looked up from the water and for just one, fleeting moment he could have sworn that he felt something move between his toes.

But it was just salt water.

The sea was long-since empty.

Interminably wise and ceaselessly sad, the old man turned around and walked back up the beach.

The biker tore down the deserted country lanes like the proverbial bat out of hell. Leaning into the tight bends at well over 100 miles an hour, Matty Briggs was daring Fate to take him; taunting her. *Come on then yer bitch. Come an' teck me.*

Then something strange happened. A sudden blur of motion; an extraordinary sense of dizziness.

From the twisted and burning remnants of his vintage Triumph Herald rose a spectre. Matty's vision locked squarely on the eyes of the apparition. Everything else fell away. The bike, the road, the sorrow…

… all the dreams, all the pain. As Matty died alone in the wreckage, he never imagined that all this could come back again; that his death would somehow… *live*. His death would go on. His violent and sudden induction into the undiscovered country would merge with that of his dead son's, and in some twisted ensemble this echo of death would live on through dreams.

Dreams that haunt life.

Dreams that have the power to change lives.

The small details would often change, but the punchline would always be the same. Either the bike or the plane would be completely immolated and then two burning eyes would invade the consciousness. The whites of the eyes would bubble, melt and flow like a cracked egg in a frying pan, but the two scorching pupils would always remain.

Even by day now, the dreams are far too real. The comfortable sense of detachment that Tommo once felt is gone. The security and monotony of the daily grind no longer holds any sanctuary for him. Even when locked in the throes of alcoholic poisoning, Tom feels his spirit thrashing about trying to free itself.

In one sickening and surreal moment bile shoots up through his throat and out of his mouth, spewing forth semi-digested pasta all over the *Studicom* standard-issue sofa. With every neuron in his head firing, his hungover and tender mind replays the previous night's atrocities to him.

Without a single ounce of self-respect he wipes the sick from around his mouth and onto the nearest bit of his quilt. 'This's just a saga now,' he whines, collapsing back into his cesspit; his place of recovery.

Through eyes wide shut Tom almost enjoys watching Anna and Gristle burst in on him with Hannah. Traumatic as it is, it is as nothing compared to his usual nightmares. He remembers tears. He remembers sadness. He also remembers relief and then…

… then it gets really painful. Something happened to Anna. She stopped crying.

Gristle made her stop.

FUTURE NOSTALGIA

JAMAL COMES TO THE CONCLUSION THAT HE is simply too soft with people. He is finding it difficult enough to concentrate on his English 'C' assignment without Tom burdening him with all of his problems. *He sits there on the edge of the sofa, malodorous and rotten, not giving a hoot for anyone else other than himself.*

'…reet, then ah comes in 'ere, an' there's that tramp…'

'You mean Will's father,' Jamal snaps. 'His name is James.'

'…yeah, reet, Will's old man, asleep on the sofa, so ah goes upstairs to gi' Gristle a knock, see if 'e could remember wheer Anna went after all o' ructions last nite. There was no answer anyways, so ah thought to mesen… that's a bit weird innit.'

'Why?' asks Jamal, feigning interest in the hope that Tom will go away and leave him to wrap his challenged mind (and even more challenged tongue) around the finer aspects of Year 4 phonics.

'…cos 'er shoes, coat an' bag are in the 'all. Which means…'

'You think she's with him? Here?'

'…well, 'e 'as allus liked her. An' at the party 'e kept touching 'er up when 'e thought ah weren't lookin!'

'And you *let* him?' Jamal is *so* appalled. Even his patience has bounds. *These people!*

Tom looks flabbergasted. 'This's fuckin' Gristle we're talking abart! Believe it or not, ah do actually value me life!'

Jamal gives Tom a look that suggests he finds that sentiment hard to believe, given the state of him.

'Tom, he should not have even been out that late. He is on a police curfew. I mean… does that mean nothing to him? Or to you, for that matter? If that young man is not very careful indeed they will lock him up before he even gets to court.' Jamal takes a deep breath and lowers his voice. 'Chances are he's going to be sent down anyway. I saw what he did to that poor cabbie.'

Tom nods solemnly. Jamal then puts his pen down, takes his glasses off and rubs his eyes.

'Thomas,' he says, allowing his head to rest on the back of the sofa. 'You seem like a really nice young man. And far, far from stupid. What are you doing wasting your time with this lot? Can you not see they're dragging you down with them? Will, Gristle, even these two – Annas, is it? Yes – both of them.'

Tom looks down at the floor. He's mildly amused that Jamal's lecture is actually making him feel quite ashamed. Jamal has headmaster written all over him.

'And I think you're drinking far too much. It makes me worry.'

Tom looks up slowly, his sniggering face suddenly betraying a flash of anger so intense that it makes Jamal sit bolt upright – he *felt* it. The look is gone almost as quickly as it appeared, and Tom musters a half-hearted smile. 'Per'aps, mate. Per'aps. Ey, d'you 'ear abart the other business last nite? It was on news earlier. They found a girl's body near uni.'

'One of those girls who went missing last spring?'

'Nope. New 'un. Killed last nite, they reckon.'

Jamal seems genuinely distressed at the news. He is not concerned with such paltry matters as his own personal security; he is simply saddened that a young life should end so abruptly and for no good reason. He looks Tom in the eye. 'Sort yourself out, Tom. Life is clearly far too short - especially round here.'

Tom grins back at him and nods. *Tell me somet ah don't know.*

Their conversation is interrupted by heavy footfalls coming down the stairs. *Gristle! Anna! It must be!*

Tom peers through the crack in the living room door and sees Anna kissing Gristle goodbye. *Kissing* Gristle goodbye! *This is not 'appenin'. The mad cow!*

Without any regard for his physical or emotional wellbeing, Tom opens the door and marches into the hallway. Gristle nods at him dutifully.

Bizarrely, Gristle behaves as someone does when they're incredibly angry with a work colleague, but don't want to make a scene. He's being *polite*. Keeping up appearances. Maintaining the status quo. *BUT THIS IS GRISTLE!!! What's 'e done? What the fuck 'as 'appenned?*

Anna's stare is one of pure malice.

Her left arm is deeply cut and through the gap between the top of her trousers and the bottom of her crop top he can see the beginnings of a nasty bruise. Mustering all his courage, Tom looks over at the monster that he shares a house with and meets his steely glaze. If he didn't know better, he'd swear that he can see *fear* in Gristle's eyes.

Probably just guilt. Tom turns back to Anna who has a single tear running down her cheek. She really is a glutton for punishment. *What 'as 'e done to 'er?* Try as he might though, Tom can't fight the future. More to the point, he certainly can't fight Gristle. The strongest protest that he can muster is a disapproving frown in Gristle's direction.

'Meow.'

Rocky trundles into the hallway looking incomprehensibly obese and not very well at all. Gristle kneels down to stroke his beloved little baby.

'Who's a good boy den? You killed any birdies today for your daddy, Rockster?' Gristle croons at his pet.

Anna sniffs into her tissue and wipes a few tears away from her eyes. 'I don't think so, Ben.'

'Eh?' says Gristle, completely confused.

'That cat is not a boy.'

'Eh? 'ow d'you know?'

'Well she's heavily pregnant for a start.'

Tom smiles to himself, secretly thinking *kittens! Fantastic!* but outwardly projecting *whatever*. With that, he turns and makes to go back into the living room and resume his conversation with Jamal.

A female voice, soft and broken, holds him back.

'Like me.'

Tom looks to Gristle, and then to Anna, and then inside himself.

He's done it now…

'Six out of ten for face!' Katie is yelling into her mobile. 'Just when I was getting to like you… then I find out my arse is better looking than my face! You're a wanker, Will. You and your stupid tally!'

Beth enters their kitchen in her dressing gown. She begins rummaging around amongst empty bottles, searching for a clean mug.

'Just go fuck yourself, and then stick that on your little chart… I don't care. You should have thought about that before you *graded* and *reviewed* me like one of Tom's pornos!'

Beth raises an eyebrow as she lifts a filthy cereal bowl and a rusty spoon out of the kitchen sink.

'I don't want to hear it. I don't have time for losers. Listen Will. Get your pet Chav… yeah, him. Him with the ankle tag and the collection of ASBOs. Get him to go out and buy you a twelve-inch pizza and a bag of jelly babies. Wolf the bastard lot down and then puke it all up you SAD FUCKING FREAK! And to think… Oh fuck you!'

Katie tosses her phone onto the table with venom, throws back her head and lets the tears flow. 'The fucking fucker!'

Beth walks across and hugs her friend, spooning cereal into her mouth from a bowl that she is holding precariously behind Katie's back. *Well I'm starving!* Sometimes it feels like her sole purpose in life is to console.

'Ah pet…'

It wouldn't be quite as bad if she didn't have to piece together the whole dreary saga from muffled sobs and incoherent, hysterical ranting.

'…and now I've even broke my new fern!' Katie wails.

'Dad! 'ave you been using me *Mach Three*?' Will protests, a blunted blade in his hands.

''od thi' 'osses lad. By 'eck, tha's not backard at cummin' forrard. Ah only borrad it for a bit. Ah'm off down ta bookies wi' tha' mate Ben, then mebbe for a few jars down t'old railway carriage. Ah 'ear it's good in theer on a Satdee aft.'

''ave yer sorted yersen anyweer out yet?' Will asks, considering precisely where he'd like to stick his blunted razor head.

'No, son. Ah think we'll be alreet 'ere, tha knows. Sample a bit o' this student life o' yours. Might even get mesen a nice dolly bird like that Katie lass o' yours. Phwaorh! Where's it anyways?'

'*She*'s…' Will gives up and heads back towards the bathroom. 'Busy,' he whispers to himself. He opens the bathroom cabinet so that he can put a splash of - *oh for fek's sake!* 'DAD! 'ave yer been at me aftershave an' all?'

* * *

Gristle and Jim Surewood sit on a bench in the back of the train carriage cum cheap 'n' nasty pub. Whereas Will and Tom tend to stand out like sore thumbs in there – *poncy students!* – Gristle has never been a slave to fashion, and even after a shower, a shit and a shave Jim Surewood looks like a strategically-shaved ape - at best. Suffice it to say that the pair looks completely at home nursing their pints amidst the local scum and villainy.

Every conversation in the pub is about the murder; word travels fast in these parts. One Leg Larry is convinced that it was *'them Kosovans'*. Slow Racist Randolph Regan the Third couldn't agree more. Old Bent Nigel blames *'the gays'*, which most of the barflies find a little odd, given his patent inclination, while 'Clever' Colin Cuthbert says that it was their own fault for being outside. *Young 'uns these days, eh? Walkin' abart in broad daylight like theer's no tommorra.* All the while, Smell-My-Cheese Leonard runs around the carriage in nothing but his slippers and a pink nightie, informing all who will listen that he did it; it was all him; that he is the killer; and that he is really, really sorry.

Leonard is doing pretty well on the old not-getting-your-skull-caved-in front; at least he is until he points a toy gun at Gristle's head.

Gristle hold his pint in his left hand, casually taking a swig every now and then. In his right hand he holds Leonard by the throat, paralysed.

'So e's got 'er up the duff then?' Jim says, chuckling to himself. 'That's 'is life ovver! Ey, 'e might move out. 'is room would be up for grabs!' Jim strokes the blotchy red shaving rash on his face, considering the possibilities. 'Anyways, Ben lad. Yer said yer wanted me 'elp wi' somet. A few quid in it, yer said.'

Gristle nods and leans towards Jim conspiratorially. 'Me and me mate Jay Mannin' got this nice little earner, but 'cos ah got me curfew ah can't risk goin' out too late at nite. Last time woz really chancin' it, but last time ah 'ad one o' veese stupid fings on me ankle it never started workin' reet 'till after the first few days so, touch wood, it'll be reet.'

Jim leans in closer. 'What kinda earner?'

'S'easy.'

'Come on, young 'un. What kinda earner?'

'Me curfew starts at nine. Come wi' us tonite 'bout sixish. Ah'll show yer the ropes. Piece a piss, 'onest. It should get your kid off yer back an' all if yer can pay yer way.'

Jim smiles to himself.

'Bitta elbow grease nivver did no 'arm, ah suppoz. Cheers, son.'

Jim charges his glass.

Gristle turns to Smell-My-Cheese-Leonard, whose face is beginning to turn bright blue. 'You 'eard nuffin' sunshine,' he grunts as he lets the limp transvestite madman fall to the ground.

Jamal, Tom and Will are walking through the university campus. Breathtaking beauty stands directly beside concrete-block architecture. Concrete paving surrounds immaculately-kept greenery. The whole place exudes life and learning. It's more than just a library and a series of lecture halls, labs and theatres - it's a way of life. And many of those that leave that way of life behind just can't let go.

As they sit in their offices typing away on their keyboards, they look out of the window and see the sun shining on a beautiful September afternoon. They nurse their RSI and wear spectacles to protect their VDU-ravaged eyes, all the while remembering how the patches of grass about campus were used by scantily-clad freshers to sunbathe. They can smell the barbeques. Taste the cheap bitter and chip spice. Recall the closer-than-brothers friends that they haven't had time to call in six months.

Jamal, Tom and Will are having the seeds of such future longings sewn right now. Today, Tom is not at all happy. Nor is Will, for that matter. Jamal is just pretty average. On the whole, it could be argued that they comprise a pretty despondent group. Yet somehow, if they were all to live to be ninety-nine they would undoubtedly look back upon days like this one and recall just how fantastic their uni lives were. Even though they weren't.

September is Tom's favourite month by far, even considering the events of 2001. The weather isn't too hot, but it's not too cold either. He also likes May, but September wins hands down because it's the start of the university year. To students, September is like a Friday night whereas May carries the bittersweet tang of a Sunday evening.

Jamal is relishing every day spent on campus before being sporadically thrust into local schools from November onwards. He spares a moment to consider just how much of an effect living with these guys is having on him. Not only did he have a lunchtime pint yesterday, but today he deliberately lobbied both Will and Tom to come to the library with him, knowing full well that they were both so depressed that they would be easy pickings. He never used to be so manipulative.

He used to be such a nice person.

A beautiful redhead appears out of nowhere, swinging around Tom's waist and making him jump nearly all the way to Scarborough. Jamal has to admit that she's physically very appealing in an obvious sort of way, especially in that summer skirt and vest top. Very pretty, very curvy – very confident. A different league to those Anna girls that Tom has been messing about with of late.

Bethany.

'Hello stranger,' she says as she circles around to stand directly in front of Tom. 'Somebody never text me back.'

Tom instantly feels his mood brighten. After unloading all his emotional baggage onto her, this fantastic specimen of womanhood is *still* interested. It's almost enough to put Anna's pregnancy and his Hannah fixation out of his mind. 'Ah 'ad no credit,' he lies, wondering why he's lying. Why hadn't he text her back?

Oh yes – guilt. Obsession's constant companion.

Beth grins. 'Yeah right, buster.' She pokes him in the chest. Tom tries to tense up before the finger makes contact but he is too late and her finger ends up prodding his flabby, clozapine man-breast. She neither notices nor cares.

Beth turns her attention to Will. 'As for you, chief,' she says in the sternest voice that she can muster, 'I think you owe a certain friend of mine an apology.'

'Like it would get me anyweer,' he says, sheepishly kicking at a hydrangea. 'She's proper got the face on.'

'You'd be surprised what a bottle of wine and a box of chocs can do,' Bethany says with a grin. 'Seriously - she's done nowt but cry all morning. She's really fallen for you. A bit of grovelling is all that's needed.'

Will doesn't look convinced. Even if he believed Bethany, it would take so much effort to worm his way back into Katie's good books. Part of him – the bitter part – is ruthlessly waging war on the good bit. *This is what yer get for bein' 'onest*, it says. *Yer might as well 'ave fucked 'er an' chucked 'er. At least that way yer wouldn't be feelin' like this. An' what abart all them other birds yer missed out on 'cos yer were only knobbin' yer Katie…*

SUCH WASTE! All them lovely freshers, poked by some other sausage.

'Boxa chocs. Bottle of wine. Stupidly expensive stuffed bunny rabbit. I know her. She'll lap it up,' Bethany promises Will (both aspects of him).

'Um, where yer off to now, like?' Tom asks hopefully.

'Going to do a bit of work on my essay,' she says. Her expression shifts slightly. 'That's if I can concentrate. You hear about that girl last night? Britney Simpson?'

All three guys nod gravely. 'Still. Can't live in fear, can you? *Don't let the murdering bastards grind you down*, that's what I say... and so on that note, I'll be in the Union tonight getting *fucked*...' she says, completely over-egging the last word in that sentence as she stares at Tom. 'As will Katie,' she adds for Will's benefit.

Tom smiles. His blood seems to run warm and tingly for a moment; so much so that he forgets how to speak. *Adrenaline? Lust? The last kick of the hangover?*

It matters not. She's buggered off. That's what you get for standing around over-analysing life.

'Seeya later boys,' she shouts over her shoulder, disappearing off towards the unsightly oblong of cement that is the university's library.

'Inabit,' Tom calls after her. *Lust*, he decides finally.

Lust and, 'opefully, no more. Although...

'Fancy a pint, lads?' Will asks, a smirk having once again found its way onto his face.

Tom can't tear his eyes away from Bethany's shapely arse as she saunters through the turnstile and into the library. Will isn't the only one smiling now.

'Why not?' says Tom the Cheshire Cat.

Tom and Will nurse their pints of snakey b, Jamal having held his ground and gone to complete his Science 'B' assignment in the library.

'Ah can't believe we didn't meet 'em before! Just think; they must've been out on all the same nites as us lot. She could've walked ret by me an' ah'd never 'av known,' Tom says to Will, a huge feckless smile now etched on his face despite all of his worries. 'Ah! She's gorgeous! An' cute! An' sooooo sweet!'

Will just shakes his head, giving Tom his infamous *'ere we go again...* look. 'Don't screw it up then, *dickface*! Try an' pull 'er again. She obviously likes yer.'

'Naaah...' Tom whines wistfully. 'Knowing my luck she probably likes you... she said more ta you than ta me!'

'Yeah, abart me Katie! Anyways, it's me what should be worried. Katie 'ates me fekin' guts at the minute, an' she's the mucky one, not yours. You've seen what she's like – all this *sex-ay* shit.'

Tom suddenly remembers something. 'Fuck. Ah deleted her number an' 'er text, didn't ah?'

Will smoothly pulls out his flash flip-top phone and casually peruses the contacts list. 'Lucky ah got 'er number then wonnit, mush?'

Tom's eyes light up. 'Ar! You're a legend, mate. A proper ledge!' He reaches into his pocket and pulls out his brick of a mobile. 'What is it then, mate?'

Will opens his mouth to begin reading out the number, but he's interrupted before he can even get the 'O' out.

'What am ah on wi'? Ah love 'annah. Ah couldn't ever pull anyone else,' Tom moans.

'What about vat other 'un - that one ah knobbed first?'

'Anna? Ah never liked 'er; yer can't count 'er! Anyways, ah was pissed.'

'*For two months!* C'mon mate,' says Will, losing patience. 'You've been after 'annah for ages an' she keeps feking yer abart. If she did love yer like she says she'd just be wi' yer. Ah mean, why didn't she tell you she was back in 'ull when you saw her wi' that Winston bloke?'

'She was gonna… She just forgot.'

'And where's she now? For fek's sake! She'll be wi' that Winston guy. 'e'll be ruttin' 'er senseless!'

'Nah…she's gone to Manchester wi' a *'select few'* friends today,' Tom says, quoting her verbatim and finally realising just how pathetic the whole Hannah situation is. 'The stuff she was comin' out wi' though in *The Room*! She means it this time. She'll put the effort in. She wants it to work. Ah've gotta give it a shot, mate. Ah've gotta.'

'Nah.'

'You just don't like 'er 'cos she said that you're a smarmy little cocksucker.'

'Look mate. She only said that 'cos ah wouldn't gi' 'er one! She's dog rough anyways. For fek's sake man, ah wouldn't touch 'er wiv Jamelia's! Ah wouldn't touch 'er wi' Gristle's, or even Phil the Greek's shit-stabbing love-lolly! Yer can do so much better. Bethany is really cute. If it weren't for me Katie ah'd…'

'You better fuckin' well not!' Tom says, scowling at his *un*trusty old friend. His scowl soon turns into a smile as he pictures Bethany in his head. She's quite a short girl, shoulder-length red hair, a pretty face with an absolutely gorgeous smile and really deep, piercing green eyes. As for her body… His dream woman, he reckons. *Twenny-seven an' all. Never 'ad a bit o' old.* Twenty-three was his record, but he was eighteen at the time and so it seemed impressive back then. Good ol' *Shagaluf*…

Will holds up his hands. 'Look mate; 'ow many birds 'ave you managed to screw things up wi' at uni?'

Tom shrugs his shoulders. 'Dunno. A couple?'

Will raises an eyebrow and begins to count on his fingers. Luckily for Tom, he only has ten fingers. 'Maggie, Liz, Steph, Alex, Jamie, Fiona, Rosie, 'annah, Anna…'

'Your point being?'

Will speaks slowly as if he is of the definite opinion that Tom is some kind of retard where women are concerned. 'Nowt will 'appen wi' 'annah. She'll just fek you up again. Beth seems nice.' He sighs and shakes his head. 'Ah don't know why ah'm bothering. You'll only screw it up an' go runnin' after that bitch again.'

Tom puts his hands together as if he's praying. 'Ah won't. Ah promise. Text 'er for us an' we'll go out wi' 'er an' your Katie tonight. Just the four o' us. You can beg Katie for forgiveness…' A thought strikes Tom. ''ey - what did yer do by the way? Sorry, scrap that. *Who* d'yer do?'

Will's brow furrows in resentment and he takes a hearty swig of his diesel. 'No-one.'

'Come on,' Tom goads. 'Ah know yer too well, mate. Who was she?'

'No-one! If you must know, she found me tally! The stupid feking thing is in the bin where it belongs now!'

'Must be love! Anyways, ah 'ope things do work out wiv 'er. It'd be ace going out wi' two birds who are mates.'

'Aye,' says Will, thinking about it. 'Might get a foursome!'

'Aii!' High-fives.

Tom puts his empty glass down on the table and rises to his feet. 'Besides, even if like yer say ah screw things up wi' Beth, if you 'ave a bird we can re-open Will Surewood's *Bureau o' Love* like when we was at school an' you wor wiv that 'olly. You charm 'em; ah'll pull 'em. Everyone's a winner! Text 'er! Text 'er! Text 'er! Text-'

'Reet,' Will smiles, also rising. 'You can have 'er number.'

Tom smiles and punches towards the sky. 'You're a ledge!'

He pulls out his phone and stands poised, ready to input the magic number.

'O seven-' Will begins.

'Yep,' Tom nods in acknowledgement, waiting for the next number. When it doesn't come, he looks up to see Will smiling and closing the flap on his phone. 'Tell yer what. Ah'll give yer one digit every 'afe 'our.'

Tom's jaw drops. He looks like a lost puppy, or a child after his first day at school, when he realises that he has to go back every day for twelve years.

'Will,' Tom whines, hot on the heels of his best friend.

Will walks towards the bogs but spins around to face Tom before entering. 'Consider it punishment for the *'who did yer do?'* thing. *Ah find yer lack o' faith disturbin'.*'

Five hours later Will, Tom and Jamal are sat in the back garden in the evening sunshine, drinking a few beers, having a barbeque and generally being lazy bastard students. 'Five,' Will finally says.

Tom punches the final digit into his hungry phone and composes a lengthy text message dancing around the vague idea of Beth and Katie potentially meeting up with them possibly later. *Mebbe.*

Tom sits back in his chair, takes a bite of his barbequed cow nostrils in a bap, washes it down with some lager and generally looks very pleased with himself. The pregnancy scare pushed to the farthermost peripheries of his mind, Tom is relaxing in the sunshine and enjoying his anticipation of the night ahead. All is well with the world. That is, until Jamal's phone beeps.

'Tom? Is this text off you...?'

'WILL YOU FUCKIN' BASTARD!!!'

CLOGS'LL SPARK TONITE

To: spadgewalker@happyloans.tv
From: Annabelle_69@mail.ac.uk
Re: Me being pathetic

Hi Spadge,

I just wanted to drop you a line because Ive been trying to ring you all week and your mobiles been off. I hope everything is OK and you and Becks have managed to straighten things out down in Swindon.

Unfortunately things are a bit of a mess at this end. Ive really, really fucked up and Ive lost Tom.

Im really worried about him. If youve heard from him this last week please let me know. Some serious shit has gone down and I cant cope.

Even if you havent heard anything from him please ring me or text me. I know this sounds sad and pathetic but I need to speak to somebody and there isnt anyone else but you.

All my love (for what little its worth),

Anna xXx

Jim is getting too old for this. That much is clear as Gristle gives him a bunk-up over the wall. Gristle looks around him. He's on red alert. He nods to his friend's father and points towards an open kitchen window.

"ow d'yer know they ain't in?' Jim whispers. Gristle glares at him menacingly with an index finger on his lip. *Fingers on lips*. It's just like being back at school, and that seems like a long, long time ago for Jim.

Gristle clambers through the small window with surprising ease for a young man of his bulk. He lowers himself gently into a sitting position just above the sink, careful not to catch the tracking device on his ankle. He drops silently to the lino, and within seconds has identified a few targets. One advantage of these long, terraced streets is that all of their houses have the same interior layout.

Gristle knows what to look for; he knows what sells. Within sixty seconds he has the scart leads out of the back of the DVD player. Another sixty seconds later he is clambering back out of the window one DVD player, thirty-six CDs and eight DVDs heavier. Too easy.

'So this is what ah'm gonna be doin' tonite?' says Jim, a sudden childish fear taking hold of him. *Ah might get in trouble.*

Gristle nods, putting his swag down as he hoists Jim back over the wall. 'S'easy. We get a squid for a CD, two squids for a DVD an' fifteen ta twenny squids for owt decent like a DVD player or an 'i-fi or mp3.'

'Is that it?' Jim asks with surprise. To think he's risking God alone knows what for a miserly few...

'It's a nite out. That's all yer need up 'ere, old 'un. Cheap as chips, 'ull!'

Jim nods with resignation. 'I suppoz. Wheer theer's muck theer's brass.'

Outside one of their popular haunts just by one of Hull's busiest crossroads, Jamal, Will, Tom, Katie and Bethany wait for a taxi to take them over to the Union. With a few pints inside him and one more in his hand, Tom's mind is once again full of images of violence. However, rather than tortured images of his father or brother, Tom is allowing himself the luxury of imagining himself pushing Anna down the stairs. *That'd learn her.* It's a good job guilty thoughts aren't a crime…

Tom glances across at Katie and Will who are kissing passionately. 'Ah guess 'e's forgiven then,' he says awkwardly to Bethany who is looking at him in the same way that Captain Birdseye looks at a fish.

The night has turned quite nippy. Tom is glad of his coat. Not only does it provide him with warmth, but it also allowed him to sneak a pint outside the pub to drink whilst he waits for a taxi.

'So what are you studying then?' Jamal asks Bethany.

Tom rolls his eyes back in his head, necks what's left of his pint and then yobbishly throws the glass over his shoulder – a show of defiance against Jamal's innate blandness.

As he does so, all five of them turn around suddenly as they hear brakes screeching and the sound of shattered glass. Tom laughs at a taxi windscreen covered in pieces of his broken pint pot.

'C'mon you lot,' he says to the others as he runs over to the cab in question. They are all frozen in shock.

Cautiously, he opens the passenger door and addresses the driver.

'Y'alright mush? Yer booked?'

In the back seat, Will slowly takes his right hand and places it in Katie's. She turns to him and smiles, squeezing his hand tightly. 'How are the kittens?'

'Noisy!' Will laughs. 'There's six of 'em in all. They're just like little balls of ginger fluff!' He tries to convey to her the infinitesimal size of the kittens with his hands, but ends up just gesticulating like a madman, much to the amusement of all.

'Have you given them names yet?' asks Bethany. She is sat snuggled up to Tom, resting her head on his shoulder and casually draping her arm around his waist. Tom stares impassively forward. The war rages on.

Hannah is losing.

Tom reaches into his coat pocket and pulls out a miniature bottle of whisky, which he downs in one.

'Go on my son!' yells Will yobbishly.

Despite her ever-tightening grip on Tom's waist, Bethany can't help but feel that he is drifting further and further away.

'So driver,' says Jamal, comically-sandwiched into the small space between these two pairs of unlikely lovers. 'Tell me: have you been busy?'


```
To: Annabelle_69@mail.ac.uk
From: spadgewalker@happyloans.tv
Re:Re: Me Being Pathetic
```

Hi Anna,

I'm really sorry I couldn't take your calls - we've had a bit of a flap on at work; this new place is horrendous.

Don't worry about Tom. I don't know if you know, but he's been through some shit in his time and he's hard as fuck. You worry about yourself.

Look I've gotta go straight back out, but I promise I'll give you a call tomorrow.

Hang in there princess,

Love Spadge x

Inside the Union, Tom is enjoying the jealousy of the other males almost as much as he is the attention from Bethany, but his mind is still clouded with thoughts of Hannah and Anna. He can't get last night out of his head. Nervously putting his hands on Beth's hips so that he can circumnavigate her person, he ducks, dives and worms his way to the front of the bar queue with the expert precision of either an alcoholic or a fourteen year-old glass collector.

'"ow much 'r' shotsa vodka?' he slurs at the poor barmaid.

'A pound,' replies Charlie (for that is the barmaid's name). Working in this place you quickly get used to faces. Most of them look alike, but a few, like this guy's, aren't easily forgotten. It wasn't that long ago that they were cleaning up at the end of the night, waiting for their staff pints, when they discovered this guy spark out underneath a table wearing a smart cream suit covered in purple sick; his tie fastened around his forehead like it was 1989. *What in the blue hell is he doing?* He rummages deep in his pockets, pulls out a cloakroom ticket (which he drops on the floor... *no ticket, no coat!);* a ticket for the evening's festivities, which has been ripped down the centre to signify his admission; some house keys precariously attached to a miniature laser-sword key ring; and, most outrageously of all, a half-empty metal flask. *The cheap sod.* Charlie's heard of sneaking a miniature bottle of vodka in, but c'mon... *a full flask!*

'Ah! There we go, luv.'

A couple of notes and a pocket full of shrapnel hit the bar; coinage sprays in every imaginable direction. 'Can ah 'ave... ummm,' he says drooling, pointing at each coin with his index finger as if to count them. 'Twenny-six please.'

Charlie makes a mental note to hand her notice in.

* * *

Will has his pint in one hand and Katie's arse in the other. His tongue is firmly rammed down her throat. He can't believe his luck. How many girls could you confess all of your sins to and still have them want you? He makes a silent promise to himself that he will make this work. This is his chance to stand up and be a new man, not an old, homeless loser like his –

'Dad! What the fek you doin' 'ere?' he shouts at the cautionary tale incarnate that is walking towards him with a pint. 'An' where d'you get the brass for that?'

Beth, meanwhile, has had enough for one Saturday night. If she wanted to spend the evening babysitting, she's sure that with her two years' experience of *au pairing* in LA she could probably get a job doing the same thing in Hull if she so desired - but she doesn't. She kisses both Tom and Jamal on the cheek and then goes to collect her coat before the queue for the cloakroom spirals out of control, leaving her one drunken 'friend' and her one sober friend stood by one of the huge cylindrical columns near the entrance.

Jamal is clearly disgusted with the state that Tom has got himself into. How Beth can be attracted to such a gibbering, dribbling yobbo he has no idea. Even in his moments of relative lucidity, all Tom can do is shout loudly and unintelligibly in people's faces, showering them with drool.

Suddenly though, Tom's eyes are once again alight with the glimmering of intelligence; the light of recognition. Jamal knows what, or rather whom, he's looking at. Walking towards the dance floor is one of those Annas – not the pregnant Anna, the other one. She is wearing a tight school uniform with knee-high boots, has her bleach-blonde hair up in pigtails and freckles pencilled in on her cheeks with make-up. As she descends the steps and makes her way onto the dance floor, she looks behind her, as if she senses something. Her mouth sucking on her lolly and her eyes roving, she fails to see the drunk staring a hole straight through her.

'She *sh*aid she woz goin Manchesta!' Tom yells, Jamal holding him back. 'She's a LIAR!'

'Calm down,' says Jamal sensibly. 'You are supposed to be here with Bethany, remember?'

Tom's voice quietens and he waves a hand dismissively. '*Sh*we're just *sh*mates. Bestest fwends…'

Tom allows his body to relax, then as soon as Jamal loosens his grip he makes a break for it.

Tom dives into Hannah's group of friends who suddenly appear to have changed their minds about the guy they had been allowed to meet just once – the guy who they thought seemed, I quote, *really sweet*.

'LIAR!!!' Tom shouts across Hannah's friends' shoulders.

Surprisingly quickly a bouncer (and then, a split-second later, Jamal) appear and together haul Tom's dead weight away. The bouncer quite leniently warns Tom to keep away from Hannah or he'll be out. Tom does the sensible thing and walks away.

For about two minutes.

Jim Surewood takes a sup of his – what did they call it? Diesel oil? – and gestures towards the bar. 'Ben bought it for us. Sharp as Sheffield, that lad.'

Will puts his head in hands. 'Gristle? 'as 'e got no fekin' brains at all–' He stops himself mid-sentence. 'Sorry. Stupid question,' he says quietly, purely for Katie's benefit.

Gristle struts over carrying three pints of snakey b. ''ere tha' guz, Will,' he says, passing him a pint. 'An' annuver jar for you old 'un. Toast a job well dun!'

'Cheers, *son*,' Jim says to Gristle, emphasising the term of endearment whilst maintaining eye contact with his biological spawn.

Katie wearily rubs her forehead. 'Shall we go home? I can't see us having much fun here, and I don't fancy the idea of Beth walking home on her own.'

'Yer,' Will says, resigned. *Bloody families. Bloody friends.* 'Text 'er an' tell 'er to get me coat an' all, allus we'll be queuing for fekin' *howers*,' he says, desperately trying to speak with any inflection other than the one that people may think he inherited from his father.

Katie does as Will asks, but she is perplexed as to how someone can ignore practically every aitch in the English language, yet pronounce a silent one.

Tom tears back onto the dance floor only to find Hannah dancing flirtatiously with some guy; one of the American Football team by the looks of him. His drunken thoughts aren't that he's livid about her dancing with someone else; oh no. He's more enraged that she doesn't seem to care about him having caught her out. There she was, dancing away merrily as if nothing had happened. The rusty Yale that holds back the anger gives way.

He just wants to make her *understand*...

Jamal has the raw deal of being sat in the front seat of the taxi. If Ben tries the same trick again he will... well, *they* will throw away the bloody key. He shouldn't even be out after nine! To think, in a little while he is going to have a classroom full of mini-Ben Davises to contend with.

Tom, meanwhile, is sat in the back seat next to Jim nursing a swollen eye from his short stay in the club's 'security room' (unofficially christened 'The Beatings Room' by staff and students alike). He hopes and prays and begs and pleads to the Gods that Gristle doesn't try his usual trick.

Jim is having the time of his life.

Get me own digs in town? What's that lad o' mine on wi', ey? Gi' up the life o' riley? All them fit young dolly birds? Ah's not sa green as cabbage lookin'. 'ow can tha gi' up this? Free ground rent an' easy money to be 'ad just for a bit o' 'onest thievin'? It's not even thievin' really; all these student types are insured up to the eyeballs. Victimless crime, innit?

Katie and Will walk hand in hand through the dimly-lit back streets just off Newland Avenue. Bethany is walking just a few steps ahead, talking back over her shoulder at the two lovers.

Walking these streets, Will actually feels quite anxious. He's not so much worried about himself; it's the two girls. What if something happens and he can't stop it…?

'I know I'm being soft,' Bethany says to them, 'but… ah don't know. There's something about him. It's retarded, ah know. He's too young, too… And who's this Anna girl he was moaning about earlier?'

'Which one?' Will says sarcastically, before immediately wishing that he hadn't. He glances over his shoulder again, just as he has done every three or four seconds for the entire journey thus far.

'I dunno,' Beth sighs. 'Something about a bairn or something?'

Will just shrugs his shoulders, neither lying nor giving anything away. 'If truth be known reet, Tom's me bestest mate an' ah love 'im, like, but… if ah was a nice, gorgeous lass like yoursen, it's…'

Bethany blushes. 'Gorgeous - as if!'

Katie frowns and squeezes Will's hand. Hard. *Don't push it.*

'It's not worth it, luv. Ah shouldn't really say owt, but 'e's proper got depression. 'is brother, 'is old man, an' some ovver relation 'ave all died in the past few year. Ah just... 'e just... ah don't fink 'e can give yer what yer want off him. 'e just ant gorrit ta give.'

Beth nods soberly.

Katie begrudgingly releases Will's hand, runs a few steps back and puts her arm around her slightly older and much more world-weary friend's shoulders. 'There's plenty more out there, darlin'. You're beautiful. You could have almost anyone.'

Beth frowns. *'Almost?'*

Damn it! She breaks. She swore she'd never break. Not in public.

'I don't want anyone. I want T...' she says, but stops herself. *NO.* She's never been the type to blubber about a guy and she won't start now. She breathes in deeply, hoping that she can suck the tears that are welling underneath her eyes back up into her tear ducts. 'Yeah. I know, pet. I know.'

'Now then,' says Will, clapping his hands together. 'Who's up for pizza?'

Exhilaration.

Jamal runs and he runs and he runs. With this every Wednesday and Saturday night, at least he'll be in shape for his PE lessons! A silly smile flickers across his face as he stops, panting for breath at the bottom of Black Hill. He's starting to believe that there may be more to life than lesson plans and pedagogy texts, and it scares the living shit out of him.

Tomorrow, sober, he would look back on this moment with colossal regret and shame. He would then immerse himself in the hyperlinks of some online *OFSTED* report just so that he can forget this… madness. But for now, for right now, Jamal is on top of the world.

He's alive.

Somebody has to pay for her sins.
Nobody will see this one coming.

Hedge-hopping over fence after hedge after fence, Jim finally snags his jeans (well, jeans stolen from Will's wardrobe, to be pedantic) on a stray nail and collapses in a heap in the dirt underneath a rhododendron.

He glances about himself. Under the harsh illumination of the security light he can see a *Barbie* trampoline, a road works sign, and the remains of an old telly - one of the ones his mam used to have with a coin slot in for the telly man. That takes him back. For the first time in his life, Jim puts two and two together and makes four.

'Thissiz a student 'ouse,' he mutters to himself drunkenly, unbuttoning Will's thirty-two inch waist jeans and unleashing his gargantuan gut.

Moving on from advanced mathematics, he notices that the kitchen window is open. A cruel smile creeps across his drunken face.

Unlike the rest of his little group, Tom doesn't run like hell as the taxi pulls to a stop. Chances are Ben would only go and twat the driver anyway, so why attract attention to yourself by running? Anyhow, Tom has more on his mind. So much, in fact, that he feels completely detached from the events unfolding around him.

He just isn't there.

How has he become the bad guy in this whole thing? He's never been a violent man… has he? He'd just gotten… angry. Hannah's ridiculous behaviour and his bad temper aren't a match made in heaven, are they? *Damn her.* That bitch has once again manipulated circumstances so that he looks and feels like the bad guy.

At almost three o'clock in the morning, a very inebriated and a very irritated Tom rings Anna's doorbell. Alcohol may not be an excuse for an act, but it's certainly one hell of a reason. It gives you confidence. Ideas. Determination.

One problem could be solved ever so simply.

Jim is impressed about how he manages to enter the kitchen virtually in silence. Without paying too much drunken thought to what he is actually doing, with his ripped jeans over his arm he begins to noiselessly ascend the stairs in his socks, boxers and shirt. He leaves his shoes along with everybody else's in the hall.

He pushes open the first bedroom door a crack. It's empty. No good.

The second bedroom has a young man asleep in it. No good.

The third room contains just what he's after. Just what he needs after one too many jars to satisfy his desires. *Clogs'll spark tonite.* He slowly peels off the rest of his clothes and slips into bed beside the young, firm brunette in the superhero pyjamas.

Another for the tally.

* * *

After repeated rings, Anna opens the door wearing nothing but a white dressing gown and looking awfully upset.

'You up the duff then or what?' Tom forces out in the midst of several noxious alcohol fumes. She slams the door in his face.

Shaking his head, Tom walks back to the pavement, his destination home. Then a thought strikes him. *Ah'll go back, an' ah'll put me 'and in th'door so she can't slam it on me. Then ah'll get some answers!*

Two minutes later he is nursing an inflamed and bruised hand to match his budding black eye. At least he managed to keep the door open long enough to speak.

'So are yer preggers or not?' he asks for the third and final time.

She shakes her head slowly. 'No.'

Tom can breathe again.

He turns to leave. 'Is that it?' she calls after him.

'What more d'yer want from us?' he asks in return. Anna looks on the edge of tears. Anna looks on the edge of starvation. Anna looks like she's on the edge of the precipice. Skinny, bony and broken.

'You were only worried about that mucky Hannah slapper finding out!'

Tom shrugs his shoulders and wobbles uncertainly. 'So?'

Anna just looks down at the welcome mat, with which she has much in common, shaking her head. 'Tom: don't ever treat anyone the way you've treated me.'

'Alreet. Inabit,' Tom says, as if nothing has happened. And with that he leaves, a free man in most senses of the word. Free in the sense that he is single. Free in the sense that he has no 'love' child in the pipeline. But in the sense of being free from the confusion that surrounds his feelings for Bethany; in the sense of being free from his feelings for Hannah - *no chance in hell, sunshine.*

It has turned into a total and utter obsession. The world pushes and it pulls but the feeling remains constant. It overrides everything.

The call came in just before six. The milkman had found a body; or at least, what was left of one. It had been dumped in an alley just off Newland Avenue, just a few short metres away from an abandoned black cab.

BY INFERNO'S LIGHT

THE SOUND OF GIGGLING ACCOMPANIES WILL
and Katie as they tumble out of his bedroom, tickling each other. They notice Jamal - wearing a patchwork dressing down, slippers and carrying a bundle of papers under his left arm - and immediately restrain themselves just a little bit. 'All 'e needs now is a pipe an' 'e's there,' Will whispers to Katie. She stifles another giggle, which does not go unnoticed by Jamal.

'You're so childish, Surewood,' Jamal says matter of factly as he makes his way down the stairs. When he reaches the bottom of the staircase, he can't help but smile to himself. *So I'm nearly there then…*

He walks into the living room to face a curious sight. The psychopath with whom he shares the house is knelt down on the floor, dangling a very unconvincing toy mouse in the air above a small thatched basket. Like clockwork, a fraction of a second after each 'dangle' a tiny little ginger paw swats at the empty space.

'Morning Davis.'

Gristle almost falls over himself trying to get to his feet quickly. 'Er… Morning Jamubis. Ah was just… um… tha knows. Learnin' em to kill and that.'

'Indeed.'

Jamal walks over to the basket and crouches down just beside it. Very gently, he places his hand inside and tickles the nearest of the six kittens under its chin with his index finger. 'Hello there little one. What's your name? Are you a good boy?'

'That un's Tyson. Look what 'e did to me 'and.'

Gristle holds out his hand. Jamal has to adjust his spectacles to be able to make out the faintest outline of a minuscule scratch. Gristle laughs his laugh. 'Gonna be 'ard as fuck, that 'un.'

With all due caution, Jamal very gently places his arm around Gristle's shoulders and walks him slowly away from the kittens. This is not for their ears.

'You know that they'll have to be re-homed soon. We can't possibly look after them all here. We might not even be living in this house next year, and cats are very territorial. Best to find them homes now, while they're still young.'

Gristle looks down at the ground wordlessly. He doesn't quite know why, but Jamal makes him feel like a child. Very slowly he raises his head to look at Jamal. 'Yeah but… no, if…'

Jamal shakes his head. 'I think that they've had enough excitement for one day, don't you, hmm? You should go to your room and look for a cattery on the internet. It may also be worth contacting a local pet shop, or even the RSPCA as a last resort.'

Gristle nods gravely and walks towards the door. At the precise moment of his crossing the threshold and entering the hallway, the kittens all mew in unison.

For a moment, Gristle looks as if he isn't going to leave the room, but with a tearful, parting glance, he does so.

Tom's top secret super bumper action packed uni Diary of ~~adventure~~ epic adventure. Friday 5th November 2004.

Focus. Drive. Positivity. I know what I want.

I want to see Episode 3!

The teaser trailer came out this morning! They aired it

on breakfast TV and it looks AWESOME. They start it off with a few random shots from the last couple of films, and they're playing old Ben's voice over the top talking about his fallen apprentice. It's AWESOME. It's gonna be the best film of all time, easy. Me, Spadge and Will have already booked our tickets for the midnight premiere.

I want Hannah!

And what's more, Hannah wants to be with me. I feel like I'm overflowing with positive energy and optimism. For once in my life, I'm not focusing on the negative. My heart is so full I think it's gonna burst, and my mind is clearer now.

I don't think that anyone I could ever meet, or anything I could ever do could make me change my mind about how much I love Hannah. I've found that special someone who understands me, who actually loves me back and wants to be with me as much as I want to be with her. There is no holding us back.

If I could rip open my heart and let her look inside, I would do it gladly. If I could take her inside my mind and show her what she means to me, then I would. I'd show her it all. It's gonna work this time. It's really gonna happen.

It's gonna happen because she wants a happy ending too. She told me she does. 'I want a happy ending too,' she said, bright and breezy and beautiful.

It feels like magic, like a gorgeous dream.

It's just that...

...now I'm with her, I'm terrified of losing her. After my behaviour in the Union last month I thought that was it. But she still came back. She still forgave me. And if she doesn't really love me, then why would she forgive me? She must do. She does. I know she does.

But where does she go for days on end? Why is her phone turned off so much? Why is she always so ill? Did she really lose a kidney? I want to believe her, but I'm not stupid. Pig-headed — yes. An unwillingness to put two and two together — fully — functional. A total refusal to look facts in the face — present and correct.

I can only take us half of the way there, though.

Oh fuck why! Why! Why do I waste half my life sat at my desk with a pen, turning myself inside-out? Is this catharsis or is it just... sickness? Even now, look at me. I'm happy. Will's happy. Jamal's lovin' his course, which I reckon is about as close to happiness as he can get. Even Will's dad is smiling twenty-four seven. And Gristle seems to have calmed down. So why do I still feel shit?

Maybe it's because I handled the situation with Anna so poorly. I did wrong and I knew it. However, just because I know that doesn't make me any less determined to cling on to Hannah. After all my efforts over the last God-knows how long we are finally together, and Anna's stupid lies were threatening it all.

Mind you, it's hardly been smooth sailing with Hannah. She finds any excuse to argue with me or fall out. A few weeks ago in LA she fell out with me because I was talking to another girl, Katie's friend Anne. She then went on to verbally abuse Anne and start a fight.

Since then though, she did start to show me some genuine affection but then she got this 'illness.' There's always something going wrong for us.

That weekend she phoned me several times on her train journey back from her dad's in tears because of the pain that she was in. She said the pain was that bad that she wanted to die. I felt so powerless. I wanted to wrap her up in a blanket and make all her pain go away, but I couldn't. As Hannah said herself, there was nothing I could do. Nothing anyone could do.

She spent that night in hospital apparently, then the very next night she came around to see me. I met her half way between my house and hers. She looked fine. She didn't seem to be in any pain at all. If anything, she was horny. She was groping my arse all the way to my house, then as soon as we arrived she dragged me upstairs.

Upstairs, she was back up to her old tricks. As soon as she got what she wanted from me, she said 'oooh....stop babe....my kidneys hurt.'

A likely story, I thought, but I said nothing. I couldn't complain. It wasn't her fault that she was ill. I would just have to live with my frustration. After all, she was in hospital the night before with chronic kidney pain and tonsillitis.

We were both laid there in my huge bed and I felt happy. It didn't matter that she was ill or that I barely saw anything of her. At that moment, Hannah was falling asleep in my arms. All those months of unrequited desire had been fulfilled, if not sexually, then at least emotionally. As her eyes closed and she fell silent I closed my eyes, a portrait of a man who couldn't believe his luck. I didn't just love her. She loved me back.

I was in love. But just because I felt the love, didn't necessarily mean it was there.

Over the last few weeks she's been far too ill to go to lectures, so I've been to each and every one of them for her. I took notes, then went round to hers to give her a 'mini lecture.' Whenever I'd be there though, her phone would always be ringing with Winston on the other end. One night I confronted her about it when I was walking her home before she went to work. 'Why does Winston keep phoning you? I thought you weren't even talking anymore,' I asked her, flatly. No anger or anything — I asked as if I was merely curious.

'We're still friends. He's like family.'

I wasn't happy.

'Oh right,' I said. We walked in silence for a few minutes before I brought the matter up again. 'Does he fancy you?'

'Probably,' she answered snappily, before adding, cheekily. 'You can't blame him.'

'Do you reckon anything will ever happen between you two?' I asked, expecting a negative answer. I only asked so that I could at least try and put my roving mind at rest.

'I don't know, our relationship is hardly concrete is it?'

'What d'you mean by that?'

'I'm just not happy having a boyfriend that's all. It's

not fair on you. I don't have the time.'

'Why not?'

'I'm too... erm... ill and that. You know. I have enough problems seeing all my mates as it is. I sleep about sixteen hours a day I'm that poorly. I have to squeeze everyone in. It's not right. I don't have time for Winston or anyone. They're all bugging me to see me and I just don't have the time.'

'Okay fine. Whatever,' I said.

'Oh! Nice one, babe! Thanks for upsetting me before I go to work,' she said. I just shook my head at her and walked away.

I was gonna drink myself to death. That'd learn her.

Within half an hour of walking away from Hannah, I was at home downing bottles of fizzy green shite out of litre jugs. I did four in a row I think, then headed to the Union to down pint after pint of diesel and do a few shorts with Gristle and his mate Jay.

The next morning I woke up in LAs on a very damp floor in the manager's office. I had absolutely no memory of getting there – hell, LAs wasn't even open on a Wednesday night! I figured we must have had a lock-in or something 'cos this Jay is the manager. Anyway, I walked out of the office and straight into a very frightened cleaner. Panicking, I just shoved her over and ran off before she could ring the police or anything. I think I got away with it.

I would later learn that after the Union, I got into a taxi with Gristle, Will, Jay and this kid called Pete. We went back to this Pete's house where I had a piss in the middle of his living room. We were then chauffeured by a very stoned Jay to LAs for a lock-in where I passed out after a matter of minutes. They had left me in the manager's office to sleep the drink off, but as they were so pissed themselves they totally forgot about me. Apparently in the middle of the night I got up and was wandering round the club. I set all the alarms off, so Jay had to come back to turn them off and put me back to 'bed.' The bed consisted of two large doormen's coats.

Of course the next day, with me at death's door with the hangover from hell, Hannah appears. Since other Anna broke in, it's like having a bloody revolving door. I can't believe we haven't been done over proper yet! Maybe people know Gristle lives here and not to mess.

Anyway, Hannah casually slips off her shoes and then gets under the covers, snuggling up behind me. I feel a slight pang of arousal as she ventures south with her frosty hands. 'Just checking,' she says, kisses me on the cheek then falls asleep.

And she's still asleep now in my bed.

My girlfriend.

And so on bonfire night, against all the odds, our fire still burns.

'Do you believe in God then, Spadge?' Anna asks him.

'Quite a question for this time in a morning,' Spadge answers without looking her. He is busying himself looking for a brown shirt, but in extra small. As usual, there aren't any on the rail. 'I'm just gonna nip and find someone. I won't be a minute. Typical, innit? In your face as soon as you walk into a shop, but if you actually *need* any assistance you can't find 'em anywhere.'

Anna sighs and trawls through her handbag, more motivated by a desire to look like she's doing something than because she actually needs to do something. She just can't stand waiting around without fidgeting. People look at you when you aren't fidgeting. People judge you. If you have a mobile, however, you are always saved.

Anna pulls out her mobile, flips it open and just as swiftly flips it closed again; only a full battery and a full signal stared up at her. *No new messages.* Cue three minutes of accusatory stares from shoppers.

A few minutes later, Spadge emerges from the dressing room in a very trendy, scruffy-style white shirt. He looks almost handsome. 'What about this one? Shall I get it?'

'Yeah. Then can we have lunch per-lease? I didn't come all the way down here to watch you shop, gay boy.'

'Oh yeah… sos. Five minutes. Honest.'

Spadge vanishes back behind the curtain for six minutes. He'd lied.

Anna wishes that she could vanish behind a curtain, but unfortunately the puppet-master supreme is pulling her strings too fast. The act isn't over yet.

'Strictly speaking, the answer is no.'

Spadge shovels a forkful of tuna into his oral cavity. Anna looks at the red-raw flesh around his mouth and decides that ginger stubble is attractive in a peculiar sort of way.

'You don't believe?'
'No. But I don't *not* believe.'
'Oh.'
'I think that atheists are just as narrow-minded as religious people, if not more so.'
'Oh.'
'Why d'you ask?'

'Dunno. I've just been thinking about stuff recently. Meaning of life and everything. That sort of shit. I guess I'm just down. It's making my face hurt.'

'It's all in your head,' Spadge responds dispassionately.

'You say that as if it makes it all okay.'

Spadge frowns and puts down his fork. 'God no,' he says, chewing. 'It makes it all the more serious. It makes it much harder to conquer than something physical. Trust me, I know.'

'You confuse me, Spadger.'

'Thanks. More wine?'

'Mmm.'

As Spadge pours a thought strikes her. 'Did you hear about Wednesday last?'

'No. What happened?'

'They found another body.'

'Oh no,' says Spadge, feigning concern and concealing a guilty rush of adrenaline.

'Yeah. Scary, innit? People don't even seem to care anymore. It barely got a mention on the news. Front page of the local rag, though. What was her name? Aley Griffiths? Something like that. I think she must be the fourth one now, including that taxi driver last month.'

Spadge puts down his fork and looks out of the window.

'What's up?' Anna asks, quite naïvely. 'Spadge?'

'I knew an Aley once.'

'Yeah but… there's loads of Aleys, surely?'

'Aley Gs? In Hull?'

JUST A SPACE AWAY

AS TOM OPENS THE CURIOUS, SLIGHTLY-
scented envelope he feels his heart thud inside his chest. It's been weeks since he last spoke to her.

'Don't ever treat anyone the way you've treated me.'

Words from their last few conversations torment his mind.

'Die if yer want to!'

Numbly, he begins to read the letter.

Dearest Tom,

Sorry about the way I have treated you over the past few months. I know I have said some very silly and hurtful things. I hope you do not think I have turned in to some kind of Evil Monster. I finally hit the bottom of my life I wanted everything to end. Now I am seeing doctors and I am undergoing counsiling as well as getting help off of my family and friends, Trying to make me feel good abut myself and get over my problems that finally got way out of control I hope you now may understand Why I have been like I have. I hope I have caused no distresse to you. Enjoy yourself while you can. I will be intouch very soon. You have not got away from me that easy.

Love
Anna (Hartley) xXx

Tom runs his fingers through his short scruffy brown hair. The skinhead that he had recently sported is gone (or some of the hair that he had shaved off is back - it all depends on who you are and how you look at it, I suppose). Not that it matters. What matters is the sense of responsibility that Tom feels towards Anna's plight.

He is remembering making love to her. He is remembering her kindness. Her devotion. He is remembering her being sick in a cardboard box, half-dead, only the diligence and care of Jamal keeping her from choking to death on her own vomit. He is remembering standing over her, feeling powerful and superior; no doubt exactly how Hannah feels towards him. He is remembering being nauseated by the smell of her vomit, her frail and weak frame, her face so pale and gaunt from malnutrition and alcoholism. He is remembering his indefensible desire to spit on her; to stamp on her. She was in his way, dragging him down, holding him back. She was something he'd stepped in.

He is remembering being on top of the world and not coming down. He is remembering crouching down beside her, grabbing a handful of her hair and yanking her head up off the floor. Her eyes barely open, sick flowing out of her nose.

He slammed her head back down into her box of vomit, and stood back up. Had he done this to her? Had he brought her down to this? How could he be so callous? This wasn't like him.

He had whispered into her ear. 'Ah'm wiv 'annah now. Just be 'appy for us.'

Tom remembers standing up, turning off the light, leaving the room, shutting the door, and looking for his new girlfriend - the real Hannah. It was official. They were together. He had never felt such contentment.

Tom remembers his disinterest in Anna's life. Hell, if she died with her head in a box as a result of her own excessive drinking, he was off the hook. No more tearful pleading phone calls at all hours.

'Die if yer want to!' he'd spat vehemently as he'd walked out of the room. After all, as he'd learned, nice guys finish last. Now, however, he's learning another lesson: *not everyone is cut out to be a cunt.* Bad guys are beset by guilt and self-loathing. Lifetime baddies learn to deal with it; some don't even know it's there. For Tom though, it's harder.

He has everything he ever wanted. Hannah is his. He should be happy. He should be happier than ever. But he's not. It's not that simple. He just can't be happy. Not just like that.

His all too intelligent brain has begun to unravel not only Hannah's duplicity but also the world around him. The value of everything - the value of *everyone* - is crashing faster than late-twenties' Wall Street stock.

Meat puppets.

That's all they are.

Flesh and bone and muscle and sinew somehow imbued with consciousness.

Of course, he can't prove that part.

Just the flesh and bone.

The existence of his own consciousness, however, is one hundred per cent incontrovertible - the mere fact that he is pondering upon his own potential existence is proof in itself, at least intrinsically. But even if he were to accept that the meat puppets around him were somehow *ensouled* like him, not one of them would be in synch with his fucked up head. He's either too pissed, too stoned and mad for it, or way too low.

Mania. Comedown. Mania.

And it's the Mania that's killing him.

Memories of things he's never known have started manifesting themselves inside his head. Memories of a cold autumn night. *Gristle made her stop... and I...*

Tom is beginning to realise that he may never find true happiness; 'eudemonia'. Perhaps he's destined to just sail ships in the night, hear voices in the darkness, and put bricks in his wall. That's the heart of it. That's at the heart of him.

Deep inside himself, Tom longs to be right by Anna's side in the loony bin, withdrawn and isolated. All the pressures, trappings and aspirations of modern life willingly torn from him; his mind bent over and taken to brown town. Therapist. *The rapist*. Just a space away.

Instead, he's reading a poorly-spelt letter with tears in his eyes whilst Anna probably has bars in her window.

Even with his over-zealous attitude and boundless enthusiasm for the cause, Jamal finds it hard to understand how some people can become so consumed by teaching. They seem to forfeit their entire lives. He is only a little over two months into his course, and already the weight of the nine thousand words that he has to write before his next teaching practice and the constant barrage of bureaucratic triplicate form-filling is beginning to take its toll. Life is passing him by.

Life is also passing his fellow trainee Nita by, but, unlike Jamal, she doesn't care. She is blissfully lost in the safe and rigid confines of a highly-structured, highly-ordered world where essays demand no less than the sacrifice of one's very being and the post-lesson evaluation forms reign supreme. Jamal finds it hard to even talk to her without wanting to beat her with a very large stick... *dear me, I really have been spending too much time with those roguish housemates of mine!* Nevertheless, if nothing else, Jamal is a tryer.

'... then I just concluded by saying that the daily routine imposed by the excellent three-part lesson structure of the strategy has resulted in pupils responding positively and enthusiastically, and that under the strategy pupils continue to better understand their strengths and weaknesses in maths better, as well as the progress they are making, which let's face it, is the key to mastering their own learning – the key to raising the bar that extra two per cent,' Nita drones in a chirpy monotone before slamming her paper down on the desk emphatically.

'I'm convinced it's rubbish though,' she goes on, and on… 'I think tonight I'm gonna have to sit down after tea with a glass of wine and start the whole thing again from scratch. I think I needed to read more widely because on paper, it looks like all I've done is review OFSTED reports from the last five years without paying enough attention to the NNS itself. Mind you, I'll not be able to get anything done if Hannah is staying in again. Last night I didn't get a wink of sleep; I just had to listen to her pretending to have orgasm after orgasm all night!'

Jamal's brain leaps to attention upon hearing the word 'orgasm' twice. *Dearie me, I am becoming uncouth.* 'Hannah, did you say? With an aitch? Is that the girl you're sharing with?' asks Jamal.

'Yeah, she's supposedly doing politics here, but I've never seen her lift a finger - or go to a lecture for that matter. She's a bit of a nut-job if you ask me. Always either out on the piss, or in bed recovering - or not, as was the case last night'.

'You live on Driffield Court, don't you?' Jamal asks despondently. He has a bad feeling about this.

'Yeah,' Nita answers, becoming slightly troubled by Jamal's rather aggressive line of questioning. 'Why?'

'Oh no,' Jamal says softly. He now has a *really* bad feeling about this. 'I don't suppose her surname is Drake, by any chance?'

'It is actually, why? What's up?' Nita's face drops. 'Oh no! You don't know her, do you? Oh - don't tell me! You're not one of her fancy fellers are you? If you are I'm really sorry! I didn't realise she was shagging you as well as every other-'

Jamal rises to his feet, quickly sweeping all of his meticulously positioned stationary into his satchel. 'I have to get back to the house. I've... um... forgotten my-'

'What? Why? You can't. *It's not allowed.* Victor French will be here in a minute, you can't miss this. If you miss any professional studies lectures you won't be able to meet all the TTA standards listed in your Professional Development Profile!'

Jamal walks out of the Primary Centre, for the first time in his life putting friendship before professionalism.

'I won't be long, Nita. Make an excuse for me,' he says over his shoulder as the door closes.

'What a total nut-job!' says Nita, shaking her head. 'Nutty as a fruitcake. Absolutely crackers. He'll never be able to tick off all the qualifying standards now.'

Nita cannot believe this. Wait 'till she tells Alex.

Jim stands in line beside several mature students, each of them eager to earn fifteen squid. Fifteen notes. Fifteen dumps. Eight point three seven nine lovely beer tokens.

Jim isn't there for the money, though.

In fact, he's the only one not getting paid.

He looks into the dark side of the one-way mirror unsafe in the knowledge that on the other side of it the girl's eyes will be locking onto him. How could he have been so stupid? He was battered. He thought that they were all up for it, these student types. That's what his kid told him. He reckoned that he was doing her a favour...

Now the police have a positive identification made by a girl whose house Jim had broken into and whose bed he had invaded. If it wasn't for her boyfriend coming in from the night shift, she may well have ended up being the latest murder victim of this sick pyromaniac instead of just his sexual toy for the night.

That's right - the police have evidence linking Jim to at least one of the deaths. The cab driver was horrifically killed after picking up a James Surewood from the Union. Forensics placed him in that vehicle, as did the witness statements of Jamal Prakash and Thomas Briggs.

Upon his arrest, the police's search of the accused's clothing had revealed both a lighter and a flask of liqueur about his person. Detective Inspector Brooman had felt an ambiguous surge of both anger and satisfaction as he slapped the cuffs on the sicko. To think that in spite of all the evidence, he still had the gall to deny it. Oh, he admitted breaking into the house and raping the girl, but how could he not? He was caught red-handed. He even admitted responsibility for three robberies that same night and mentioned an accomplice.

They finally have their man. All the pieces fit. Now it's just a matter of linking A to B to C and they can peg the lot on him.

Pieces of shit like this make Brooman wish that this country still had the death penalty. Now if only he could get the name of this 'accomplice' out of him…

LAST MAN ALIVE

NOT ONCE.
Not even for a second.

It was supposed to be a bloke's greatest non-sexual fantasy. An empty world. All the people and animals gone; all the buildings and technology left in tact. But even after the truth had finally sunk in, the last man alive hadn't felt any sort of emotion at all, positive or otherwise.

Not once.

Not even for a second.

He'd inherited all the lands, all the chattels and all the treasures of the world. He could do anything he wanted; *anything*.

And so he'd wandered aimlessly through Hull city centre, shouting and screaming and singing. He'd gotten his cock out, and waved it about underneath the big screen in the square. The screen was blank, and nobody was there to be amused or appalled.

He'd stopped dead in his tracks and spun around three-hundred and sixty degrees. Eyes roving madly. Lungs breathing heavily. Anything he wanted. *Anything*.

He collapsed into a heap on the floor, sobbing. He'd been wrong. The world isn't black and white. It's not even greyscale. Life is in glorious technicolour, and if you act like it's in black and white you're only ever going to see its outline.

In spite of the heavy cloud, from his lofty vantage point atop the university's library the last man alive could see for miles. Everything was so quiet and so still from up there. At first, he'd thought that he would never be able to get used to the calm. Despite only a very abstract awareness of exactly who or what he was, he felt more acutely than ever that he was a social creature, and as such the silence unnerved him greatly. This land of plenty was obviously made for a large number of people, so where had they all gone? Why had he been left behind? It was all so familiar. So realistic.

In a world where there was no-one and nothing to harm him, the man was consumed by cold terror. He didn't fear death or pain or poverty... it was far less tangible than that, and infinitely nastier.

Initially, he'd been afraid of being alone forever; the puniest speck in an infinite pool of darkness. In more recent months though, his solitary existence had become a more contemplative one – after all, you can only run riot in shopping centres trying on knickers for so long before it becomes old hat – and he had begun to ask questions that made him freeze right through to the core of his being. There was no-one to anchor him; to *define him*.

He tentatively held one foot over the edge of the building. He managed to hold himself steady for a moment, but before long he felt himself stumble back as his natural defences kicked in. The adrenaline. The fear. The survival instinct.

He let himself fall backwards onto the gravelly rooftop and cursed the sky, angry at his lack of conviction.

It mattered not.

His life had ended long, long ago.

And this is the story of how he died.

* * *

The lights are out. The curtains are closed and there, by the window, there's something. Does it have a name?

Does it even deserve one? It has a penknife clutched in its hand. This is getting dangerous. Where is the danger though? Is it stemming from the knife, or from the solitude? The point is academic as it hears the door. It could be anyone.

This person stood knocking on the door could be the person to change its life forever. It retracts the blade, puts it back on the shelf with its CDs and trundles down the stairs to see just who the mysterious caller could be.

Pulling back the Yale and slowly opening the door, it narrows its eyes. Its eyes don't like the light. They haven't seen light for four days. Four long, lonely days. Four even longer sleepless - though not dreamless - nights. Everyone needs to dream, even the man on top of the world. But not these dreams.

The mouth moves. Well that's new, at least. It can't have moved for days. If this is what life's like after not even a week, imagine it in a year's time. Unthinkable.

Why won't she call?

The caller enters and follows the other upstairs, berating it for having double-locked the door. 'Can't be too careful these days,' the other says. 'Especially considering who – *what* – we've 'ad wi'in these walls.'

Upon entering the other's bedroom, the caller is already opening the curtains and a making nuisance of himself, upsetting the lighting and the mood. Ruining the atmos. Why the other is trying to cultivate such a gloomy ambience escapes even him. *Just is.*

The caller turns to face the other.

The caller speaks.

'Tom,' Jamal says. 'I've found out something that you won't want to hear. Please take a seat.'

'What?'

'Your girlfriend has been unfaithful. I understand that last night, while you were holed up in here, staring at your phone, she had... *relations* with another fellow.'

Gristle and Will burst into the living room. They'd legged it back as soon as they'd received Jamal's text. 'LIAR!' yells Tom at Jamal. 'You never liked 'er!'

Jamal instinctively puts his hands up as if Tom is holding a gun to his head. Slowly he lowers them, opening them wide to signify that he's being as open and as honest as he can possibly be. 'Ring Nita. She will tell you the same. She lives with her. Why would she lie?'

Will steps forward and puts his right hand on the shoulder of his best friend. First his dad gets banged up on charge of mass-murder and sexual assault, and then his best friend completely loses the plot over some whore.

'Mate,' Will says softly. 'Ah'm sure it's true. Ah never wanted to say owt before, but last week in Spiders, when you was in the bogs, she tried it on wi' me again. Me Katie went mental.'

Tom grabs Will's hand and stares perplexedly at it.

'You're all fuckin' liars! It's a conspiracy! You don't want us to be together. You never 'av! Bastards. Fuckin bast-'

Gristle's fist meets Tom's face with such power and pace that not only does it knock him out cold, but it also knocks him into Jamal's precious bookshelf. Books fly across the room in all directions as the flimsy, MDF unit collapses on top of Tom.

'For 'is own good,' Gristle grunts, flicking on the TV to check the racing results.

That punch felt good. Better than usual. He'd wanted to do that ever since Shabba's party when he'd... *well. Don't bear thinkin' about, duzzit? 'e's lucky they is mates or ah'd 'ave… as if ah ain't got enuf to think abart. If that daft old sod Jimbo oppens 'is gob ta the cops… ah mean… If ah af to, ah'll face th'music for me nickin', but ah ain't gettin' drawn into this rapin' an' killin' shit…*

Gristle ain't goin' down for what some other fucker did… YES! Go on my son! What an' 'oss! Fifteen ta one! An 'oss an' 'afe!

Tom comes round only to find Jamal right in his face, offering him a mobile phone.

'Call her,' he says gently. 'She will tell you what she told me. Then it's up to you whether to believe it or not.'

One day Jamal would make a damned good Head.

Tom takes the mobile phone and presses the green button.

It rings the number stored as *NITA mob*.

Tom had heard the accusations but he didn't believe them for a second. How could he believe what they were saying about his Hannah. About *his girlfriend*. How could he believe it? It would mean the death of him.

But then why would they make it up? Jamal has always been caring and honest if nothing else, and there's nothing in it for this Nita lass. Everything that they have said certainly fits with the rest of the puzzle. Still, there's one thing that doesn't make sense. If she's such a slapper, then surely she'd have put out long before she did?

Tom's world finally collapsed completely that bitter November evening. Everything that he once held dear, everything that he had been living for, was crushed in one swift and brutal blow. And the worst sting of all was that he should have known. Deep down he did know, but he'd been blinded. Every intuition had failed to find its way. Unheeded warnings; he thought he'd accounted for everything.

Looking but not seeing.

Then having his eyes prised open, and wishing for blindness.

The Darkness finally took its hold of Tommy Briggs that night.

Winston seems surprisingly genial, despite all of Hannah's horror stories about him. She'd managed to program Tom into thinking that this intimidating bouncer look-alike was a complete psycho – probably to discourage him from ever doing what he's about to do. For all Tom knew, Winston had been fed equal and opposite propaganda.

As Jamal's friend had promised, Tom receives a text from Winston telling him to wait by the crossroads.

I'll be the one in the pink carnation, the message concludes.

Perhaps 'e is a psycho after all...

The two *beep-beep-beep, beep-beep, beep-beep-beeps* of Tom's mobile make him jump a mile. It's a text. It's Hannah.

```
If u think that u & him r gonna sit together
in a pub & talk about me ur a fucking idiot
ill never speak to either of u again if u
do. u both want me u wud both take me back
ne way.
```

Tom feels nothing. He just stands, and he waits.

For an hour Tom and Winston sit by the pool tables in the nearest pub that they can find, share a civilised drink and exchange Hannah stories. To both of them, today is totally surreal. Both suspected that something was going on, but neither could have ever imagined something so... so audacious... so callous... so *twisted*.

Once Tom has finished telling Winston the whole 'Hannah saga' – the full, feature length, x-rated version – Winston details, point by point, exactly how they have both been misled, manipulated, and used.

Firstly, Nita had been right when she had told Jamal that Hannah and Winston were far more than just friends. What their relationship is – was – exactly even Winston doesn't know, but they were certainly together in every sense of the word. In fact, they had started shagging during Freshers' Week last year, right at the beginning of uni. In all that time, certain people had said that Hannah was also having a relationship with a guy Winston only knew as 'Polish Paul' and, even more shockingly, that she'd been pregnant twice. Twice she'd miscarried. *Rumours,* Winston had thought.

Until now.

So that's what 'er bouts o' unexplained 'illness' were.

Against their better judgement, Tom and Winston compare dates. Last year, Hannah shagged Winston the night before she first slept with Tom. That very same night she was shagging Winston and bombarding Tom with filthy messages - Winston even found them on her phone. They hadn't used protection either, and Hannah had made a big fuss about the likelihood of her being pregnant. The next day she shagged Tom, unprotected, less than twelve hours after she'd had Winston up her.

Tom runs into the toilet and throws up into the urinal.

For the first time in years, Tom's puke is neither purple nor alcohol-induced. He feels like he's been violated. Normally full of a youthful and healthy sexual energy, the very idea of intercourse with *anyone* – such an intimate act – makes Tom's guts wretch.

Animals.

Meat puppets.

The stories go on and on. Hannah had reportedly told all her friends that Winston beats her up. Once upon a time, not too long ago, she just started to scream in the street for no apparent reason. Winston had said something that pissed her off, and so she screamed rape and bloody murder. She even told people that Tom had hit her and tried to rape her. She'd only managed to restrain the backlash of Winston and his mates by spreading stories about Tom's unstable psyche and fictional collection of guns.

Last month, Hannah had got Winston beaten up by the bouncers in the Fez. Tom had actually heard about this from Hannah – well, he'd heard *a version* of this from Hannah, but in light of this evening's revelations, Winston's version sounds far more credible to his sceptical ears.

According to Hannah, Winston was acting like a possessive maniac and threatening the bar manager because she was flirting with him; curious behaviour for a mere 'best friend', to say the least. Winston says, however, that she – his girlfriend - was getting off with this bar feller right in front of his face. Tom can see why he may have got a little cross.

Winston's final story is the one that shakes Tom out of his comfortably numb coma. One night in the summer holidays, she went down to London to stay with Winston when, for no apparent reason, she told Winston to go home and ended up shagging his best friend in a one night stand. In a hotel that Winston paid for.

After all her preaching to Tom. After all her self-righteous speeches to him about fidelity, she went and shagged one of her lover's best friends.

All those lies.
All those fuckin' lies!

The sheer scope of the delicate web that she has weaved is astonishing; it truly beggars belief. What is really amazing though is how she got away with it for so long. But now the shocking truth is laid bare, perhaps embellished a little on both sides, but nevertheless the testimonies of Tom and Winston constitute a far more accurate account of the past fourteen months than Hannah is ever likely to give. And so say both of them.

Tom's top secret super bumper action packed uni~~ Diary of adventure~~ epic adventure. Saturday 20th November 2004.

... half a bottle of Southern Comfort later (which I drank the Lion's share of) Hannah appeared at Winston's house. She strutted into the living room with a huge smile on her face and sat down on the chair in the corner, just looking at us both. She sort of lifted her hands up. 'You two having fun slagging me off?'

I remained silent.

'You're a clever girl, I'll give you that,' Winston said with a smile. She almost broke into tears. Winston's so cool.

She pointed at me. 'What's he been telling you? It's lies! He's a liar! He just wants me to himself! He thinks you're the only thing standing in his way! He's trying to turn you against me! Don't listen to him! He's a liar! He's a psycho!'

Winston just shook his head. 'No Hannah. No he's not. I've had enough this time. You can't keep treating me like this.' I can't remember exactly what was said, but he mentioned her shagging his best friend, Sam. I couldn't keep quiet any longer.

I looked up at her with a sneer. 'I thought you had to be in love with someone to have sex with them, hmm?'

No response.

'I SAID, I thought you had to be in love with someone to fuck them. That's what you always say, innit sweetie?' I hissed at her.

She scowled ferociously. 'I'd had about ten Es so I was pretty loved up,' she said, laughing to herself. 'I thought you'd have learned by now, there's no such thing as love you fucking idiot!'

Within minutes she was on her knees in front of the

sofa where Winston was sat, prostrating herself before him and begging for him to marry her. 'I love you... let's go into town now and get married... I mean it...'

I didn't know whether to laugh or cry. I was just sat there, drinking my whisky, watching the world disintegrate around me, every second I spent in that room scarring me for life, if not for longer.

'How can you say that with him sat there, the other guy you're shagging?' Winston said, I think out of pity for me, more than anything. And to think I'd hated him for so long. He's just a young bloke like me. A decent enough sort. And so cool.

'Come upstairs,' she asked him.

'No,' Winston answered resolutely.

'Please... I want to talk to you away from him,' she said, looking at me with a look of utter contempt. 'I love you.'

'Why?' I stepped in. 'So you can tell him more lies about me? So you can tell him that I hit you, that I forced you? What more shite are you gonna fill him full of? Oh yeah, and I thought love didn't exist. Make up your mind, love.'

With tears in her eyes and her voice full of rage she got right in my face and yelled 'Fuck off! This is the guy I want to marry. You – you're nothing! You were just a plaything!'

I got up and looked straight into her twisted face. 'You're sick.'

She looked back into my now almost equally warped face. 'What yer gonna do about it?'

I shook my head at her and slumped back down into the armchair. She got in my face again screaming. Now it was Winston who didn't know whether to laugh or cry.

'Are you gonna hit me, Hannah?' I asked, smiling to myself, because that looked like exactly what she was gonna do. 'Just like I supposedly hit you?'

My harsh words didn't do me any good. Hannah dragged Winston upstairs for about half an hour, maybe forty-five minutes while I sat downstairs and polished off the scotch.

I could hear her begging to Winston upstairs, but it wasn't that I was listening to. 'Plaything,' wouldn't dislodge itself from my thoughts. I couldn't get the vision out of my head of going down on her only hours after Winston's (probably stereotypically massive) black cock had just been in her. I could see them both in the pub laughing at me as I sat in lectures or in the library copying out notes for her.

I had thought that I loved her. I thought that she was the one. That day, I saw the real Hannah. My true love wasn't anywhere to be found in the girl who called me a 'plaything.' My true love must have just been in my head, somewhere lost in cuckoo land. After everything I had been through with her, all I had left to show were a few dregs of whisky, a scar that wouldn't heal and a heart that had been broken because I'd seen the real Hannah Drake.

I'm utterly sick of this all. Life's shallow. It's empty. And worst of all I've squandered over a year wasting all my affection on someone who is lower than scum; nothing more than a cheap, ugly, fat-assed, specky, four-eyed bitch who would prostitute herself to get her uni work done.

And now I sit here. Words flowing around in my mind. What am I anyway? I mean really. How am I alive? How is my heart still beating? After so many injuries, so much alcohol, so many drugs? After every punch. After every kick. After every fall. How am I even walking? My mind... just a brain... an organ. Cells, molecules, atoms, neutrons, protons and electrons. Even from my rather arrested perspective it seems that I was handed rather more electrons than protons.

Unbalanced.

Damaged.

Deluded.

Or maybe it's like old Spadge says, I'm not deluded. I'm one of the few that can bloody well see. And I can see far too well. Far too fucking clearly.

The amazing gift of consciousness was the cruellest gift of all. I wish I was like Rocky. No worries, no trauma. No feelings per se. I wish I were a creature of pure instinct, just living one day after the other, blissfully unaware of... well. Blissfully un-self-aware.

Now I know how Dad must have felt.

I guess this is the end.

I've taken the pain as the world laughed and smiled. As everything slid down the pit into forever. The steep gradient, dripped in grease to make everyone's descent faster. From the cradle to the grave; all those hopes and dreams of all that I wanted to be. And no-one will ever remember my name.

I feel like I know all the answers but yet I know nothing.

How could I have been so stupid?

How could I have done all those...

I couldn't have.

I shall now bring my journey to a comma, not a full stop. A hopeful piece of punctuation that will see me ascend, or see me perish.

I wish she could hold me until the world disintegrates around us, but in the morning when she wakes, I'll be gone. Carried away with the rising sun to parts unknown. I don't want to go to heaven. I just want to go...

But she never really existed, at least, not in the conventional sense. She exists in the same place that the aeroplanes and motorbikes do. The domain of dreams and fire.

Why do I have this little voice in me? This thing I can't adequately articulate nor even hope to express now. Why did I adore Hannah so much? And why did I loathe Anna for showing me nothing but love and affection? And why do I still fear Bethany? Are we all part of some massive cosmic plan, fated to be together by God? Does he write the pages our story, relishing the drama in every agonising twist of fate? Or do I?

Maybe I'm just as I appear to be, a composite of flesh, bone, muscle, and water. Maybe those feelings I had for Hannah were just different chemicals running around in my brain. I guess it's all just semantics.

It doesn't matter whether these feelings are chemical in nature or somewhere in my soul. It doesn't matter whether Hannah is just a notion in my head, a pleasing alignment of atoms or whether she lives her life as just another no-one like me, not knowing who she really is, what she really is, or in fact anything at all. What matters is what is within my soul. If I am more than the sum of my flesh and blood then my Hannah is indeed an integral part of my soul, someone I truly love, and someone whose face I will see again, somewhere other than behind my eyelids or in my darkest night terrors.

If I am just flesh, blood and nothing more, then everything I was; everything I am; and all my thoughts, feelings, hopes, and dreams are nothing but chemicals being balanced out in my brain. If that is true, then it would mean that Hannah was merely the chemical that completed me, that brought balance. And chemicals can be replicated...

I have to be conscious you see, of the fact that many people suffer from similar disorders and go on to live long, productive and happy lives, and I should not fall into the trap of using my weakness as a self-fulfilling prophecy of destruction. Sometimes I can feel it just above my eyes though. I can hear the demon's voice. I can feel his black hatred seize their lying, philandering little throats. And I see what his hatred does to them. It consumes them like fire.

It could be this placebo effect that the Psychologists bang on about. Or it could be madness, pure and simple.

Believe it or not, I'm aware that my thoughts are a danger to me, and as I write this right now I can actually feel them wrestling for control. At the moment the Darkness has the Light on the ropes. I long to be free of the persecution; free of the heinous master plans that Hannah has hatched against me, but it's too late now. I can't stop her plans. I don't even want to.

Did something evil ensnare my mind long ago, reel it in and then let it simmer slowly in a pan? Did it direct knock after knock after knock against me, just so I'd be weak and it could take me, and make me...

The Bible says that the Devil entered the heart of Judas Iscariot. The Bible says that the Devil made him betray Jesus Christ. And when Judas saw what the Devil had made him do, he committed suicide.

I've gotta admit, I've had it with being used by things that I can and things that I can't see. Dying doesn't scare me any more. It can't be worse than what I've been through today. I don't want to kill myself — I want to be run down by a lorry, contract a fatal disease, fade away slowly from all the hurt that she has knowingly and willingly inflicted upon me . . . and leave her burning in pain.

I'll make her pay for what she's done!

My mind's clearer now.

I understand Truth.

I look in the mirror and see the empty eyes, the dying body and the broken heart.

I should take the money and start to gamble.

I should take the money and start to drink.

I should max out the overdraft and die in Amsterdam in a drug-fuelled sex orgy.

But I can't be arsed.

Staying alive just isn't worth the hassle, or the risk.

'It's better to burn out than fade away' – who wrote that . . . I mean originally? I know Kurt nicked it. I can't even think of anything to nick first-hand, so I guess it'll have to do.

I'm sorry Mam

xxx

ONE OF MY TURNS

TOM CINEMATICALLY DROPS TO HIS KNEES in the heavy rain, clutching the wilted rose tight. He feels its thorns cut deep into his hand. Drops of blood drip down onto the tarmacadam and run with the rain into the gutter. It's all that his blood is fit for. The sharp red of the blood stands out from the blues and greys of the scene; it's an image torn from the pages of a graphic novel.

The dark clouds continue to bombard Tom with heavy rain, soaking him to the bone. His hand is bleeding and his jeans are (genuinely) ripped and dirty; his heart is black and broken. His soul is in tension. His anger rattles at his skeleton, desperate to break out of him. It's not even aimed at anyone anymore - it's just pure, indiscriminate rage.

Tom hears the voice, calling to him.

He feels it enter his heart. Again.

Just like with Judas.

If he were able to look upon himself he would see the slightest of movements in his thorax, precisely in synch with the words ringing inside his head.

Take her. Slice the smile from her face. Cover her with methylated spirits and watch the lies smoulder on her skin. Take the power she has over you and break it. Use your power.

Destroy her.
End it.
End her.
End her now.

… but… that isn't 'annah… ah don't know who she… it's not her fault… it wasn't her…

THEY ARE ALL THE SAME! They all laugh at you. They all have the potential to bestow the most excruciating suffering imaginable upon you. Stop her before she gets chance. Let the flames be her Jury! You are but the Judge.

Do what must be done.

'No...' Tom cries out internally, his lips unmoving; his throat in spasm. 'Not again... Ah'm not...' the words come hard but they come. They hurt.

'... your...' Pain.

'... puppet...' Fear.

'... anymore...' Release.

No more excuses.

No mucky halo to cling on to.

The truth of what you are and of what you've done. Of what you could be.

Of what you could never be.

A bolt of thunder crackles high above and the sky dances with electric light. A single tear burns into Tom's face like acid. He takes the specially sharpened penknife from his pocket and slices vertically down what he reckons must be a major artery – *that should do it.*

This isn't a cry for help.

This is a cry for a release.

As the blood flows, a sense of giddiness surges through Tom's nervous system and he laughs out loud. For some reason, futile romantic imagery floods into his mind.

It's Bethany.

She's running towards his prone body that is now collapsed in a pool of blood not a hundred metres from her house. He'd not even realised where he was; not consciously, anyway. Bethany scoops him up into her arms, into the most explosive big screen kiss of all time, and suddenly he's fine. The blood has gone. He's more than fine. The pain has gone.

All of it.

But deep down in the innermost part of him, he knows it's only a trick of the mind; the demon's last roll of the die.

Shaken, yet strangely excited, the old man ran further and further away from the city centre as landmine after landmine exploded in volcanoes of blue flame. The floating glass shopping centre went *bang-bang-a-boom*. The giant TV screen exploded in a surfeit of sound and fury.

Ah'm not doing this! he thought. *Ah can't be! Ah'm the last man… alive?*

But if he wasn't doing it then… could it be someone else? *Please God…*

God. That's a word that's played on his mind often since… *before*.

The old man stopped for breath beside a small playing field. He felt like he'd been running forever and for all that he knew, he may well have been. Words like 'forever' didn't seem to carry much weight in a world with no real sense of time.

A playing field.

A playing field without any children.

A playing field without even a light breeze blowing across it.

Of all the strange things the man had seen, this was the strangest. Every single molecule seemed to be frozen. When he reached out towards the grass, he felt his entire body lock. His heart began to beat that little bit faster.

Panic.

PANIC.

PANIC!!!

He glanced in slow motion over his shoulder to see a passenger jet falling from the sky. No smoke. No flames. Not even the slightest hint of sound.

The old man wrinkled his brow, almost annoyed that the plane wasn't hurtling towards the ground in an epic blaze of glory. Instead it dropped silently, gracefully.

Well, he'd wanted to know for a while now.

Time to find out.

Dead or alive?

As the passenger jet bore down upon him, the old man became even more determined. The plane's cold glass eyes drew ever closer, but to the man's surprise he saw that his reflection in them showed no fear. His own eyes were alight with passion; he could almost feel the heat from them burning his eye sockets from the inside-out.

The sheer enormity of the craft closed to within metres.

At the last moment Tom's resolve broke and he threw his arms up in front of his face.

He was hit hard; overcome by a strange dizziness that eventually became nausea. He pictured himself as a swatted fly, buzzing around insanely and about to die.

And then he died.

Again.

And the world fell away in a bath of flames.

Again.

He looked up at the burnt remnants of the young women and the taxi driver trapped in purgatory with him. Bound to him in warped apocatastasis.

His sorrow growing in direct proportion to his increasing wisdom, old Tommy turned around and walked back up the riverbank.

Now he knew.

THE TRUTH

Tom's top secret super bumper action packed uni Diary of ~~adventure~~ epic adventure. Friday 24th December 2004.

Time for a catch-up. Where to start? I didn't really know what had happened. I was laid on my trolley, waiting for the Doctor, so I said 'you don't have to wait with me yer know,' to Will, so he didn't. Selfish twat.

I was alone.

Before long an attractive young female Doctor was checking me over, inspecting my bandages. The work of mere seconds had left me with a four-inch long laceration running down my left forearm and the likelihood of a long hospital stay courtesy of section six. The days of dismissing my condition as prodromal and medicating me up to the eyeballs were over, I feared.

I have never been as happy to see anyone as I was to see Will, Jamal, Spadge and Katie a few hours later. I was hurt that Bethany wasn't with them, but apparently she was visiting her parents in Newcastle.

On the same note, I have never been as angry to see anyone as I was to see Hannah show up just a few minutes later. As soon as she arrived, my friends all left. Will had to restrain Katie.

Hannah sat on the edge of my bed. 'You see now,' she said. 'I hate to see you like this babe, but this is what I knew you would do if you found out about Winston. I should have told you. I'm sorry. I'm so sorry.'

I tried to look away but I couldn't. I'd played right into her hands. Now, she could turn around to Winston and say something like 'I only slept with him because he threatened to kill himself,' and she would have a credible story. Yes, I'd hurt her, but I had also given her the means to win Winston back.

It wasn't worth it.

I verbally abused her for a little while. When the nurse came over to change my bandages, I even said 'it's all her fault I'm in here.' After suffering an onslaught of abuse from me, Hannah got up to leave. I grabbed her hand.

'Please don't leave me.'

After everything, I couldn't let her go. I couldn't allow her to walk away. I didn't want to be alone in that hospital. I didn't want to be alone full stop. I couldn't bear it.

'Stop it, or I'll be in that bed with yer in a minute,' she said with a smile, the dirty bitch. I remembered Winston telling me of how he shagged her in a hospital bed once.

'Why?' I snarled at her. 'So I can try and rape you again? Isn't that what all your friends think of me? Tommo the psycho rapist? Alright then bitch. Get in this bed now. Get naked. If you don't I might just slash my other arm!'

She shook her head. 'I won't give into this.'

It went quiet. All that either of us could hear was the rolling of wheels, the rustling of bed covers, and the noise caused by her mobile phone interfering with the hospital's life-preserving machinery.

She burst into tears again. 'I can't believe I have actually made somebody want to die. Don't you get it? This is so big. Do you get that? It could've been the end, and I . . . I made you feel so bad you wanted to die, didn't I? This is all because of me.'

I said nothing. I thought that my silence would hurt her far more than me acknowledging the truth of her last statement.

'You wouldn't be here though, if it wasn't for me, would you?' she repeated.

I said nothing.

I was remembering another voice.

A voice that told me to do something...

I can't think of anything more terrifying than memories that I can't quite unlock.

Terrible memories.

My memories...?

Its memories...

Hannah stayed for a few more minutes dramatically apologising to me, but soon after a suspicious beep of her mobile she stood up to leave. 'Don't go,' I begged her.

'I'll come back,' she promised. She seemed like my Hannah again, not the evil monster that I had seen the night before. I wanted her back. I wanted to marry her, to chain her up and hide her away from every man on the planet. But it wasn't feasible.

I couldn't forget what she'd done, and she could never forget this. We had gone too far. So far that we couldn't get on in this world anymore. Deep down I knew this as she took me by the hand and squeezed hard. And then she was gone.

Still, I couldn't help wishing that she would come back. I couldn't bear the thought of never holding her again, never kissing her again, and never telling her that I loved her again. It was a thought, though, that I would have to bear.

Will had told her not to come back. I was furious with him, but for once he was right — it was for my own good. She was no good for me. She was scum. I just couldn't see the light at the end of the tunnel. I couldn't see the women on the other side. The only light at the end of the tunnel that I could see was the great beyond opening up before me. What made it all worse was the fact that I'd done this to myself.

The clock seemed to tick backwards. I had nothing to do and nowhere to go, and all I could feel was pain in every possible meaning of the word. I was alone with my thoughts and my feelings, perhaps the worst possible situation for me to be in at that time.

'Poor old Judas', I thought to myself. He had the Devil in his heart.

I didn't know where this sentiment had come from, but the more I pondered on its meaning the clearer things became. For the first time I felt that I could touch upon certain memories that weren't mine. Foul horrors gnawed at me as I felt my mind beginning to unravel. Deep inside my heart I could hear my voice that had once screamed so loud fall into nothing but a whisper, while in its place a dark spirit rose slowly from my guts, wrenching every primal instinct, fear and desire up along with it. Gradually it took control of all my bodily functions. All my higher brain functions.

Thought.

Reason.

They were all enslaved to this demon.
Poor old Judas.
Poor old Tommo.

Perhaps this was the onset of my 'positive' symptoms — a curious turn of phrase, I've always thought. Perhaps that's why I'm here. Perhaps it won't be long now until I'm just a dribbling spastic in a straightjacket, wandering through town in my slippers, haunted by visions that aren't there and tormented by paranoid delusions of being the pawn of some satanic beast. But how am I to know that this illness isn't the delusion? How am I to know what's real and what's fake? I could just be some sad old entity, roving and alone. Sat on a beach, amusing myself with this make-believe life to pass eternity. Who's to say?

Well at least Hannah was right about two things. One — there's no such thing as love. Two — I shouldn't have put my whole life in her hands. Either way — sick or possessed —

there is something very wrong with me. The illness... the monster... it feeds on need and hunger and desire.

And fury.

And fury is borne out of love.

Maybe I just love people too much. Maybe I don't really love myself, and that's where it all falls down. That's the final indignity. As long as I'm beset by this... curse... no-one can ever truly love me. Not all of me. Not even me. I can't love myself, even though as long as this disease ravages my mind, myself is all I'll ever have.

I lay awake that night looking around the ward. So fucking depressing. Just ill people. No telly. I looked at the bloody earwig Nurses who now thought I was a blackmailing son of a bitch thanks to Hannah's excessively bombastic dramatics. I looked up at the 'turn off all mobile ferns' sign (honestly, it says 'ferns') just as I felt my mattress gently vibrate.

```
1 message received
```

I read it with a lump in my throat. It should have all been so *straightforward. It should have been her, not Hannah. Why wasn't it her?*

thank god ur still alive, ive been so worried and upset.u do whatever it takes 2 get urself better.if u need anything don't hesitate 2 let me know.take care love B xXx

SENDER: fit beth mob

SENT: 05:13:01 22-11-2004

I read that message and felt the first positive emotions that I'd felt for a long time. Bethany is one of those people who when you think about them they just make you smile. That night we texted each other loads. No-one else bothered to text me. I even sneaked into the shower room — dragging my drip-feed by my vein — so that we could speak on the phone, and then again the next night while the Doctors debated my sanity.

Being kept in there terrified me. Although I hadn't been officially sectioned, I had the distinct impression that that would change were I to try and discharge myself. Beth was the only thing that keeping me going. I had to believe in her positivity. I had to believe in her optimism. I think if it wasn't for Bethany cheering me up, I would've ran out of that hospital and I'd probably be dead right now.

I didn't even realise how far I'd fallen until I reached the bottom. But it was climbing time, and Bethany had thrown down the rope ladder for me to start climbing. I'll never be more grateful to anyone for anything in my whole life.

And so there you have it. It took five weeks but I finally got it down and out of my system. And I'm happy to say that this year I won't be spending the most wonderful time of the year alone.

While Gristle is probably living underground in some cesspit like Rotherham or Swindon selling pills; while Jamal is back in Lancaster with his lass; and while Will's dad rots in jail, leaving his son having to spend Christmas comforting his poor, broken mother; I will be here in Hull spending Christmas Day with the loveliest, most beautiful creature in the world! I will be spending the day with a girl who no longer evokes fear in me because for the first time in years I feel like I can face the future.

I look forward to it.

It must be a sad life when its most outstanding moment is standin' on an old stone bridge in the pale moonlight. The tall an' polished trees cast shadows over the river below, an' ah'm kissing the most beautiful girl in the world.

Ah look into her eyes an' tell 'er that she is the loveliest girl on the planet, and that ah want to scoop 'er up an' run away, get married an' shack up wi' 'er in some 'ermit 'ole down south wi' digital an' broadband.

In just ovver a month she 'as made me feel more emotion than anyone 'as been able to in years. It's not love... yet it is. It's a flight o' fancy on a winter's night. It's probably more romance than love, but in me drunken 'eart it feels as real as real can be. So cold... so drunk... yet such a sense o' overwhelming contentment an' 'ope. We might just meck it. It could all work out alreet.

Ah wanta feel like this forever.

'I love you,' says Bethany to Tom.

'olding 'er tight in me arms, wi' the river ebbin' an' flowin' beneath us, as she says 'I love you' me whole life seems like no more than a build-up to this moment. Me whole expanse 'ad allus been geared towards this moment on the bridge. Ah never wanted anything but this. She probably doesn't believe me, an' she probably never will, but ah wish ah could stay on this bridge forever wi' 'er.

My 'eart thrashes around in me chest, but ah won't let it punish me any more.

'annah is the past.

So is Anna... an' ah wish 'er well.

But one question remains.

Is this love... or is this me longing for an 'appy endin' clouding me judgement?

Ah, Beth. You're the most beautiful, sexy, sweet an' lovin' girl in the world... but are you the cure, or a symptom?

* * *

Oh fuck me, I think I've fallen for this one big time. When you can see somebody's blatant imperfections and you still think that you love them... well, you're in deep shit.

Oh bugger. I've got my Weight Watchers *class tomorrow night. I'm gonna be pissing and shitting all day long just to make sure I'm a pound or two-*

'Ah think, just maybe, ah love you too,' he says to me.

When it feels so right, why do I have such a bad feeling about this?

Lost in time.

I could have been in these arms for days.

It feels like a dream.

It feels like 'that' dream.

It feels like forever.

'Tell me number three,' she asks him.

Toms looks at Bethany curiously. 'Number three?'

'You told me about your brother. About your father. We never finished the game. Remember?'

Tom looks downcast.

Bethany suddenly looks guilty. 'Oh! I mean, um, the three worst things *before* the whole *kiss kiss slash slash* thing last month.'

'Such tact,' he smiles. 'Look... ah... ah don't want you to think ah'm crazy. You must already think ah'm a total fuck-up.'

Bethany shakes her head. 'I don't... I mean, I won't.'

Tom lets out a deep breath. 'Ah'll tell you, but only 'cos it's you, an' only 'cos ah want us to be close-'

Bethany nods, then leans into him, resting her head on his shoulder.

'*-er.*'

Tom is thankful that he doesn't have to look her in the eye. Not for this. He gazes up into the night sky and picks a star. *Alpha Centauri… Wolf 359…*

His eyes eventually fix on a constellation; *Orion.*

'Ah was still reet young, ah'd not been at the comp long. Ah think it was abart 1997 when it began. Yeah; *Song 2* had just come out. Ah've allus loved movies, an' back then me an' a mate o' mine, Sean the Prawn, shared the interest an' managed to worm our way into usin' the school's media studies room at dinner to meck our little films under the oh-so-clever pretence o' enterin' a competition.

'The media technician, Andy, was a total pushover. Sometime before that Christmas we'd 'ad 'im let us crawl underneath the school in the asbestos-filled tunnels for our own fun wi' 'is neck on the line. Ah 'ear 'e got the sack last year for being a paedo. That explained a lot.

'Anyways, after we'd filmed about forty hour o' our intergalactic adventure *The Dentist of Time,* wi' both me an' Prawny teckin' it in turns to play the mysterious Dentist, our movie ideas ran a bit dry. Soon the school's prized media room became nowt more than a dossin' room for the school's academic elite… an' Will.

'On the verge o' puberty, our interests were slowly bein' pulled away from the pressures o' the 'movie business' an' were instead becoming more interested in impressin' the media room's resident girls… in my case, it was Sean's sister Sarah who 'ad me undivided attention. Me first proper love, ah reckon.

'Anyways, in one o' the school's dreaded breaks – you 'ad to watch yer back for the 'death merchants' as we called 'em - guys like Gristle! – ah remember Sean approachin' me an' tellin' me that a *ouija board* 'ad told 'im that 'e was gonna die wi'in three month.

'At first ah dismissed it as soundin' like the sorta object Rolf 'arris would own, but ah wanted to become the centre o' the girls' attention by 'avin' a séance mesen. That was me first mistake.

'The next day in the media room Sarah opened up the feebly constructed paper board an' nicked a glass from the dinin' 'all. We all put our fingers on the glass an' attempted to summon the spirits. We weren't summonin' the spirits o' Robin 'ud or JFK; oh no. We were summonin' the dispossessed - the spirits o' those in the limbo between 'eaven an' 'ell; those in their own, personal purgatory; those who 'ad shuffled off this mortal coil in pain. Ah sceptically watched the board as it failed to provide me wi' any amusement, an' ah was gettin' well pissed off at the 'spirit' only trying to meck contact wi' Sarah who, to be 'onest, really didn't gi' a shit – she just wanted to eat 'er dinner in peace away from the death merchants in the dinin' 'all.

'Before long the board 'ad piqued me interest though. It began to toy wi' the emotions o' those foolish enough to lay their grubby little paws on the glass. O' the seven youngsters who each 'ad put a frightened but excited finger on the glass, only Fat Rob mocked it. As we all asked the board for dates o' the world's end an' our own deaths – we were a cheery lot, as you can imagine – ah could feel a whole, alternative world openin' before me, one where the dead are alive. An' dreams...

'Fat Rob's continued 'eckling angered Beef, who was particularly touchy about these supernatural matters. Beef was Prawny's cousin, built like a brick shit 'ouse, but the sort o' lad to allus cry whenever 'e 'urt 'imsen, even in the comp. 'e also 'ad an intense fear o' the witchcraft takin' place yet 'e couldn't drive 'imsen to be torn away from it. Suddenly Beef just cracked, liftin' Fat Rob up wi' one arm an' throwing 'im towards the door. Fat Rob 'it 'is 'ead on the door, an' then as we watched in awe, Beef ran ovver, opened the door an' through 'im straight out. Funnily enough, poor ol' Fat Rob was thrown straight into

Gristle an' Bayonett who weren't best pleased when Fat Rob came crashin' into 'em. They kicked the living daylights out o' the poor bastard.

'Anyhow, that's neither 'ere nor theer. Beef slammed the door behind 'im. For a moment, the iron man looked like 'e was going to cry, but 'e managed to compose 'imsen an' return to 'is chair to continue the séance.

'Finally it got to my turn an' ah'd come up wi' a vast array o' questions for the board that only ah could possibly know the answer to. Once again the board asked to speak to Sarah, but ah 'ad to 'ave the attention. Sean's tales about how the board 'ad predicted the death o' 'is Uncle Warren fell upon deaf ears, so ah 'it the board wi' me questions. Ah asked the board whether the prophet what Sean an' me were fascinated wi', Nostradamus, was a fake or not. Slowly, our fingers were dragged by the glass from 'N' to 'O.' Ah then asked whether the end o' the world would occur wi'in our lifetimes, as it said in Nostradamus's prophecies, an' once again our fingers were dragged by the glass from 'N' to 'O.' Wi' it seemingly contradictin' itself, me faith in the board was dwindlin'.

'Sean then asked if the Devil existed. Our fingers were dragged from 'Y' to 'E' to 'S.' Givin' up on the board, ah walked into the control booth o' the media room. Unbeknownst to the others, ah 'ad the cameras all trained on the board, an' wi' a sly flick o' the switch they began to record everythin'.

'Ah sat back down wi' the others an' placed me finger once more on the glass. Some part o' me longin' for adventure, longin' for something to reach up at us from beyond the grave an' say 'yes, there's more,' ah shouted at the board "'ave yer got the ability to manifest yoursen in one o' us?'

'The others went ballistic, an' before ah knew it ah was 'urtling towards the floor wi' Beef's fist buried in me ribs. The gentle giant 'ad snapped again. Wi' everyone but Sarah an' Sean's attention on Beef an' me, no-one 'ad noticed the board - Sarah an' Sean were still usin' it. 'Y' 'E' 'S', it said.

'Angered by Beef, an' 'opin' that somehow ah would be taken over, just aching for the adventure an' attention, ah shouted 'go on then.'

'Like in a bad fifties' b-movie, the lights in the room flickered. Seriously! Ah wouldn't lie about this. Ah ran into the control room, an' found me video 'angin' out o' the machine, the chewed up tape 'angin' through the plastic casing. Ah 'anded it to the bemused Andy an' told 'im to sort it out.

'The bell rang an' we all left the room, Beef givin' me an *ah'm gonna kill thee' loo*k an' do you know what ah said?'

Bethany smiles and says what Tom wants her to. 'What did you say?'

'So much for manifestation.'

Bethany raises an eyebrow. 'And then...?'

'Then what?'

'And then what happened? Who got zombified?'

Tom shakes his head with a stern look pasted onto his furrowed brow. 'Nobody.'

'So what was the point of that little tale? After what you were saying last time, I thought...'

'Look,' Tom says in a teacher voice - he's been spending too much time around Jamal. 'It could all just be coincidence. There are loads o' power cuts in comps. Teens act up. It's just... well. To this day no-one admits to fakin' that board, an' ah know ah saw wi' me own eyes that damn glass whiz around the board wi'out any o' us touchin' it. An' what bothers me... it's somethin' Sean used to say, about his Dead Uncle.'

'What did he say?'

'That if yer get a bad spirit, it can stay wi' you for life. It can manipulate you. Consume you. We were playin' wi' things what we didn't understand…'

Bethany looks concerned and pulls away from Tom so that she can look him square in the eye. 'What are you saying?'

'That just maybe,' Tom sighs. 'Ah know it's fuckin' stupid, but ah think this demon might've… manipulated me entire life from that point on. *Possessed me.*'

Bethany can't help but laugh. Even Tom realises how daft it sounds when he hears himself say the words.

Yet even now *he can feel it.*

Just behind his eyes.

'It's not funny!' Tom snaps defensively. 'It's been one disaster after another. Tragedy after tragedy…' suddenly he breaks into tears. 'Ah lost me baby brother. Ah lost me dad… an' now ah… ah…'

Bethany quickly pulls him into a warm embrace. It wasn't fair of her to laugh at him after he'd poured his heart out to her. 'I'm sorry, pet,' she says softly.

'It's not my fault ah know… It's a chemical imbalance, easily corrected wi' a few pills an' a couple o' 'ours talkin' shit to a psychologist every time…'

To his surprise Bethany pulls him close to her once again. 'It's only natural, sweetie, after what you've been through.'

'No… You don't understand,' Tom protests, pulling away again. 'Ah 'ear things. Ah'm scared that the Doctors are *wrong*; that ah'm *not* depressed, or suffering from schizophrenia… Ah'm worried that ah'm no more than a vessel for that fuckin' *ouija board* demon!'

Bethany pulls him back to her again and laughs.

'But that's it ain't it?' he says to her, calmer. 'Thinking up stuff like that. *Believin'* stuff like that. That's why ah'm ill. That *is* ill. Ah mean what if…'

'What if what?'

'What if ah've done bad things because o' this, an' then blamed them on somet what don't even exist. An' all the time it was me. Just me. *What if it was all me?*'

'You daft sod. *I fucking love you.* You're right. You can't blame demons an' monsters for what life has thrown at you; you just need to blame God, 'the man' or George Dubya like the rest of us.'

'Ah've never told anyone about me being ill,' Tom mutters. 'Only Will. You wouldn't…'

Bethany pulls his head towards her chest.

'Course not, pet. Course not. Although, I reckon after the whole hospital thing they might've suspected something was up…'

After only twenty minutes or so Tom can feel his right arm going dead because it's underneath Bethany, cuddling her, but still he refuses to move it. He knows that there's never been a night that lasted forever and that one way or another she'll be leaving him in the morning, no matter for how short a time. Thus he holds her as close and as tight as he possibly can without hurting her - he knows he won't be holding her for long.

His mind runs over a lot of things. All the events in his life have brought him to this point, and he doesn't know where he's going to go from here. Right now, at this moment, he's totally and utterly besotted with Bethany. He loves her to pieces. He thinks the world of her, and would do anything to be with her properly. A proper couple. *'is an' 'ers.*

He feels the same way about Bethany as he did about Hannah, and as he did about many others before her. Nothing has changed. Nothing ever really changes. Maybe he's starting to learn something after all.

He lifts his head slightly to look at Bethany's sleeping face and gently brushes the thin strands of red hair away from her eyes. He stares down for what feels like only a second, but in reality is probably hours. He was wrong; something has changed. Looking down at that face, he knows he'll always deeply care about her. He may not always feel as passionately about her as he does right at this moment, but he knows she'd do anything for him, and that she would never, ever hurt him.

She is now the most precious thing in the world.

Tom reckons that his biggest problem is that he either loves people too much or they mean absolutely nothing to him; they're just animated slabs of meat as far as he's concerned. He had loved Hannah far, far too much, and now…

He closes his eyes and holds Bethany tighter than ever. He can't believe she doesn't wake up, he's holding her so tight. Tom promises himself that he'll do everything that he can not to ruin this special relationship. This way, at least a little part of his furnace heart can always stay with her. He couldn't bear to lose her. He'd lost so much already. Ghostly images dance before his vision but they don't faze him at all. Not anymore. His mind is deaf to the voices; his eyes blind to the dreams. He just holds Bethany even tighter still. He would get better. He would beat this illness. He'd do it – and he'd do it for her.

He opens his eyes for a second, just to take in where he actually is and what is actually happening to him. The bottom line is simple. He is trying to fall asleep with a girl that he loves deeply in his arms. Whether he loves her as a friend, or as a lover, or in whatever way, doesn't really matter anymore.

Bethany has given him back the life that he had almost extinguished. She has given him what he could never have asked for. This night, Tommy Briggs is truly happy. For the first time in years, he feels not only hopeful for the future, but free.

'Perhaps there's 'ope,' he whispers.

THE DRUNKARD AND THE TRAMP

MAY 2005

'WANT SOME CHEESE MATE?' THE DRUNKARD asks the tramp.

'No fanks,' says the tramp.

'*Ah said*, d'yer want some cheese?' the drunkard asks again emphatically, waving his cheese under the nose of the tramp. The tramp – a young, stocky man wearing some old jeans, a winter coat, a hat and sporting one hell of a beard – aggressively swats the drunkard's hand away.

'If yer fuckin' starvin', you'll eat me cheese!'

'Ah'm not fuckin' starvin'; ah 'ad an all-yer-can-eat petezer 'ut earlier. Now fuck off before ah cane thee!'

Gristle is not a happy tramper. Life on the run isn't all it's cracked up to be. *Fuckin' Jim Surewood an' is big lyin' gob. A bit o' 'onest nickin' an' the pigs try an' meck out you're a murderer. This country!*

As the drunkard gives up and wanders back inside the offy, a lean tabby cat approaches the tramp with poise and rubs around the bottom of his legs, purring.

'Eyup,' says Gristle to the cat and, careful to ensure that he's not being observed, he gently begins to stroke it. The cat arches its back as Gristle smooths down its fur. Resting a single paw on Gristle's leg, the cat extends its claws – testing the ground, as it were. As soon as it's sure that Gristle's leg is neither soft nor wet, it hops onto his lap and closes its eyes.

'You remind us o' our Rocky,' Gristle whispers, resting his head on the cold, hard, brick wall behind him. *Wonder 'ow the ol' girl's doin'?*

Not bad at all is the answer to the question on Gristle's mind. She's rolling on her back in the lads' house on Worthington Street with her legs in the air, having her still more than ample tummy tickled by Jamal.

In the kitchen, Tom is sat on the top of the washing machine finishing off his chicken vindaloo and can of special brew (which rhymes). Will is doing the washing-up - 'proper domesticated an' everything,' as Tom takes great delight in pointing out.

'Yeah, well. Gotta grow up eventually, 'ant yer?' Will retorts.

'Ah suppoz mate. Ah suppoz. Wanna bit o' this?'

Will winces. 'No, ah'll be reet. Ah had a ryvita the other day.'

'You'd better be jokin' me!'

'Yes. Ah'm jokin' yer. Don't worry yersen; ah'm alreet now. Our lass 'as sorted us out.' He lifts up his t-shirt and feebly attempts to pinch an inch of non-existent flab. 'Look at Little Elvis 'ere.'

Tom isn't impressed. 'Ah'll believe yer when yer twenny stone, and not before,' he laughs, shaking his head. 'What lives we lead.'

'Aye.'

'Come on, mush. Yer need cheerin' up.'

Tom grabs Will's arm and drags him into the living room half-heartedly. He points at Will's favourite chair – the one with the barbeque sauce stain on the arm. 'Sit yersen down theer an' suck on this,' Will's told, and before he knows it, he's supping a can of super strength lager and watching *Episode V,* all thoughts of his father; of Gristle; and of girly eating disorders about as far from his mind as they could be.

Tom sits down on the floor by Jamal and casually offers him a small white tab, one of several that he has in the palm of his hand. 'Wanna try one o' veese?' he asks.

He also points towards Will, sat quietly in his chair drinking. 'An' offer one ta laughin' boy an' all. 'e needs it!'

Will turns to face them, shaking his head. 'Ah'm alreet, cheers mush.' Will turns back to face the TV.

Luke's right hand is cleanly sliced away. No blood. The heat must have instantly cauterised the wound. Which hurts more, the loss of the appendage, or the knowledge that your father is an evil killing machine?

Will stares at the TV. He stares into it. He stares through it. He isn't in the room. He's in that cell with his father.

Jamal chomps on the chalky substance. Not very minty at all. 'Are these those new slow-release breath-freshening things, Briggs?'

Tom scoffs. 'Yeah, reet! They're Es. Ah found a few o' 'em in Gristle's room when ah was looking for 'is porn stash.'

'By the cringe!' Jamal proclaims at the top of his voice. He turns and runs for the bathroom, spitting the contents of his mouth into the wash basin. It's too late though; he's already swallowed more than half of it. He's certain that he can already feel it polluting his body – *or is that just the panic? Confusing and powerful stuff, adrenaline.*

You hear every day of the ecstasy horror stories. Of how some poor young lass died writhing around in agony with her lungs exploding; all that pain and suffering caused by one little pill. Jamal doesn't want to be the guy that parents warn their children about. He can see Nita stood in front of him, lecturing a classroom of children. 'Never take ecstasy, or you might end up dead like silly Mr Prakash.'

Jamal doesn't want to have lived his whole life just to end up as the main character in a cautionary tale for children. *Damn Tom! Damn Gristle! Damn them to Haedes!*

Little does Jamal know, but his life will change forever on this cold and stormy night. As Tom rushes out into the darkness, no doubt to escape his inevitable scalding from the others; and with Gristle still off in parts unknown, desperately trying to avoid the authorities; Jamal sits himself down with the coolest, most fantastic guy in the world – Will Surewood. His best chum. He loves him so much.

The overwhelming sensory input galvanises Jamal's existence. Pleasure that you can't measure quashes his every fear and nagging fret. *This old fool has wasted his life on text books and exams while this lot - this wonderful bunch of scallywags - have held the keys to the kingdom all along.*

Warmth and love take their hold of Jamal Prakash, and they won't him let go.

The cold talons of Death tenderly caress the back of Gristle's neck. Someone walks across his grave again and it wakes him, suddenly. As he hits the waking world with a definite jolt, the cat jumps from his knee and sprints away into the night.

Into the night.
Into the road.
Straight into the path of a speeding white van that has apparently accelerated in order to get through the lights while they're still on amber.

Without thought for himself, the big hard man leaps to his feet and with - quite aptly - cat-like agility, dives into the path of the vehicle and knocks the cat out of the way.

The eyes of the driver stare straight into Gristle's.
He doesn't slow down.
He puts his foot down.
In both their heads the moment is stretched out forever, but in reality Gristle only has time to furrow his brow ever so slightly in surprise.

WHEN I DIE, DON'T LET THEM TAKE MY EYES

THE JOURNEY HOME HAD MADE BOTH TOM
and Will feel uneasy. Although no great distance at all from Hull in any real sense, their old stomping ground feels like a world away to them now. For Tom it reminds of him of what he once had: a brother, a father, a family. And for Will it's much the same, the principal difference between the two being that Will doesn't have the luxury of having buried his father - his lives, in Doncaster Marshgate Prison no less, on remand. But both friends have damaged but devoted mothers. Both friends are in loving relationships. And neither friend has the 'protection' of a living Ben Davis. Not anymore.

Gristle is dead.

A rather small gathering crowds around a tiny hole in the ground.

Gristle's dad, Dave, and his seventh wife, Di.

Gristle's mam, Morag, and her nineteenth husband's brother, Billy, who is her current live-in lover.

Gristle's best friend, Will, and his paramour, Katie.

Gristle's old friend Tom, and the latest "love of his life", Bethany.

Gristle's housemate, Jamal, and Gristle's affectionately tolerated archenemy, Spadge.

All of the above wear black with the exception of Spadge who has instead elected to wear a cream suit and brown loafers. He's a twat.

Not one of them knows how to feel or what to say. It's hard to miss somebody that nobody really liked and that everyone lived in constant fear of. It's also hard not to notice the absence of such a person, as Spadge points out in his uncharacteristically short speech. For once the appropriate verbiage eludes even him.

Ironically, the one who misses Gristle the most couldn't make it to the funeral. She's otherwise engaged prowling around the lads' back yard on Worthington Street, sniffing around the damp mattresses by the shed and eating mice. Wondering where 'Daddy' has gone. When he'll be back. When she'll be fed.

Rocky aside, Will had taken the news the hardest. Unlike Tom, Will had known Ben since his infancy, and it's remembrance of those days, not the depravity of more recent times, that provokes the ceremony's first tear. Seeing his best friend cry, Tom can't help but break down too. From there, the domino effect kicks in and, before long, almost all in attendance are weeping.

Jamal was surprised to find that in spite of his institutionalised loathing of Ben, since his disappearance he has really missed the old scoundrel. Ben - this larger than life 'Gristle' caricature - had helped him to open doors and cross thresholds that he was too afraid to admit even existed. Ben had made him harder and better-rounded. More human. Ben had helped to make him a better teacher. He had helped to make him a better man.

Katie worries about Will. In recent months they have grown closer than she'd even have thought possible, but he's really been through the meat grinder of late and she fears for him. From time to time, she still hears him being sick and somewhere deep inside her, she remembers what he once was and how he used to be. She can't shake the feeling that it's only a matter of time before he strays and she loses him forever.

And although he won't talk about it, she knows what his father might have done weighs heavily on him and Gristle's death has only stirred these feelings up all over again. The extent of Gristle's involvement in Jim's crimes is still unknown, and will probably never be discovered now.

Katie tosses dirt into the grave; not for Gristle, but for Will.

Bethany is the last to toss dirt, *or 'muck' as yer calls it round 'ere*, into the grave. She considers that she is alone in appreciating the irony that the biggest, loudest, dumbest and most intimidating ape that she has ever had the misfortune to meet shuffled out of all their lives in a mere whisper; even the controversy of the police's lengthy hunt for him overshadowed by... well, overshadowed by more pressing matters closer to home.

She looks at the man beside her, the man that she loves with every fibre of her being. A man plagued by mental illness? A man tortured by his own private demon? Or a man with a furnace for a heart who's made her feel more loved and needed than she could ever have imagined. She squeezes his hand tightly.

'Pet,' she says in a whisper, her eyes still fixed on the six foot hole in the ground. 'You know I have an organ donor's card...'

Tom turns to face her, bemused by the apparently arbitrary statement.

'When I die, don't let them take my eyes.'

Tom says nothing. He just looks deep into her blazing green eyes and squeezes her hand, and suddenly the statement doesn't sound as random as it first appeared to. Bethany *is* her eyes. Her beautiful face; her sexy body; even her red hair, which she now wears in a cute bob. It's all nothing but an extension of her eyes. Her heart, her soul, her essence - it all lives inside those eyes.

Tom hopes that her wish isn't one that he'll ever have to grant.

*　*　*

With some trepidation, Tom pushes open the door of his family's surprisingly lush and modern ancestral seat. It hasn't changed one bit. His friends allow him a moment for reflection before barging their way into the hall.

'Are you certain that it's alright for us to spend the night here?' Jamal asks. 'Mrs Briggs won't mind?'

'Course not, mate,' Tom replies, still looking around him as if he's entered some ancient temple. 'Me mam's livin' wi' our Unice, 'er sister like, down in Sarfampton. Ah'm surprised she ain't flogged this ol' place yet. It's been on the market for a fair old bit now... A couple o' 'undred thou 'ere now, ah reckon.'

Bethany touches his arm gently. 'You okay, pet?'

He nods and whispers to her. 'Yeah. It's just... y'know. Memories. That's all. It's all so *untouched!* Ah expected... ah don't know. A paint job! A laminate floor! Anything but... the same... sameness. It's creepy.'

'When were you last back here then?' Beth asks.

Tom sighs. 'Ah 'onestly don't know. Years ago.'

Bethany examines a photograph of a chubbier, youthful Tom; an older, bearded man wearing a leather jacket and a bandanna who she assumes is his father; a young and wiry dark-haired kid, presumably his brother; and an older, kind-faced woman. His mother. 'Am I ever going to meet your mam, Tom?'

Tom ignores the question. He has found his way into his dad's old study, a large dining room that he used to house all of his motorcycle memorabilia.

Bethany and Spadge appear behind him. 'What's that?'

Tom reaches out and touches a scabbard hanging from the wall. 'Some antique sword. Me dad bought it when we were little. 'e's... that is 'e *was*, a bit of a collector. We… me an'… *ah* used to pretend that it was 'aunted. Weird.'

Tom wanders back into the hall and beckons Jamal. 'These are your lodgin's for the night, matey,' he says with as smile, pointing towards the guest room. As Tom helps Jamal in with his bags, Spadge and Bethany tease Jamal about spending the night in a haunted room. For a man of science and reason, Jamal looks far too troubled by their gentle wind-up routine.

He's got this horrible feeling, you see.

The woman behind the counter at the supermarket will only serve Anna two boxes of paracetamol and ibuprofen. All that pretending to be well to get out of hospital only to be confronted with a fifty-something fat Doris who enjoys enforcing the rules rigidly. *Cow!* There's always something going wrong. No wonder she wants to die.

In the end, Anna has to go and buy another four or five bottles of paracetamol from the newsagents just to make sure - they're not fussy. That should really do the damage. It will be the ultimate fuck off to everybody for not making this world a better place; for treating her like shit; and finally, most damningly, for not helping her when she needed help the most. She will be gone, and there will be nobody for everybody to say sorry to.

She sits in her bedroom and pours all the paracetamol and ibuprofen into a huge pile. It's like a small mountain. She finds herself playing around with the pills with all the wonder of a child on Christmas Day, but all too soon she feels the weight of the world bearing down upon her again and the harsh realisation that her life is about to end hits her.

She takes the pills one at a time at first.

Then two at a time. Then three at a time.

She washes them down with pint after pint of water.

No more tears. No more broken hearts.

Anna doubts that Jesus felt this euphoric as he waited in the garden for Judas to betray him. Betrayed with a kiss. Tom betrayed her with something far dirtier.

They say that Satan entered Judas's heart and *made him* betray his friend for the silver pieces. Anna scoffed at such an idea. If Judas did betray Jesus for personal gain, then it was he that made the choice to do so. Not the Devil. The 'evil' that men do is of their own making. To blame it on devils or demons is sheer cowardice; it's just passing the buck. As they nailed Jesus to the cross, driving the nails through his flesh, he said that he forgave Judas. He didn't say that he forgave the Devil.

This situation is very different, of course. Anna is no messiah, and Tom is no disciple. And, try as she might, as Anna feels the life ebb out of her she does not forgive Tom as Christ forgave his alienated apprentice. Jesus in his wisdom may have preached 'turn the other cheek,' but today Anna preaches 'fuck you all; every last bastard one of you.'

The ibuprofen is really working its magic now. The term 'painkiller' is spot on because in her euphoric haze, Anna doesn't feel the slightest ache. She feels giddy. She's going to face her greatest fear; a far greater fear than living alone: dying alone.

Jesus said it himself: 'to conquer death, you only have to die.'

But as he found out the hard way, it's easier said then done.

Anna suddenly panics. It was alright for him - he could come back!

I've changed my mind! I want to live!

She dials every number in her mobile but not one of the selfish fuckers answers.

I don't wanna die like this.
But then she gets lucky.
Someone answers his phone.
Someone who likes to talk…

'Where'd Spadge rush off ta?' Will asks Tom, pulling up a pew and sitting beside his (now) oldest friend in the pub where they first tasted beer together.

''e 'ad to leave suddenly,' Tom says broodingly. He ruffles up his bleach blonde, mullety hairdo. ''e did give a sufficiently long-winded explanation; ah lost track about 'afe way through. Ah got the impression 'e was keeping somet from us.'

'What?' asks his friend with the matching hairdo.

''ow should ah know?' Tom pushes his empty pint glass from the edge of his table into its centre. 'Ah'm gonna call it a nite an' all. It's the… oh you know. *The usual.* Crazy boy shit.'

'Shall ah get Beth for yer?'

'Naw, it'll be reet. Ah just need a time-out. Look, before ah go… ah know recent months 'ave been 'ard for me… for you… *for Gristle.* But they're gone now. In the done pile, innit? Everythin' else might've gone to bollocks but we got Beth and Katie, young Spadgewalker, and even the Professor over theer,' Tom says, pointing at Jamal who has cornered two young ladies by the quiz machine, no doubt trying to impress them both with his primary school teacher's massive general knowledge base. 'What ah'm sayin' is, well, could 'av been worse cunnit?'

Will nods, and looks towards the bar where Katie and Bethany are both giggling. They're happy. 'You know what?'

Tom shakes his head.

Will grabs him and roughly pulls him into a firm embrace. 'Fekin' love you, crazy boy.'

'Love yer too, man. Look at us! Gristle would be callin' all us both queers. Turns his back for five minutes and we turn into two gret big poofs!'

Tom wipes his watering eye. 'Enjoy the rest of the wake, mate. Inabit.'

Tom had lied. He hadn't had any hallucinations for a long time. Even the voice had been curiously silent since… well, for a long time. He'd just felt compelled to leave the pub; to spend some time alone in his cradle of memories.

Rummaging through his old wardrobe, Tom discovers an exercise book backed with an old Trippie the Trampler wrestling poster. After rolling himself another joint, he opens it and allows himself a chuckle at the pages within. It's his old diary, from way back in '99. The greatest summer ever.

Tom reads through the diary at an amazing speed, relishing every page of angst-strewn action and adventure. How monumental it all seemed. And now… now it all seems so trivial.

The final entry gives him pause, though:

Tom's top secret super bumper action packed Diary of ~~adventure~~ epic adventure. Saturday 14th August 1999.

It was in the early hours when he confessed it to me. We were both pissed. He told me about it as if it was just another one of these women that he had pulled behind Holly's back. I could tell as soon he told me that he regretted doing so. He saw the anger in my face.

'Don't get angry with me!' he shouted in a defensive, aggressive way. 'I didn't think you liked her anymore. You never said you did.'

'No,' I snapped back. 'I didn't say that I'd gone off her either, did I? You assume too much. I haven't spoken about her because I was trying to forget about her and move on.'

'Well you can now you know she doesn't like you,' he said, and I was unsure whether this was meant as a comfort to me, as an insult, or whether it was just him bragging.

'Look, you're my best friend, you're more important to me than any woman,' he went on. 'If you don't want me to go near her again I won't. I promise.'

'Okay, fine.' I answered. 'Don't go near her again.'

'What?' he whined. 'That's not fair! What's the point? You can't have her, so why can't I? I only want to take her virginity.'

'WILL!' I snapped, beginning to walk away from him.

'Look I'm sorry. Just do what you think is right mate.' I walked away in awe of what he had done with no thought for me, or for Holly.

I should tell Holly. Then he'd hurt like I'm hurting, but what would it achieve? Absolutely nothing. Maybe he's right. She obviously doesn't want me. Why am I being so selfish in stopping him going near her? Perhaps because I'm human, and don't want my best friend sleeping with the girl I fancy. I won't even go into him blatantly cheating on Holly again, who has also been a good friend to me recently.

I got home about three am, poured myself a glass of strawberry milkshake and opened up the Monk's autobiography to the page I was at. I threw myself into the life story of a crazy hardcore wrestler rather than face the harsh reality of letting another girl I wanted to be with so badly walk away from me. When my drunken and weary eyes got to the stage where I couldn't make out the words anymore, I just pulled the knife out from between my shoulder blades, rolled over, and fell to sleep.

Tom rests his old diary on his lap, saddened by the memory and remembering the pain. It hadn't happened just that once either. Three... four... was it even five times that Will had stolen a girl away from him?

For the first time since his thwarted bid for oblivion, Tom hears a voice calling to him. For months Bethany's love had at kept it at bay, but now his fear had unleashed it. His greatest fear. His fear of losing her...

You should have trusted me.

I told you all along that he was a threat, and yet you allowed sentiment to get in the way. Now what have you done?

Where is your precious lover now?

You are a fool, boy.

She is with him!

Anna is wrapped up in a big cardigan as the medic examines her in the back of the ambulance. 'Man trouble is it?'

She nods. *'Yeah.'*

She shivers. It's getting cold.

Katie staggers out of the toilet, her world spinning. Too much wine.

Dirty old rough men all eyeing her up... *cheeky fuckers... and Will? Where's Will... he's got his arms round Bethany... he's... I knew it was only a matter of time... It's his nature... Bastard! Fucking cheating bastard! And her, the bitch! Supposed to be my friend...*

Katie spins around on her left high heel and very nearly falls out of the pub, screaming for a taxi. Will and Bethany don't even notice her leave; they're too wrapped up in their own private little world.

Will releases Bethany from his tight embrace.

'So you fink ah should then?'

'Definitely!' the new-born romantic inside Bethany proclaims, a huge smile on her face. 'Oh! I'm so happy for you, pet. You make such a bonnie couple! When you thinking of asking her?'

'Week after next, it's 'er birthdee, innit?'

'Oh that's fantastic! I'm sure she'll say yeah!' Beth squeals playfully, leaping on him again. When did she become such an idealist? Whatever happened to the old cynic?

Time can do so much.

And so can people.

People like Tom.

'Tha ne'er knows – might be you an' Tommo next!' Will says, putting her down again. 'Thinkin' on... where is Katie? Is she still in the shitter? She's bin ages!'

Tom listens carefully to every word that the voice has to say. Tom listens carefully to every word that Katie has to say. Tom ignores every word that Jamal has to say.

His last anchor to reality severed, Tom's rowing boat finally clears its moorings and drifts away into the fog. The face of the boat's solitary occupant is scared and hardened.

You never can win.

The voice drowns out all else.

It is no longer a question of influence.

There is no disparity.

There is no Tommy Briggs.

The voice no longer speaks.

The voice simply *is*.

A fast and astonishingly powerful elbow to the face floors Jamal, and Tom's blood-red eyes focus on Katie. He makes no move towards her, but the fire burning in his eyes scares her into complete silence. Complete stillness. Eyes wide open, Katie cannot do anything but look on in horror at the set-piece about to unfold.

It's unlike anything that she's ever seen on TV or in the movies. Most of the dialogue is inaudible and the sound mix is all wrong. It's too hard to even follow it all; it's all just crying and shouting and noise. And it all happens so fast.

Their whole world. The five of them. Changed in a moment.

The door opens and in they stumble, laughing and drunk.

Will and Bethany.

Entr'acte.

It's over quick. The back of Tom's hand connects viciously with the face of Bethany and like Jamal, she falls to the ground unconscious. Instinctively Will punches Tom square in the jaw, tears of confusion in his eyes as he is forced to try and knock his friend down.

As soon as he does so, Tom's boot catches Will's jaw in a flash of movement so fast that it denies both gravity and reason. Tom's eyes smoulder with purpose.

Will's normally steadfast hands are shaking. *This is Tom. Me best mate. 'e's like a bruvver. But it ain't 'im…*

Will's hand rises to strike the monster that is advancing along the hallway towards him, but the inhuman power behind Tom's simple double-hand push repels his whole body. The sheer force of it sends Will hurtling into the banister which collapses and splinters behind him. Even after the pain of his fall, Will doesn't miss Tom's eyes wandering towards his father's study, his steely gaze releasing him, if only for an instant.

Will's head buzzes. It's getting darker.

Tom pulls down the rusty scabbard from the wall and examines the old, blunt sword resting within. A moment later he is in the hallway looking down upon Katie's beloved, his face contorted into a gruesome mask of evil.

What had Katie said to unlock such... such... *evil?*

What is this thought that strikes her? *Oh my God. Oh my God! OH MY GOD! It was never Gristle or Jim - it was him! Poor Jim! Oh my God...*

Tom smiles at the sword as he hovers over the semi-conscious Will. Katie must stop him. Nothing has ever been more important in her whole life. But her legs won't move an inch. Every muscle is jelly. She's a prisoner of fear.

After the storm, all is quiet. A cold, detached voice poses a question to its apparently unconscious prey.

'Are you scared?'

Tom raises the sword and thrusts it towards Will's chest, but at the last moment Will manages to roll to the side and the blow only just misses his heart.

There is one blistering moment when Will realises that the sword has sliced through his wrist.

Katie looks on, sickened, as the blood flows and Tom struggles to remove his aged weapon from her boyfriend's forearm.

Tom twists and pulls on the sword as Will writhes around in agony behind a crimson veil. The entity within Tom's mind notes how blood is a wonderful leveller. Will looks no better now than anyone else after sustaining a horrific injury.

No woman could want him now.

After a microcosmic eternity the sword finally comes free. It is drenched in thick, browny-red rivulets of plasma. Were any part of Tom still present, he would have been confused as to why the sword didn't slice cleanly through the arm. This isn't a city in the clouds, though, and this sword doesn't cauterise wounds. This is... *horrible*. He should have stuck to burning people, bagging up their ashes and then scattering them in the Humber. *Now there's a thought...*

Will holds his half-severed hand up in front of him and stares at it in shock. Possessed by a cold dread, his mind tells him to try and push it back on. He does so, and then clasps his other hand around the haemorrhaging join. Blood seeps through his locked fingers.

Katie vomits down herself. As she sees Tom and his sword bearing down on her, her impotence is only magnified. She can't even breathe. So this is how it feels to be terrified. She'll never say she's 'scared' of a film again.

Tom is distracted by a low, female groan emanating from just behind him. He turns sharply to see Bethany struggling to her knees, wiping the blood away from her nose. She's too frightened to look up. Her mind is spinning. Her heart is broken.

Her world has been destroyed.

'*You...*'

The word slithers out of Tom's mouth with unqualified malevolence. 'You were wi' 'im all along. LAUGHIN' AT TOM! Just like all the others.'

He kicks her hard in her stomach; so hard that she spits blood. 'Treating 'im just like a puppet from day one. *A plaything.* You're just like the rest! All,' kick, 'your,' kick, 'fuckin sick,' kick, 'master plans!'

Tom reaches into his back pocket and pulls out a lighter, his eyes darting around the hallway scanning for alcohol or some other inflammatory.

Bethany looks up at her lover. She now wears a mask of blood on her face and her eyes are tormented with bewildered sorrow. 'I didn't do anything, pet,' she splutters, bleeding from the mouth. 'I love you so much...'

The hollowed-out shell of what was once her lover kicks her hard in the face.

He's feeling almost merciful.

He might only take her arms.

Anna is wheeled into the ward and hooked up to a drip that will coat her liver with glucose in order to protect it from the paracetamol. As for the painkillers crippling her kidneys, that's down to luck.

She holds up her right arm slightly and observes at all the wires and machinery that are apparently grafted onto her very body. She feels more like machine than woman.

She throws up inside a cardboard egg-box.

Bethany comes round. She is looking through the window of a car; a car travelling at an incredible velocity up the M62. She lifts her head and looks out through the driver's window. Her eyes focus on the imposing image of the Humber Bridge coming honing into view. It sparks the happiest of memories within her.

'Ah think, just maybe, ah love you too,' he'd said to her. Almost as an afterthought, she looks at the driver. She looks at what was once Tom. *Fuck! Where am I? Where he's taking me? My clothes... Where are my clothes...? Did I imagine...? Did that really happen? Whose car...?*

'Slow down, pet,' she breathes deliriously, her eyes opening and closing rapidly. 'Where are we going? Why are you-'

Tom's eyes hold her still.

Tom's eyes hold her silent.

Bethany realises that it did indeed happen.

A furnace burns within each of Tom's pupils, but neither belongs to Tom. The man whom she loves just isn't there. His body is just the engine. His body is just the vessel. *Oh God, he was right. He was right all along. This can't be happening...*

Bethany's bleak realisation is her last as the car careers into the side of a medium-sized people carrier and lights up the night sky for miles around. *The biggest explosion ever!* At least, that's how it feels from the inside.

Out of the broken glass of the front offside window, the fingers of a charred hand clench into a tight fist, then fall open again, limp. Suitably theatrical.

This vehicle has served its purpose.
Now it can be consigned to the inferno.

FLIGHT THROUGH ETERNITY

immolate im-mo-late (ĭm′ə-lāt′)
Transitive verb. Im-mo-lat-ed, im-mo-lat-ing, im-mo-lates.
 1. *To kill as a sacrifice.*
 2. *To kill (oneself) by fire.*
 3. *To destroy.*

CHATTER... VOICES.

'...third degree burns to the head and arms, internal haemorrhaging...'

A dash of blinding light. A sharp and excruciating inhalation of oxygen.

'...intravenous cannulation...'

A shadow leans close.

'Thomas. Thomas Briggs. Can you hear me?'

The shadow is beautiful.

'Thomas?'

But the blonde, bespectacled shadow is not enough to hold you in this waking world.

'Thomas, can you hear me? Doctor Spyrou, his eyes are opening...'

You are my prize now, Thomas Briggs.

You feel nothing but pain.

Every nerve ending was scraped off by your own instrument of torture, but every nerve survived. The fire ran just deep enough to keep you here in agony. Every hair, every tattoo, every last nuance of every subcutaneous layer. Every single distinguishing mark has been ripped away by the conflagration which has consumed every last part of you.

Indiscriminate and unforgiving. The weapon of a fool.

You try to speak, but for the first time in your life you are truly aware of the meaning of the word thirst. The most unbearably tender reflex in the back of your mouth accompanies every syllable that you utter and every last word is accompanied by a mouthful of your own blood.

Be... Bef... Bethany...

Why do you even ask? You know what we did to her. She had to pay for what she has done to you. For what she planned to do. At best she is in as sorry a state as you are - burned, crippled and broken.

Moribund.

BETHANY!!!

You killed her. Just like <u>you</u> killed all of them.

But ah love her... Ah could never...

You are a murderer, Thomas Briggs.

A mass murderer.

A serial killer.

Boy, have I made you famous!

And now you are going to die.

This is the end; the final act. Are you scared?

Three.

NO! Please... please don't...

Two.

The plane is coming for you.

Coming to take you away.

The twisted wreckage of an airy-waz besides a burning motor brum-brum.

It's getting bigger... no... please... it feels different this time...

One.

There is no dizziness.

There is no nausea.

274

You will stand forever embraced by the conflagration as the inferno slowly chews upon your weak and mortal flesh. You cannot stop it now.

Conscious for every agonising moment you will be forced to look into my eyes and, locked in my brimstone gaze, your dead soul - just as it did in your insect life - will belong to me.

Ah'm walkin' down the street where ah grew up. The street where ah spent the first eighteen years o' me life. Ah stop at the foot o' our old driveway.

Ah'm pushin' me baby bro around on a tricycle.

Ah'm laid in the back garden wi' an old, gold Labrador layin' on me.

Ah'm in the garden, buildin' a snowman wi' me parents.

Ah'm inside, sat beside the roarin' fire eatin' bacon sandwiches an' drawin' make-believe cities in the front room. They're cities which ah enjoy complete power over; where no-one ever gets sick or 'urt an' no-one ever, ever, dies… unless… unless ah… ah… unless they melt in the 'eat o' the roarin' fire… unless…

… *you* melt them.! Like *you* melted those girls.

Like you melted your Bethany.

It was you.

It was all you.

Ah turn to walk away from me past, but out o' the corner o' me waterin' eye, as clear as a bell, ah can see Bethany.

'My love,' ah say, rushin' towards her. 'You're safe. Thank God you're alreet. Thank God! Ah love you so much.'

'Tom,' she wails as she collapses into me. 'I love you too, pet… So why did you kill me? How could you kill me after all we… no… You're doin' it again. You fucker! You sick fucker. And I… I… loved-'

She crumbles wi'in me asbestos cuddle; little more than black ash remains o' 'er.

Me remorse burns 'otter than any fire ever could.

Ah'm walkin' up Black Hill when ah'm 'alted in me tracks by a six-foot tall version o' a teddy bear that me dad bought for me when ah was about a year old. Neddy the Teddy was the only childhood toy that ah 'ad ever kept; a scruffy, fleabit creature wi' an 'alf-chewed ear an' a suspicious brown tail.

But Neddy's right 'and has been sliced off. Thick red blood is sprayin' from the wound an' 'e's cryin' out to me. Is that Irish?

No. It can't be.

'An' ah thought yer was me best mate. Look at me. Crippled. Deformed. Ah'll never get a woman now, will ah? Ah can't even wank!!! Ah 'ate yer! 'ow could yer do this to me?'

'Neddy!!!! Nooo!'

Ah burst into tears as Neddy multiplies an' surrounds me. Giant, grotesque parodies o' Will Surewood close in on me. The Neddies' eyes are afire wi' an infra-red light that, in this cruel imitation o' life, slices up me body like a sci-fi laser beam.

As ah collapse to the ground, limbless an' helpless, the mobile phone in me pocket begins to sing to me.

'You're goin' to die tonight,' it chirps in Anna's voice.

Ah beg an' ah scream an' ah plead an' ah cry but they can't 'ear me.

'You're goin' to die tonight,' it chirps again.

'Ah can't even remember! It wasn't me! Ah didn't change 'er message. Ah wasn't there! Please!'

'You're goin' to die tonight,' it chirps.

'AH CAN'T REMEMBER!!!'

Oh, but you can. The memory is there, you are just too afraid to touch it. Just like you were afraid to touch the others. You dismiss them as nightmares, voices, schizophrenia. You are wrong.

You are a *bad 'un*, Tommo. A killer, plain and simple.

It was <u>you</u>.

It was all <u>you</u>.
There was no demon.
I'm not real.

Ah'm in me C:\ drive walkin' between C:\Program Files\ an' C:\Documents and Settings\Thomas Briggs\My Documents. To me left, the folder details are goin' through the roof. The incessant whirrin' o' the 'ard disk is deafenin' as it processes file after file, unable to determine just 'ow many terabytes o' data are stored in that one folder. Ah double-click on a file randomly usin' the sheer power o' me will as a mouse. The file is a record o' a memory; digitised, compressed an' encoded. The detail is phenomenal. This particular memory is nowt special: ah'm sat at me computer alone, wearin' me old 'in the 'ouse' trackies an' 'oody that ah wouldn't be seen dead in outside, doin' a pleadin' e-mail to 'annah. Ah feel exposed to think that moments like that 'ave been observed, recorded an' stored. Ah don't wanna be remembered as someone who wore trackies an' an 'oody – someone who begged like a dog.

Soon ah'm able to navigate the sub-folders. My mind double-clicks a spreadsheet entitled 'Girls What Ah've Been Obsessed With.xls.' 'undreds o' names suddenly cloud me vision. Some are so small that ah can 'ardly read them; others are in such a large font that ah 'ave to teck several steps back to read 'em. Certain names, such as those o' 'annah an' Anna, are represented not by text but by large, naked, dancin' images; each one trapped inside their own private glass booth for me viewin' pleasure.

Next ah open a spreadsheet entitled 'Friends.xls' which is far shorter than ah'd 'ave 'oped. Some o' the other titles range from the mundane to the perverse. 'Books Ah've Read.xls', 'Pornos Ah've Seen.xls', 'Lies Ah've Told.xls', 'People Ah've Idolised.xls', 'People Who've 'urt Me.xls', an' 'People Ah've 'urt.xls'; to name but a few. This one has pictures an' hyperlinks; even the odd video clip. Nasty.

'ell, ah 'aven't even lived seven an' an 'alf thousand days, yet ah'm faced wi' billions o' files. The sheer volume o' it all over-

whelms me. No wonder brains get screwed up carryin' all this data about in 'em all day long.

One file is isolated from the rest - 'The Tally.xls.' Password-protected. Ah know deep down that it ain't a tally like Will's. It's burnt — an' not in the CD-ROM sense. Digitally charred; digitally black. The thought o' what it might reckon up mecks me blood run cold.

'Time to leave,' ah say to mesen, but there's nowheer to go. After walkin' backwards through the directory for ten long, subjective years, the files finally begin to fall away. In their place are millions upon millions o' old-fashioned index cards. These must be from before ah got me first computer.

Each card is written in me own handwritin'. Except one, that is. In handwritin' specifically designed to emulate me own there's a card readin' 'Money Ah Owe Will,' wi' a fake signature on the back which closely resembles Will Surewood's distinct, childlike scrawl. Dickhead.

After a further subjective century o' restless searchin' ah finally find what ah'm lookin' for. The card that ah'd dreaded findin' the most. It's labelled 'The One Ah Love.'

A chill runs through me body. Ah can't bring mesen to look at the card an' so ah just decide to slip it into me pocket in readiness for a time when ah might 'ave the courage to go that last mile an' look into that final part o' mesen. If that time should ever come in this hideous simulacrum, that is.

Ah thrust the card deep into the side pocket o' me white combats wi' the purple stain - the Bethany stain. From the first time we met. She almost fell into me, remember? She steadied 'ersen at the last minute but still spilt a bit o' 'er purple snakey b down the back o' me kegs. Ah barely noticed at the time; nor did she.

And then we died together.

'ow do ah even know this…?

A scowl hardens across me face.

Many a night ah'd laid awake, frightened that ah wouldn't leave me mark on the world. Me greatest fear was that ah'd be forgotten - another no-one. Not a single trace o' me journey through this world left behind.

This place has taken that fear an' turned it on its 'ead.

Ah want to be erased.

There must be no records; no evidence.

The 'ard drive must be wiped an' the 'ard copy files burned. An' no, ah do not mean onto CD-R.

Out o' me pocket ah pull out me lighter.

Ah set to burn, but no flames return.

Ah smash me 'ead against the wall an' let out a long, self-pityin' sigh. Ah just want an end. Any end. Ah'll tear this place down wi' me bare 'ands if need be; ah'll teck me computer an' throw it outta the window.

But where would it land?

Nowheer. Anywheer!

Where am ah?

Nowhere anywhere.

Ah might as well be in Swindon.

And ah'd rather be anywhere else.

Doin' anythin'.

Ah spin around to see Gristle. 'is body is covered from 'ead to toe in deep lacerations, an' not a single inch o' 'im is unbruised. 'e is the walkin' personification o' soft tissue damage; a personal injury lawyer's ticket to retirement. Wi' every single bone in 'is skeleton broken, the seventy per cent o' his 'ead that remains in tact wobbles precariously on 'is shoulders.

'is remainin' eye stares grimly at me.

Fuck, 'e knows.

Somehow 'e knows.

And ah didn't think 'e saw!

Ah was doin' seventy! 'ow could 'e 'ave seen?

Me behind the wheel. Joyridin'? Anythin' but.

'e walks towards me, slowly an' deliberately. Ah've nowhere to run.

'e grabs me 'and an' once more ah feel the atoms vibratin' wildly as the burnin' 'eat transfers from 'im to me. Trust Gristle.

Even when ah'm dead 'e'll kill me. Ah should've known! O' everyone in the world ever... trust him to kill me back.

After a few seconds though, 'e just lets go.

Ah'm not dead.

Well ah am, probably, but just from the first time.

What ah mean is that ah'm not dead again.

Ah'm not deader, daft as it may sound. Ah'm not dead 'ere.

Ah look down an' in the palm o' me 'and ah see a new lighter. Gristle's lighter. The putrid mass o' gore that was once me friend winks at me an' vanishes back into the nothingness from whence 'e came. An' wi' the merest flick o' me thumb, the flames erupt around me wi' orgasmic vengeance.

Ashes an' dust is all that will remain o' me passage through this life. Nowt of Tommy Briggs'll remain but the 'ollow innards o' a man, sat inside a burnt down room beside a broken computer inside his own 'ead somewhere between life an' death; somewhere just behind the world.

Probably.

And ah'll never escape this 'ell, will ah? What 'as 'appened is done. Recorded in starlight, me birth now bein' seen almost twenny light years away. That starlight'll never die. It'll go on an' on in an endless flight through eternity.

It'll never end.

Ah look up to appreciate the total blackness o' infinity. The blackness starts to dance wi' light as the entire story o' me life plays out across the sky.

Throughout the entire performance, no matter what ah press on me mental remote control ah can't rid mesen o' that annoyin' little red button.

The whole chronicle is divided up by commercial breaks every fifteen minutes or so. Some o' these adverts would be for items that ah'd once desired; items that ah believed would meck me 'appy.

Buy this wide screen television half-price only at... ...all *Manager 2005* out now from... Get

```
the    girl   of    your   dreams,   just    drink   this
magic potion…
```

Ah can't run away. Ah can't move. Me neck is locked upwards, me eyes 'eld wide open by invisible clamps. Me life is so vast. So massive. So short.

Twenny years o' telly pass before ah'm watchin' me empty body burn beside the corpse o' me lover. It was only a matter o' time.

Ah stare up into the empty sky. What's it up in the air for? What's the point o' wallowin' in me past like this? Why is me own mind doin' this to me? All ah can see up theer are two burnin' eyes. My demon. My scourge. My master.

Footsteps approach from behind.

'God wi' 'is pen in 'and?' ah muse. Ah wonder if ah can convince 'im to meck a few revisions…

No.

Any semblance o' meanin'; any credibility whatsoever that this experience may 'ave 'ad is killed in an instant as ah spin round to see a tall, muscular man.

It ain't Jesus.

It isn't God.

It isn't even Dad.

It's Trippie the Trampler, *dressed in 'is sickly purple an' yellow ring attire. An' if it isn't Trippie, it looks exactly like him. 'e 'olds out 'is 'ands before me.*

In the left 'and is a purple pill wi' Tramplamania *written on it in yellow. In the right 'and is a yellow pill wi'* Trippie Still Rulez *written on it in purple. Ah've got to admit, after what ah've been through this last 'undred an' thirty year, ah'm startin' to get just a bit frustrated. Ah mean, 'ow can ah possibly know which pill to take? Purple or yellow? 'ow am ah supposed to know the good from the bad? Which pill is reet for me? Ah've a feelin' that this decision could affect me very soul.*

Every decision we meck 'as massive consequences. So many possible futures an' so many possible pasts, yet all we 'ave is now to guide us. Bethany used to call 'em 'what if' moments; ah don't think ah've a name for 'em.

Ah try to remember the scene from that weird Keanu Whatshisname film. Ah try to remember which one was the blissfully 'appy 'let me live in ignorance' pill. Ah'll 'ave 'afe a dozen o' them please, squire!

'Blue! Yeah, ah'm pretty sure it was the blue one... D'oh.' There is no blue pill.

Purple pill? Close enough, surely? Worth a pop...

But the Trampler clasps his titanic 'and closed.

'You'll never learn, sunshine.'

Ah look at Trippie wi' a look o' complete confusion on me face. Ah wanna say 'what?', but no matter how 'ard ah try ah can't talk. It's like in one o' those 'orrible nightmares where you need to scream, but no matter how 'ard you try no sound will come out. Ah rage an' ah scream an' ah boil over inside, but the inside no longer controls the out.

'You shouldn't take pills, sunshine. They just make you worse. They give you another excuse; create another demon.'

Suddenly ah can speak again.

'Alreet then mush. Ah wayn't teck drugs. Ah'm sure you're priceless advice will stand me in good stead now it's too fuckin' late.'

Trippie shakes 'is head. 'You never could face the truth of anything, brother.'

'e points up to the ceiling wi' the remote control.

'Don't trip. Someone might trample on your dreams.'

The Trampler turns to face me, but it's no longer the man who was once an idol to millions; the ultimate babyface. It's not even the 'eel who turned the late nineties upside down. It's the shell o' the Trampler; the steroid-enhanced carcass o' Trippie.

And the burnin' eyes o' a monster.

'One more time,' slithers an inhuman voice. 'Just to milk it.'

Please God; if there is a time when you're supposed to weck up, let it be now.

Ah'm winded. Ah'm dizzy. Ah'm sick. Ah'm a swatted fly. For one last time the world falls away in a bath o' flames an' two burnin' eyes pierce me very soul; the last thing that ah'll ever see…

… the only thing ah'll ever see…

… forever.

But it's not true! Ah don't die, do ah? Ah do see, don't ah? Ah can't do anythin' but fuckin' see!

And wi' that, everythin' vanishes. There is nowt at all. No ground beneath me feet, no air to breathe, no colour, no light, no form. Me body isn't even theer.

Is this it? Am I the universe? Am I God? Am I the writer? Am I the entity that ah so despise for me masochistic selfishness?

Ah feel nowt but fear as ah am swept on through the winds o' the void by currents ah can neither see nor comprehend. Ah'd give anythin'; ah'd sacrifice anythin' just to feel me feet on the ground, or even to feel me 'ead crack open on a pavement. Ah just need to know that there's more than me out theer. Ah'd give anythin' to weck up. Anythin', that is, except the one thing that ah 'ave left.

'The One Ah Love' card. Ah'll not sacrifice it for owt. Not again. There is no price ah won't pay to 'old onto that card. There's no sacrifice too great.

Ah teck it from me suddenly corporeal pocket an' pause momentarily, preparin' mesen for the moment o' Truth.

Ah 'onestly expect to read the name Bethany 'unt. After all, she's the person that 'as dominated all me thoughts while ah've been fallin' though this macroscopic emptiness. She's the person that ah could never've sacrificed…

… all those lies.

Ah couldn't 'ave.

Ah read the name on the back o' the card.

Thomas Briggs.

* * *

Ah'm tearin' down a deserted country lane like a bat out o' 'ell. Ah just don't care no more. Ah crash. Ah burn.

And from the twisted wreckage o' me vintage Triumph 'erald rises a spectre. Squintin' me eyes ah can just about meck out its form...

... ah know. Ah know 'im. That face...

Everythin' else falls away again. The bike, the road, the sorrow...

... the grindin' engines o' the universe.

It's just me an' a pen.

Ah storm the gates as ordered, but as ah climb the rope ladder ah feel an arrow in me back.

The surgeon puts me under, an' then it all goes black.

The terrorist says 'e's gonna shoot me next. 'e does.

A trillion deaths, an' they're all mine now. The universe as one self-contained existential nightmare. 'ow is this possible? Ah was so sure. Ah was so sure that Bethany was the one for me, even after it killed her... after it took 'er from me! That ghost... It couldn't 'ave been... The brakes lock an' me car slides before the big truck. 'CLEAR! CLEAR!' commands the Doctor an' before long ah'm clear o' it all. Ah miss even the 'arsh caress o' the flames.

Please let me feel somet else.

Anythin' but this... anythin' but nothin' and... this.

And so he finally understands!

You finally remember ALL of it.

You remember the cold fire in your blood.

You remember the graphic scenes of immolation; the silent whispers of terror.

You remember touching the two wires together and driving straight though Gristle.

You remember the green hatred that made you pull the sword from the wall.

You remember the crimson masks that you forced your friend and your lover to wear.

You remember the venting of the suppressed rage; the unleashing of the anger at the injustice that took your family from you.

You remember striking her across her gorgeous face to shut her treacherous little mouth.

You are bundling her into that car right now.

You are ripping at her dress now.

You are stripping her.

You are violating her.

You are taking your hands off the wheel so that you can touch her face for one last time.

You remember.

No, not me; I am not here. I am not real.

There is no demon.

The only voice is your own.

You did it.

You did it all.

You killed her.

You killed myself.

A thousand million centuries later, Tom kicks off his sandals and wades into the gently receding tide. His mind is very nearly blank now. An eternity of solitude has exorcised his 'life' almost completely.

As he paddles in the sea, he distantly half-remembers his irrational fear of the creatures that lurk in the murky depths of the ocean.

He finds himself trying to evoke that same feeling of dread within himself. He actually wants to feel the goosebumps as the fish swim by his toes. He needs to feel his blood turn cold. He needs to feel someone walking on his grave again.

But there are no fish.

There is no fear.

There is nothing now.

Tom turns around and walks back up the beach. He's going to have to start it all up again, but this time he'll tone down the sex and the violence.

He'll create a world with less pain. A world that makes sense. Something for the kids, with more aitches and fewer characters. Last time he felt that there'd probably been too many, each leaving only blurred impressions of varying intensity. Slightly-tweaked templates and near-clones. He wasn't entirely happy with the plot, either – it was poorly structured and appallingly paced. And worst of all, it didn't make sense. One had to work very hard indeed to read between the lines and solve the riddle of the author's intent, which of course, as always, was purely to stop himself going mad.

And there were no answers, and there was nearly no end.

He nearly lost himself that time.

He nearly lost himself in there.

Next time, though...

At last Tom opens his eyes to see a slim, beautiful blonde wearing spectacles and a long white coat looking down on him. He finally manages to mutter his last words on Earth; his parting gift to Bethany. The one thing that he can get right for her.

'Don't... don't teck... don't teck 'er eyes...'

His final moments are spent in the grip of claustrophobia as his brain sends instructions (coded in electrical impulses) to his arms telling them to rip the breathing apparatus from the remnants of his face. His actions are futile as what remains of his arms don't work anymore. His eyes begin to glaze over as they take in his final sights.

'Bef... Bethany... Don't teck 'er eyes...'

Tom gives in to the urge to leave the world exactly as he entered it.

Screaming.

He could fight for every breath, and perhaps even live on for that little while longer, but he'd only be confined to a bed in an asylum.

In the end, he doesn't even want to.

He's not even sure that this is really real anymore - whatever 'real' means.

The wonder of the world is gone, and for him, the world will follow.

FOREVER TWISTED

FURTHER DOWN THE SAME WARD, ANOTHER patient wakes to inhale the rank smells of detergent and death. She almost chokes on the taste of charcoal.

She grasps at the paper-thin sheets with her clenched fists. Looking down, she sees a drip going straight into her right arm. Anti-dose, no doubt. *Black shits for me.*

What would her devout mother say? *What would Dad say?* She can't bear the thought of their disappointed faces. *What will Tom say...?*

Anna is overcome by regret and remorse. She focuses on the sensation of the anti-dose entering her blood stream. Anything to take her mind off... well, *everything*.

Soon hardness sets in. *This'll teach him. This'll make him sorry. You can't just fuck with An-*'AAAAAAAAAGH!'

A deafening scream from nearby shakes her out of her self-pity. It is the raw scream of a young man. Lots of noise. Doctors. Nurses. Machines. Buzzing. His screams go right through her, chilling her to the bone. What's happening? What has happened to this guy?

'AAAAAAAAAAAAGH!'

'Doctor Spyrou to casualty,' the tannoy chirps urgently.

Anna feebly calls out. 'Doc, I feel a little sick...'

'AAAAAAAAAAAAGH!'

Scorched lungs scream their last as Tommy Briggs leaves us all in pain.

Why doesn't she answer? Doctor! What are you doing to that guy? Why am I here? What have I done? What have I done? I'm talking to you!!!

Suddenly there is a commotion at the desk. The nurses are trying to restrain somebody. Wait a minute... it couldn't be...

'Spadge!' Anna almost sits up, but she has to stop herself because it would tear the drip from her vein. She can't believe her eyes.

He runs over to her, his face a mask of sorrow. She grabs his hand and holds it tight. The nurses are crowding him now, telling him that he has five minutes and then he'll have to come back in the morning.

'I can't believe you came. I thought-' Anna cries, but Spadge puts a finger to her lips.

He squeezes her hand tightly and just for once, doesn't say a word.

She looks up at his compassionate yet melancholic smile.

So there is hope for this world after all. But never in her wildest dreams did Anna think that it would hail from Swindon.

Several hours later in a different hospital many miles from Hull, a stern-looking middle-aged Doctor leaves the operating theatre. He doesn't have to say anything to Katie; he just smiles at her solemnly, and gestures towards the heavy double-doors.

Two nurses follow her into the blue room.

Nervously she approaches the bed and looks at her sleeping boyfriend. He looks peaceful – minus a dominant right hand, but peaceful all the same.

A torrent of thoughts flood through her mind concurrently. How would he react? She'd never met anyone so vain! How would *she* react? Could she still...? Did she still...? She didn't even want to think about it.

She's dreading him first opening his eyes and asking the inevitable, and that's not even the half of it. She'd only got the call about an hour ago. Bethany – dead. Tom – dead *and*...

Katie shakes her head. Will's father is rotting in jail, due in part to the crimes of his son's best friend. Jim is an old, sick wanker – but he doesn't deserve that. She'll get the record set straight. Jim might still rot, but at least he'll rot justly.

Katie will save everybody.

Everybody who's left.

Who'd have though uni would have been so… *mad*. It's all just too real.

Ushering herself past the nurse she leans over Will and kisses him gently on the forehead. She can't believe how much she loves him. She will make this work. She'll make it work for Will. She'll even make it work for poor old Jim. More than that, she'll make it work for herself.

As she clasps Will's remaining hand, the strangest of thoughts brings her comfort, and she hopes that it might even offer Will some consolation in the difficult days ahead.

Doesn't Will's hero, that *Starkiller* kid from the seventies, have just the one hand?

At four fifty-two am Lorraine Simpson receives a call informing her that her husband and two sons have been killed in an accident on the M62. A couple of daft students doing over a hundred ran into them and blew them all to kingdom come. They need her to ID the bodies… or at least, what there is left of them.

Lorraine doesn't believe that they can be dead at all. Not so soon after her daughter, after her little Britney…

Lorraine can't even bear to think about it. She reaches for her big coat and empties her mind of all these painful thoughts. It's beginning to rain.

Locking the door behind her and checking it twice, she's sure that she can hear something. A voice calling to her…

In an old maritime town, a young man stands at a bar and he waits. His life already full of an almost unbelievable amount of incident, he isn't waiting for something to happen. *Au contraire.* He's waiting for something to come along and stop things happening. Perhaps he's even waiting for *someone.*

Someone new.

Someone like-minded.

Someone who can be professional by day, but at night knows how to kick back and enjoy themselves – after all, life's far too short.

It can't even be half eleven yet, but Jamal can feel the ecstasy kicking in. The warmth consumes his entire body and the beat of the music pulses within his veins. Pure energy and love flow throughout his circulatory system instead of the normal concoction of blood, alcohol and ink that his body is used to.

Jamal pokes at the scab that covers the new tattoo sat on the inside of his forearm. In *Ye Olde English* lettering it reads:

Dream as if you'll live forever. Live as if you'll die today.

That particular pearl of wisdom was passed from Jimmy Dean to Tommy Briggs and finally to Jamal Prakash.

Jamal is on top the world. He loves Hull. The mental scars and emotional damage inflicted on him last year now excite him as he looks back on them, the drug glorifying his experiences and making him feel like the sole surviving soldier of some hard-fought war.

A soldier with an interesting story to tell.

A wave of epiphany comes over him as he sups at his water, providing a revelation that he feels compelled to share with the largish woman stood to his left.

'Would you like to know why the world is such a shitty place?' he asks.

'Yer,' she replies, her eyes looking down to her drink in disappointment as she realises that she probably isn't going to get any tonight. 'Alreet.'

'I believe….'

'What?'

'I believe that God is a writer.'

Silence.

'Or,' he almost stutters, 'the spiritual equivalent.'

The woman looks unconvinced.

''ow d'yer work that out, then?'

Jamal recomposes himself, a second surge of warmth and self-assurance oozing through his polluted blood stream.

'If you were to write a story, for instance, would you fill it full of happy people? Would you have your characters be born happy, live happy and die happy? Where's the journey? Where's the interest? *Nowhere.*

'God filled our lives with pain and misery because this planet is the greatest, most tragic show in the universe, and it's the best, I should say! As an old friend of mine used to say: *'ave it!*'

At that point, a group of freshers dressed up in Alan Partridge masks, ties and blazers point out to Jamal that God is a gas. Jamal ripostes that he's a teacher, and as such knows best when it comes to such things.

After some debate the freshers back down.

ABOUT THE AUTHOR

Edward George Wolverson grew up in a mining town in South Yorkshire. In 2001 he moved to the East Riding to read LLB Law with Philosophy at the University of Hull. He now practises as a Chartered Legal Executive locally.

Wolverson has harboured a love for writing, and particularly for writing fiction, since a very young age. This first became apparent to his flabbergasted parents when, at the tender age of five, his teacher invited them into school to discuss his use of colourful language in a short story that he'd written about a band of outlaws. '*I'm* not being rude,' the young scribbler argued. 'That's how they talk.' He still relies on the same old argument today.

In his teens, Wolverson wrote a number of screenplays which he and his friends promptly turned into dreadful, CSO-driven movies in his school's disproportionately sophisticated 'Media Studies' room. On the back of these movies, in 1997 he co-wrote (and much to his adult embarrassment, *starred in*) a film funded by the local Council to highlight the dearth of facilities for young people in his town. As many pointed out at the time, the film actually cost more money to make than it would have done to improve facilities, but it did at least allow Wolverson to share a memorable scene in Leeds Magistrates' Court with an actor who'd recently sent Steve McDonald to prison in *Corrie* (and who, as it happens, was playing the Judge who sentences Wolverson's character in the film).

With the prospect of having to work for a living looming large, Wolverson began to take writing seriously shortly after graduating from university in 2004. He even read a book about it. His first draft of *The Tally* was written over several day-sleeping months working in a Hull nightclub's cloakroom (between the busy bit at the beginning, when clubbers dropped off their coats, and the busy bit at the end, when he had to tell clubbers that he'd lost them).

In 2006, Wolverson launched the unofficial *Doctor Who* website *The History of the Doctor*, which he then edited for five years. During this time he contributed the better part of a thousand reviews and articles, which is sadder than it probably sounds.

Wolverson's next project is an anthology of morality tales for children, tentatively entitled *When and How to Cry Wolf.* These are currently being vetted by his receptive daughter and sceptical wife.

PRAISE FOR 'THE TALLY'

"...driven by an angry verve that takes us from realism and comedy, through weirdness and philosophy, into the realms of horror... Wolverson can switch from graphic descriptions of snakebite-flavoured vomit to solipsist reflections on the nature of the mind, granting each a colourful turn of phrase."
- Daniel Tessier, Immaterial

"...just when we begin to chuckle with, and at, the "meat puppet" characters, we are hit with truly good writing that makes us stop in our tracks. When I die don't let them take my eyes... a writer who can take the common game of Snake and force me to consider the nature of my existence is certainly a writer I would like to see more from."
- Vicki Bolton, Amazon Customer Review (Kindle Edition)

"...an inevitable and effective contemporary tragedy but ridiculous too. You can have the main characters bearing their souls to each other, talking about loved ones' deaths and awful things like that while Wolverson focuses on one of them really needing the toilet. It's the kind of stuff that happens but no one admits to and so it makes the madness feel more real."
- "Lord Vorselon", Amazon Customer Review (Kindle Edition)

"The Tally is more than just a university comedy / drama - it's got a really dark and heavy philosophical side to it. A lot of horror comes from the terrible events that happen, and the really brutal way how the writer describes them, but what's really disturbing is the psychological horror and how the writer plays on your mind. I can't think of anything scarier than losing all sense of who you are and becoming the plaything of something evil, whether that evil's a manipulative girl, a buried part of you that you don't recognise, or something supernatural, or losing all sense of reality altogether."
- "robtrinity", Amazon Customer Review (Kindle Edition)

"Violent, perceptive and funny; brutal, subversive and sly; this is a dazzling read from a writer who punches with both hands and winks at the crowd while he's about it. Funny, macabre, edgy and utterly compelling, The Tally *is wickedly entertaining."*
- "Coldwater", Amazon Customer Review (Kindle Edition)

"The novel is at times puerile, but… it is only trying to be an accurate depiction of student life, and the thought processes of the average male student, something the novel nails brilliantly. The Tally *is on occasion laugh out loud funny, but with frequent asides of philosophical inquiry to add depth. The book, like the characters it portrays, has a superficially crude exterior but will regularly have you drawing parallels with your own experiences and forces you to ask the same questions of yourself as of the central characters."*
- "Jaymz", Amazon Customer Review (Kindle Edition)

"On his website Wolverson calls The Tally *'Bloke-lit' fiction, and that's perhaps the best way to describe it. The book's coarse, boorish exterior belies a twisted tale of psychological torment and cosmic loneliness like some wacky cross between* American Psycho *and* American Pie *(only in Hull of all places!) Reading it you almost feel like Wolverson has tricked you into thinking about things you weren't prepared to when you began. He uses a frivolous, zeitgeisty set-up to catapult you into a haunting treatise on self-determination, culpability and even existence."*
- "Mrs P", Amazon Customer Review (Kindle Edition)

"…fast-paced, written in a way that reflects the emotional and mental fragility of the characters and handles local dialects really well to create really funny moments throughout the book. The storyline itself is very dark, but the real to life characters mean that you can enjoy the comedy while reading their decent into their own personal hell."
- "Spiros", Amazon Customer Review (Kindle Edition)

ALSO AVAILABLE:

THE TALLY
kindle edition

ASIN: B006SIQN3O

CPSIA information can be obtained at www.ICGtesting.com
Printed in the USA
BVOW061457300312

286496BV00001B/2/P

9 781781 760765